TRAIN TO BARNJUM

BY

RANDALL PROBERT

Train to Barnjum
by Randall Probert

www.randallprobertbooks.net

email: randentr@megalink.net

Photography credits:

Front cover train photo ~ iStockphoto
Front cover background photo ~ Randall Probert
Author's photograph, p 272 ~ Patricia Gott

ISBN: 978-1530091201

Printed in the United States of America

Published by
Randall Enterprises
P.O. Box 862
Bethel, Maine 04217

Dedication

I would like to dedicate this book to my folks:
Toby and Alice Probert.

TRAIN TO BARNJUM

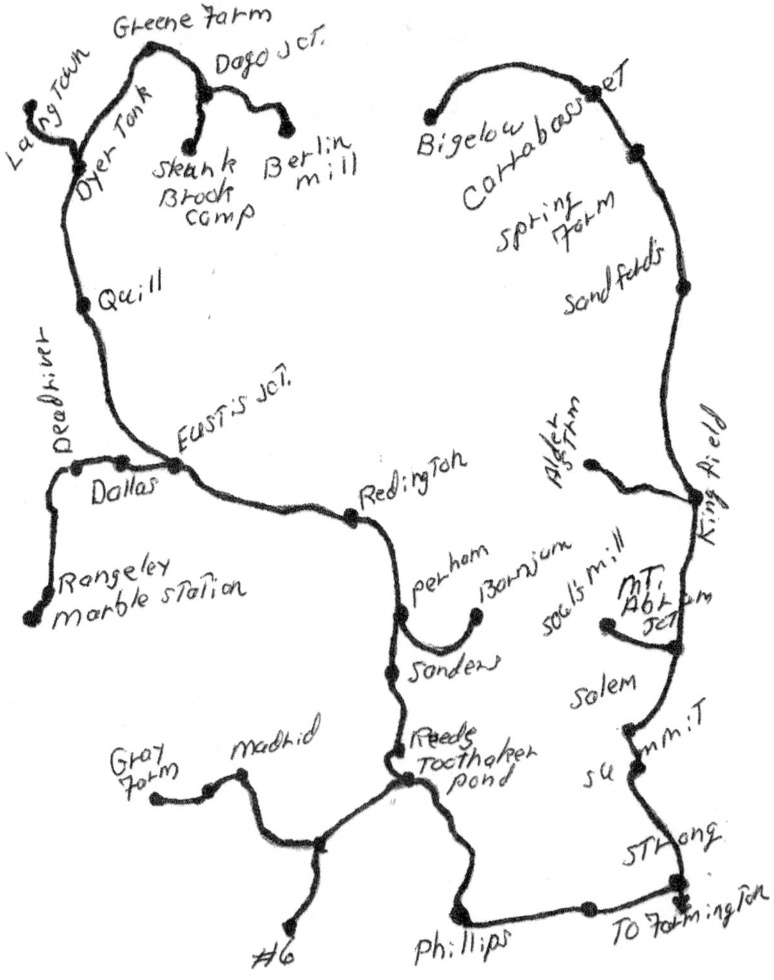

Greene Farm
Langtown
Dyer Tank
Dago Jct.
Skank Brook camp
Berlin mill
Bigelow
Carrabasset
Spring Farm
Sandford's
Quill
Deadriver
Eustis Jct.
Dallas
Rangeley
Marble Station
Redington
Alder Stream
Kingfield
perham
Barnjum
Soule's mill
Mt. Abram Jct.
Sanders
Salem
Summit
Reeds
Toothaker pond
Gray Farm
Madrid
Strong
To Farmington
Phillips
#6

Chapter 1

Sergeant Sterling Silvanus had joined the Army two years ago. He was now almost 18 years old and already an Army Sergeant. His father and mother were Russian emigrants—Knute and Yvette Silvanus. They were in love and wanted more for their children. They were married and left Moscow for America. Sterling was born two years later, 1880, in Portland, Maine.

Sterling had been a bright lad. Ahead of the other classmates, he seemed much older for his age. He stood six feet tall with broad shoulders and very strong. He was tired of book learning and wanted to experience the real world. He finished the eighth grade, but told his parents he had had enough of schooling and he wanted to join the Army and go out west before life there became too civilized.

Knute and Yvette didn't have any problem with Sterling quitting school, but Knute had wanted him to stay on the farm and work the land for farming. Knute was disappointed, but he loved his son enough, so he gave him his blessing.

Knute and Yvette soon left New York and stopped at Portland Maine, where he found work with Maine Central Railroad working on the lines as a trackman. When Knute learned of the Narrow Gauge Railroad further to the north in Franklin County, the Sandy River Railroad, he knew this was where he wanted to be.

They boarded the Sandy River Train in Farmington bound

for Strong, only a short distance up the Strong Line. There they found a small farm for sale on the back side of the river about one mile from town. The McClain farm sat on top of Lambert Hill. There were cleared fields for hay and a few crops, but it was mostly woodlands, with some very nice hardwood and spruce timber.

Sterling was ten years old and found the adventure exciting. With Knute's background in railroading, he found immediate work with the Sandy River Railroad and was soon made track foreman. Yvette was an excellent seamstress. She started making alterations and mending tears for most of the trackmen. In her slow time, Yvette made women's clothing.

Knute was also an adventurer and he would liked to have gone out west with his son.

"You probably know more than those teachers already. You want to quit school, that's okay with me. You just write to your mother and me and let us know where you are."

* * * *

Sterling was at this moment thinking of his folks and missing them. But he had to keep his senses alert and his mind on what he was doing.

Shortly after Sterling's arrival at Fort Apache in Arizona, Captain John Reeves saw how easily Sterling took directions and he could equally give directions and support to those with him. Captain Reeves promoted Sterling to sergeant. And no comment was made about his young age. Everyone at the fort naturally assumed he was much older.

A year later a new fresh lieutenant from West Point, Oliver Borden, made his appearance. Oliver was only 5'7" and weighed soaking wet, maybe 130 pounds. And he had the same character and mannerisms as a small Chihuahua dog that would nip at anyone's heels as they walked by. Everyone at the fort disliked the lieutenant and the lieutenant was offended by the respect showed to Sergeant Silvanus by the enlisted men as well as Captain Reeves. Sterling tried his best to stay out of the lieutenant's way.

There was a stray renegade band of Apaches that kept crossing back and forth on the Mexican border and raiding beef cattle. Just before Christmas of 1897, Captain Reeves called Lieutenant Borden and Sergeant Silvanus into his office.

"Lieutenant, the border raids are increasing. Tonight after dark, so no one will see you leave, you and Sergeant Silvanus will take a patrol unit of 15 men and provisions for 2 weeks and patrol between here and the border. I want you to document what you observe of Indian activity only. I do not want you to engage them in a fight, unless you are fired upon first. Is that understood, Lieutenant?"

"Yes sir, it is," Borden replied.

Once outside, "Sergeant Silvanus, you will ask for 15 volunteers and a cook. Then provision a wagon with enough food, water and supplies for 2 weeks."

"Yes sir," Sterling replied.

* * * *

Sterling looked over the top of the rock he was lying prone behind. He was hot and thirsty and too dehydrated to sweat. There was one fatal casualty and one seriously wounded, all because the lieutenant wanted to make a name for himself. . .to prove that he was as good an Indian fighter as any man at the fort.

Their scout had spotted a group of maybe 25 braves hunkered down by a spring and instead of going around them, Borden wanted to ride directly at them. Sterling knew what he was doing. The lieutenant was trying to force the Indians into shooting first, so the lieutenant could have his skirmish.

"Lieutenant, I advise you to go around," Sterling had said.

"I'm in command here, Sergeant! I know what I'm doing.

You just make sure the men are ready."

The band of Indians had seen the patrol sooner than Borden had thought they would, and just like he guessed they would react, they started shooting. And the fight was on.

Sterling had seen a few braves go down and Private Smith was fatally shot and as they were retreating, Corporal Rusty—James Russell—screamed out in pain as he was wounded and fell. When the patrol had reached the safety of some high ground and rocks, they took cover behind the rocks.

Sterling could still hear Rusty calling for help. At least he wasn't screaming. With the patrol safely positioned, Sterling said, "Lieutenant, Corporal Rusty was wounded and he's down and calling for help. I'm going out to get him."

"Negative, Sergeant. You'll remain here with the patrol. Do you understand?"

"Yes sir, I understand! But I'm still going to get him. I will not leave him to be captured or left to die!"

"You'll remain here, Sergeant!"

"You go to hell, Lieutenant!" And Sterling started crawling on his stomach towards Rusty. Pulling his haversack behind him.

The entire patrol had heard the exchange between Borden and their sergeant. And they were all glad Sterling was going after Rusty.

He reached Rusty without any difficulty and then realized Rusty had broken his right leg and was wounded in the left shoulder. Sterling bandaged the shoulder wound and then he put a makeshift splint on the leg.

As he was looking around he noticed a young Indian boy about 10 feet away. When Rusty was all bandaged up, Sterling crawled over to see if he could help the boy. He was still alive.

A bullet had creased the side of his head and the boy was rubbing his left ankle. The boy didn't seem to be afraid of Sterling, as he cleaned the wound and put a bandage around the boy's head. Then he put a wrap around the ankle. It was probably only sprained. When he had finished, Sterling pointed where the rest of his people had gone and he said, "Go," and he pointed again and said, "Go."

The boy understood and he began to crawl back towards his own people. Rusty watched as Sterling bandaged the boy and surprised when he turned the boy loose to return to his people.

"He was only 12 or 13. I had to let him go."

"That's okay with me. Just don't say anything and I won't either," Rusty said.

"You can't put any weight on your leg and we can't stand up and expose ourselves, so I'll have to pull you along."

One foot at a time, Sterling pulled Rusty back to safety.

"Sergeant, you disobeyed a direct order. I intend to put you on report when we get back to the fort."

"Yes, Lieutenant, I disobeyed you when I went after Corporal Rusty." That's all he said.

"Now, Lieutenant, it's my recommendation that we either leave now while all is quiet or we take the fight to them. They won't be expecting us to attack and we just might catch them by surprise."

"Negative, Sergeant. The men need rest and food. At daylight we'll attack. Besides Indians won't attack at night."

"Who says they won't? That's only a myth."

"Are you going to disobey me again, Sergeant?"

"No sir. That was only a suggestion."

Sterling went around to all the men telling them to be alert. "Groups of twos, and only one sleeps at a time. No fires and no loud talking."

He went back to his rock and looked out across the shadowy ground in front.

* * * *

The Indians didn't attack during the night, much to everyone's relief. In fact, when the patrol found their camp, they discovered that instead of attacking, they had used the darkness to escape.

The ride back to the fort was a quiet one. They had lost one man and one wounded. Sterling kept hearing Captain Reeves saying not to engage them. Observe only. How was the lieutenant going to justify his actions? Once at the fort, Lieutenant Borden said, "Sergeant Silvanus, I intend to write a full report about your disobedience."

"Yes sir," that's all he said.

After Captain Reeves had read Borden's report, he asked Sterling for a full report and then he talked with each man on the patrol. Ten days later, he called for Lieutenant Borden and Sergeant Silvanus to report to his office.

"I have taken it upon myself to further investigate these charges against you, Sergeant Silvanus." He directed his attention now only to Sterling. "I was very interested in the completeness of your report, Sergeant. You stayed with the facts without any opinions. This is what prompted me to investigate further."

Now he was standing directly in front of the lieutenant. He cleared his throat before continuing. "Lieutenant, where I found the sergeant's report containing only the facts, yours was opinions and innuendos. I talked with each man on the patrol and I have decided that Sergeant Silvanus's report is what actually occurred.

"Lieutenant, I don't know if it was cowardice or what, but you were willing to leave a wounded man to die without trying to rescue him. You failed to heed or take notice the advice of someone with more experience than you had. Or maybe that was your problem? Regardless, you also disobeyed my orders when I told you do not engage the enemy unless fired upon."

The lieutenant tried to speak but Captain Reeves stopped him. "Not a word from you, Lieutenant. You came out here with a chip on your shoulder. You had something to prove maybe. I don't know. But I do know that you are not officer material. Therefore, I am reducing you in rank to sergeant. And I have also added into your personnel file that under these circumstances, that you are never to rise above the rank of sergeant. You do realize that your personnel file will follow you where ever you may go while serving in the military. I don't know if you are qualified to do anything else, but it is my strong suggestion that you find it and resign."

Captain Reeves stepped over to his desk and picked something up. "Sergeant Sterling Silvanus, you showed extreme bravery when you rescued Corporal Rusty and I am awarding you this Bronze Star. And I am also promoting you to Master Sergeant." Captain Reeves noticed a peculiar expression on Borden's face as he realized that now he would have to answer to Sterling.

* * * *

The following week on the eve of February 15th, 1898, Sterling saw an alarming notice posted on the bulletin board. The USS Maine Battleship had been blown up while berthing in the Havana port of Cuba. And the war department was asking for volunteers to serve under the command of Colonel Roosevelt.

Sterling requested an immediate transfer to Washington to join Roosevelt's Regiment. As he boarded the train he noticed Oliver Borden boarding the next car. Apparently he had taken the Captain's suggestion seriously and had resigned from the Army. That was the last that Sterling would ever think of his former lieutenant.

Sterling sat alone and next to the window watching the landscape pass by. He was marveling how the United States had prospered since the end of the Civil War. In a few days now, one could ride a train from coast to coast and almost anywhere else in the United States.

The clicking of the iron wheels on the tracks had a hypnotic effect on him and he was soon sound asleep.

After breakfast, onboard the train, the next morning Sterling bought a newspaper that had come on board at the last stop. There was an article on the front page about Theodore Roosevelt.

Sterling had not known until reading that paper that Roosevelt had been the head of the Department of Navy and now he had resigned and with the help of Army Colonel Leonard Wood, he was commissioned Lieutenant Colonel and was now forming a volunteer regiment from hand picked western cowboys and western soldiers. (Soon after, Roosevelt would be promoted to full colonel as his superior Colonel Wood would be promoted to brigadier general.) Now Colonel Roosevelt would have full command of his volunteer regiment.

Four days later Sterling stepped off the train at the Washington D.C. terminal and boarded a coach that was taking men to the war department.

Sterling waited patiently in the hall while many others ahead of him were being interviewed. It was obvious that not all who were volunteering were accepted. Finally it was his turn and he was escorted into a huge office. Colonel Roosevelt was sitting behind his desk reading a report. Sterling hoped it was his report.

Roosevelt kept reading and not acknowledging Sterling's presence. Finally Roosevelt began to laugh and said, "My God! Reading this report about you, Sergeant, reminds me of me in my younger days."

Roosevelt put down the files about Sterling and for the first time, looked at him. He looked up and down and then asked, "How old are you son?"

"Eighteen, Colonel."

"I knew that. I wanted to see if you'd lie to me. You're a big brute for being 18. Captain Reeves gave you an enlightening endorsement. He says you are mild mannered but yet command respect by your actions and integrity. You set an example for others who serve with you. I like that in my top aides. You seem to conduct yourself and talk like a gentleman, but you also carry a big stick. Yes sir, I like that."

Roosevelt stood and pushed his chair back and walked around and shook Sterling's hand. "Congratulations, Sergeant. How soon can you be on your way to Florida to help Captain

Gerard train our new volunteers?"

"Tomorrow morning, sir. I would like to bathe and clean up and wash my clothes and eat a nice meal."

Roosevelt walked behind his desk and picked up some papers and handed them to Sterling. "Here are your traveling orders. Thank you, Sergeant. You're dismissed."

As Sterling was closing the door, Roosevelt said, "I hope you don't tell me to go to hell."

"No sir," Sterling replied.

* * * *

On July 1st, 1898, Colonel Roosevelt and his Rough Rider Regiment stormed up San Juan Hill. Since there were no transport ships to ferry the trooper's horses to Cuba, Roosevelt rode alone up the hill. He rode back and forth at the forefront of the charge, encouraging his men.

Sergeant Silvanus was young, rugged and in good physical condition and he was the first man behind Colonel Roosevelt. Roosevelt saw how Sergeant Silvanus was leading his men—he was way out in front—and he began to laugh out loud and he hollered, "Come on, Rough Riders! Over the top!"

Roosevelt left the Army later on and ran for Governor of New York. He asked Sterling to go with him as his personal body guard. In 1901, when Colonel Roosevelt became the 26th President of the United States, Roosevelt asked Sterling to join the Secret Service and remain on his staff.

When President Roosevelt left the presidency in 1909 to the incoming president, William Taft, he asked Sterling to accompany him on an African safari.

"Sir, I would truly like to, but I received an alarming telegraph message this morning that my folks both died last week of diphtheria and I must return to Maine."

Chapter 2

Sterling boarded a train in New York, a night express to Boston, and switched trains there for Portland. He was a distinguished looking individual. He wore a light brown suit and shoes. He hadn't worn boots since leaving the Army and joining Roosevelt's staff. He had filled out since leaving home in 1896 and there were a few streaks of gray in his hair. He was glad to be going home, but not under these circumstances.

There were a lot of memories going through his head during the ride home and he wasn't able to sleep much. Even though he wrote to his folks every week, he had not had the time to go home and visit. At least he never took the time. And now it was too late.

He wasn't sure what he was going to do once he had taken care of their affairs at home. He had saved close to $4,600 in the 13 years he had been gone.

While he waited for his train to leave the terminal in Lewiston for Farmington, he bought the morning's newspaper inside the news shop. His picture and story was on the front page. A reporter for the New York Times had interviewed President Roosevelt about his upcoming safari to Africa and instead, Roosevelt had given the reporter Sterling Silvanus's story.

"You'll find this much more interesting," he had said to the reporter.

When Sterling had found an empty seat in the coach car, a distinguished looking gentleman close to Sterling's seat said,

"You look just like your picture on the front page of every paper in the country. You are Sterling Silvanus?"

"Yes sir, I am."

"I'm Representative Howard Daggett from Farmington."

"Are you related to Albert and Washington Daggett in Strong?" Sterling asked.

"I'm their cousin," Mr. Daggett sat down beside Sterling.

"You might say fate introduced me to you. I know who you are. Hell, everyone in the country will know about Sterling Silvanus after today's newspaper. I said fate introduced us. My train from Augusta to Skowhegan had a twelve hour delay so I took the train to Auburn where I boarded this train. I'm on the Warden Service Counsel and I was in a meeting this morning with the Chief, Warden Perry. Don Perry has received approval from legislature to hire five more game wardens.

"Let me ask you this Sterling. What are your plans for the future?"

"My folks died of diphtheria last week and I'm on my way home to take care of things."

"What then? After your affairs are all taken care of?"

"I haven't thought that far ahead," Sterling replied.

"Ever since the Warden Service was created in 1880, the department has hired mostly men with a military service background. And after this newspaper article about you, I think Chief Warden Perry would hire you on sight."

"How long do I have to make up my mind?"

"Two days. If this is what you want, you can send me a telegraph at this Farmington address." Mr. Daggett gave Sterling a slip of paper with his name and address.

"I know this is awful short notice, particularly in your case. But the chief hasn't yet released the new hiring to the public. If you could let me know by tomorrow noon, I'd telegraph the chief immediately and you'll be at the front of those applying."

"If I decide to become a game warden, where would I be stationed?"

"That I'm not sure. It would be up to Chief Perry. Someone with your background, Mr. Silvanus, would have the advantage. Especially with the president as a reference. And I think this here article pretty much says it all."

"What you are saying, Mr. Daggett, seems extraordinary. Too good to be true."

"I assure you, Mr. Silvanus, everything I have said is the truth," Representative Daggett said.

They were rolling to a stop at the terminal in Farmington and Daggett left for home and Sterling boarded the little Lilliput train for Strong. He was so preoccupied thinking about becoming a Maine Game Warden, he had not been aware of the ride along the narrow gauge rails. And the train was pulling to a stop at the Strong Station, across from the Forester manufacturing mill.

Sterling picked up his gripsack and shouldered his pack. He was still wearing his brown suit. As he walked down the loading platform, a man from the inner office stepped out and Sterling recognized him immediately and began to smile. "My God, it's good to see a familiar face! How are you, Pancy?" (Erwin Newell)

"Well, hello there, Sterling. Everybody in town has been talking about nothing else since this morning's paper."

They shook hands, "It's good to be home, Pancy."

"Awful sorry about your Mom and Dad, Sterling. There was nothing Dr. Bell could do. He was with them when they passed."

"My shift is done here. I'm on my way home. Walk with you? If you don't have other plans."

"I'd like to, Pancy. I need to stretch my legs."

"What are your plans, Sterling?"

"I'm not sure. I need to take care of my folks' affairs first. Then I'll see."

"Of course, of course. Your mother and father, Sterling, were good people. Everyone in town was sad to see them taken with diphtheria. It hit other families, too. But mostly the children."

They walked in silence for a short distance and then Pancy

said, "My wife has been feeling ill for a couple of days and my daughter Helen has been keeping house and cooking for me. Here we are. Enjoy your walk home, Sterling."

"Good evening, Pancy." Sterling walked on a bit faster. There was an urge to get home.

As he walked past the Boothby Mill, he could smell the sweet perfume of the Balm of Gilead trees. That was one of spring's pleasures.

There were few people out and around as it was nearing suppertime. At the cemetery on his left he noticed someone was digging a new grave. He wandered over to inquire if the grave might be for his folks. "Hello, Runkytunk. That grave wouldn't be for my folks would it?"

"Well hello, Sterling. The paper said you were coming home. Didn't expect you this soon. No, this isn't for your mom or dad. A little girl died yesterday and she's to be buried tomorrow."

Lambert Hill always was a steep climb and today Sterling had his back pack and gripsack to carry. But the walk had inspired him. He walked on and didn't stop to catch his breath until he was at the first flateau and the Randall farm was on his right. Home would be at the top of the rise.

He walked on and little Jimmy was playing in the grass next to the road. His mom had written to him, telling about the new Randall baby boy. Now that was seeming like such a long time ago. "Hello, Jimmy."

"Hi, mister, who are you?"

"I'm Sterling Silvanus, your neighbor."

Jimmy just stood there and Sterling walked on. He was close now and he quickened his pace. He felt a new strangeness as the house came into view. How he was wishing he had taken the time to come and visit. But he had been busy with his own life. It was strange to stand in front of the house and not see any smoke coming from the chimney.

He entered the shed which led to the house backdoor entrance. There had never been any locks on the doors; he turned the door knob and he was home. He closed the door and stood there in the pantry for a moment before entering the kitchen. There were many emotions flowing through him, which brought tears to his eyes.

The entire house was immaculate. There was no dust or dirt anywhere. His folks bed was made up as well as his own. His bedroom was just as he had left it.

He found enough food to ward off hunger. Then he decided to walk out back. But as he left the shed the neighbor just up the road a piece, Freemont Allen, rode up in a horse and wagon. "Hello, Sterling. Wasn't expecting you this soon. . .and I am awfully sorry about your mom and dad. They were good people and we'll certainly miss them."

"Thank you, Mr. Allen. The place is immaculate. Mom always was a tidy homebody."

"I've been looking after the farm animals. That is except for the chickens. Young Jimmy Randall has been doing that. His Dad would bring him up in the wagon each morning after his own chores. They have been taking the eggs for the work. For taking care of the animals, your dad has allowed me for a few years now to use the back fields to pasture my own livestock. Yours are with my own."

"I need a few days. . .to take care of my folks' affairs and decide what I'm going to do. I don't see any harm in you continuing to use the pastures.

"What is there for livestock?"

"There is one cow, two heifers, two horses and a pig. The pig is still in the pen. The two horses are in a corral behind the barn.

"You are almost out of pig and chicken feed."

"Okay, I'll get some at Daggett's store."

* * * *

Sterling had had a long tiring day, but he knew it would be a longer day before he'd be able to sleep. So he sat on the porch long after the sun had set. He'd forgotten how much he had enjoyed listening to springtime sounds. Especially the frogs. The frogs and peepers in the little pond below the house were really singing a melody tonight. Maybe welcoming him home.

Tomorrow he would have to see Attorney Phillips Stubbs and see to his folks' affairs. He hadn't thought about it at all, since leaving the station house earlier, but now he was liking the idea of being a Maine Game Warden. He decided right then that after talking with Mr. Stubbs he would send a telegram to Representative Daggett. With that decision finally made, he discovered he was suddenly sleepy. His pocket watch said midnight. "Time to go to bed."

Being anxious to start the day, he was up shortly after sunrise. He wondered when Jimmy would show up to feed the chickens. *Maybe not at all since he knows I'm back.* So he went out and fed them and let them out into the outdoor pen. He collected ten eggs. There was smoked bacon hanging in the cellar. He had bacon and eggs and hot coffee.

At 7 a.m. Jimmy and his Dad did show up. Mr. Randall must have started his own chores early if he was already through. Then he remembered that farmers and lumbermen always started the day at the crack of dawn.

There were still a dozen eggs in cold storage in the cellar so Sterling gave Jimmy the fresh eggs. "Gee thanks, Mr. Silvanus. Dad has let me sell these eggs and keep the money. I have been collecting four dozen each week."

"How much do you charge for a dozen, Jimmy?"

"I get 25 cents."

"Well, I tell you what, you keep on tending the chickens and I'll buy the feed and keep only the eggs I need and you can have the rest to sell."

"Wow! Gee, thanks Mr. Silvanus. I'll be able to buy me some new boots soon."

"How old are you, Jimmy?"

"I'm five. Almost six."

"He's a big boy, Mr. Randall, for five years old."

"Yes he is and call me Dean. Mister don't sit too well with me."

When the Randalls left, Sterling went out back to saddle one of the horses. He chose the big brown quarter horse. It felt good to be back in the saddle. Once on the road towards town, the big horse wanted free rein, so Sterling let him have it and he ran at a full gallop down the first hill and across the flateau, but Sterling reined him in at the top of the big hill.

Attorney Stubb's office was above the hardware store. The door was open so Sterling walked in.

"Good morning, Mr. Stubbs. I'm Sterling Silvanus."

"Good morning, Sterling. Sit down please," he pulled out a folder from his desk drawer.

"When your father realized that he and your mother might not survive the sickness, he asked that I come up and tend to their affairs. I wrote out a will right there and they each signed it. Of course, everything is left to you. And there are no leins on the mortgage or the property."

"Your mom and dad were very proud of you, Sterling. And they never once regretted letting you leave. You have done very well for yourself."

"Thank you."

"I have an envelope here of all of your folks' valuables. Your father didn't believe in banks and he gave me this envelope of bills to be handed to you. There is $6,050.00. There is also the deed to the property and the bank release when the mortgage was paid in full. If you would sign this," and he slid a form across the desk top to Sterling.

"It simply says that I have relinquished to you the contents in this envelope.

"Neither of your folks wanted to be buried in the cemetery. They wanted to be buried on their farm, on a knoll in the back field that faces towards the east. Your father said that if they were buried on the farm, then maybe you would stay on the farm

22

and not sell the property."

Then on another note, "There were so many people at their funeral that people had to stand in the aisles. They were good people, Sterling, and they will be surely missed."

* * * *

From Attorney Stubbs' office, Sterling went to the station house to send a telegram to Representative Daggett. It was a short telegram.

> *Yes, I want to be a Maine Game Warden.*
> *Sterling Silvanus.*

Knowing there wouldn't be an answer before Monday, he returned home to look at the farm to see if anything needed fixing. There was an abundance of canned food in the cold storage bin in the cellar, along with smoked ham and bacon. The house was all okay and he checked the chicken coop and pig pen, and the pig pen could use some new boards on one side. But those he couldn't find. The well was directly behind the house and he primed the pump, and that worked fine also. The big barn door in back had broke away from the hinges and when it fell to the ground some of the boards had broken. All in all, there was only a little to do.

He had put off his next task long enough. He walked out back to find the knoll where his folks had been buried. He could see the headstones long before he was at graveside. He stood there not knowing what to say. And then, "Mom and Dad, I wished I had come back for a visit. I'm so sorry. I should have been here for you when you were sick."

He got down on his knees and said a short prayer. Afterwards he got up and walked towards the woods. He needed to walk and stretch his legs. He decided to hike out to the back line where it bordered the Doctor Brook. As a kid he would hike out to the brook on many excursions to fish.

The spruce and hardwood trees had really grown a lot in his absence. His dad had always intended to cut a few of the larger spruce trees each winter when the twitching on snow would be easier, but he had not had the time with his steady work on the Sandy River Rails System. There were a few pine trees, but not many.

On his way back he swung over towards the Allen line and there he found some nice straight white and yellow birch trees. This would be money wood—either to Brackeley's Mill or Forester's.

Across the road the property went all the way to the Sandy River. There was only about half the acreage of land on this side of the road and it was mostly smaller fir and spruce with some hemlock. This wood he figured could be all twitched down hill and piled up along the tracks and loaded onto rail cars when the time came to cut it.

On his way back to the farm, Sterling was feeling better about his circumstances. If for whatever reason he decided not to accept the warden position or he was not accepted, he knew there was enough timber on—now—his land, to make a good living from it.

Saturday morning came early and after eating breakfast, he harnessed his horse to the only wagon there was, a freight hauling wagon, and he went to town, to Starbird's Mill for lumber to make the repairs. He had found enough nails and his father had a good supply of sharp saws.

Clinton Starbird, son of Amos, in 1888 had built a new saw mill at the upper end of town and near Valley Brook and the railroad. The mill had burned in 1900 and a larger mill had been built in its place. His mother had written to him about the mill burning.

Clinton was just walking across the yard when Sterling pulled up with his wagon. "Good morning. Sorry about your folks."

"Thank you."

"What do you need this morning?"

"I need to make some repairs to the barn door and I'll need some boards."

"How many?"

"Oh, probably 20, 16-foot pine boards, 12 inches wide. That should work."

"Follow me. There're right over here."

Clinton helped Sterling load the lumber and Sterling paid him and left and headed for the bakery at Merrill and Daggett's Store.

While he was at Daggett's Store, he picked up some new hinges also. He also bought three loaves of freshly baked bread, an apple pie, coffee and potatoes. "There, that should do me, if I can get up Lambert Hill with this load."

He stopped at the bottom of the hill by the Porter Farm to rest his horse, ole Duke. Feeling sorry for the horse having to pull a heavy load up such a steep hill, Sterling climbed down off the wagon and led Duke by halter up the hill. It was a good thing he had tied the lumber on securely. He had forgotten how steep the hill was. And Duke had all he could do to pull the load up.

He started to work on the barn door and by dark that evening he had finished. The pig pen would have to wait for another day. He slept well that night with his mind at ease.

* * * *

One more board and the pig pen was fixed. It was time now, he decided to visit some old friends. There was no way of knowing how long he would be around if the game warden position came through.

When he had enough of visiting and condolences for his parents' passing, he rode his horse through the town to see the many changes since he had left 13 years ago. When he thought about that, those years seemed like another life.

25

Mid-morning Monday, he was cleaning out the barn when young Jason Humphrey came running into the barn yelling for, "Mr. Silvanus!"

Sterling stopped what he was doing to see what the boy wanted. "I'm Sterling Silvanus, what can I do for you?"

"I'm Jason Humphrey and I have a telegram for you. My father at the station house said for me to get this to you, without me dragging my feet," as he handed the telegram to Sterling.

Sterling reached into his pocket and gave Jason 50 cents. "Gee, thanks mister. I've got to go now." And he left the barn and jumped on his bicycle for town.

The telegram was from Chief Warden Don Perry. It was short and to the point:

> *Be in my office Wednesday by noon. State*
> *House Station 41.*

"I guess this is my invitation to talk with Chief Warden Perry."

* * * *

Sterling was full of anxiety for the rest of that day, and he sat out on the porch long after the sun had set, watching the stars.

Tuesday morning finally came and not wanting to miss or be late for this interview with the Chief Warden, he packed a few clothes and then walked to the train terminal. It was only 6 a.m. He boarded the 8 a.m. passenger train to Farmington. He would have to transfer again at Leeds Junction for the Augusta line. He was in Augusta by 4 p.m.

There was a nice hotel not far from the state house. "One night only," he said to the desk clerk.

The next day at 15 minutes before 12 noon, Sterling was escorted into Chief Warden Perry's office. Perry stood and walked around his desk and extended his hand to shake Sterling's.

"Mr. Silvanus, it is a pleasure to meet you."

"Thank you, sir."

"Sit down. Would you like a cup of coffee?"

"Yes please, black."

Chief Perry poured their coffee and then sat down at his desk. "I was reading the article on the front page of the newspaper when I received Representative Daggett's telegram. I don't think there is much more that I need to know about you, Mr. Silvanus. By the way, what nationality is that?"

"Russian."

"Bronze Star and Master Sergeant at eighteen and then Roosevelt's staff and Secret Service. I think you are just who we have been looking for. The article said that President Roosevelt had described you as someone who conducts himself like a gentleman and talks like a gentleman, but when needed, you can and do use your training. That speaks well for you."

They talked socially for more than an hour. "You know Sterling, most of our wardens have been in the military like yourself. We are looking for men with that in their background because of the training and experiences. As a game warden, you'll spend most of your life alone and in the woods. If you get into trouble, there won't be any help you can call on. You'll have to rely on your own training and abilities.

"After everything I have told you, do you still want to be a Maine Game Warden?"

There was no hesitation, "Yes sir."

"Good." Chief Perry swore Sterling in and handed him a badge. "There is a box over there with uniforms, shirts at least. The pants you'll have to provide. There's a wool winter coat, hats, mittens, snowshoes. You'll have to provide your own handgun, but we will issue you a box of ammunition each year. What will you carry for a handgun?"

"A Colt .45."

"Good choice." Perry handed him an envelope and said, "There is a bank form in here to have your pay sent to your bank, a pass card which will give you free passage on any train in the state and anyone that is in your company. The pass is also good for lodging and meals if you have to stay out for extended trips. There are two pairs of handcuffs in the box. Winter boots. You'll have to provide summer footwear. Before leaving for a wilderness trip, send a telegram to this office explaining where and why you are going. Then when you get back, another telegram briefly describing your activities. Then a full written report of your activities. There is also a list of courts and magistrates, Title 12, which covers all the laws you'll be enforcing. Read this and memorize it before you leave on your first assignment. Most of what you'll have to know, you will learn on the job. Nobody, not even me, can tell you what you'll be up against. Some people will hate you because of the badge you carry, while others will respect you.

"Any questions?"

"Yes. What is the pay?"

"Good question. Since 1900 we are now receiving more dedicated funding through the sale of hunting and fishing licenses. The hours and days will be long and starting pay is $150 a month payable the first of each month."

"That seems okay."

"As dedicated funding increases, you'll be paid more."

"Another question. Where will I be?"

"I understand that you now have a house in Strong?"

"Yes."

"You'll have Strong and the towns and territories along the Sandy River and Rangeley Lakes Railroad. There are many farming and lumbering villages or communities that have grown up along the rail lines because of the timber industry."

This was a sigh of relief for Sterling. In fact, this would be excellent.

"The hunting of moose, deer and caribou to feed the lumber camps became illegal in 1880 at the founding of the department. There has never been a warden willing to go into the territory to enforce those changes. Although the news has been well publicized. The law is now 29 years old.

"But first, I have a special detail for you."

"Yes, what is it?"

"Are you familiar with a past warden, Kirby Morgan?"

"No."

"Do you know anything about the Umbagog Lake and Parmachenee Lake areas?"

"No."

"Well, you will. I have received a complaint this summer from Chief Wonnocka. A band of the St. Francis Abenaki Indians. They own the land north of Parmachenee all the way to St. Francis, Canada, and there have been some white trappers on their land. I want you to find your way to Wonnocka's village and stop these white trappers. Then when you have successfully completed that task, then you can return to your new district. How you reach Parmachenee will be up to you. I'm not familiar with that area of the state either. It's big country, and I don't want any problems with Wonnocka or his people.

"How much time will you need to take care of your affairs in Strong before you embark on this detail?"

"Two weeks at least."

"Alright, let's say July 15th, you be on your way to Parmachenee. That gives a little more than two weeks."

"Fair enough."

"You are on payroll starting today though. Before leaving, fill out the payroll banking form and leave it with my secretary."

While Sterling was filling out the bank form, Chief Perry called for a carriage to be brought over to take Sterling to the train station.

* * * *

A porter at the station helped Sterling with his gear and when he produced his pass for the conductor, there was a visible sign of his satisfaction of being a game warden, as he was smiling radiantly.

"Thank you, sir," the conductor said.

On the ride home Sterling had a lot to think about. There had been so much that had happened since leaving President Roosevelt in New York. His entire life had taken a sudden turn.

The Sandy River Lilliput from Farmington pulled to a stop at the Strong terminal a little past midnight. There were four people besides himself getting off. The others would be continuing on for Phillips. There were no porters here at this hour and the night station agent, Frank Dyer, helped Sterling with his gear.

"Could I leave this gear here, Frank? I'll have to walk home. I'll be down before noon with a wagon."

"Sure thing. We'll put them over here in the corner, out of the way. Nobody will bother with it."

"Thanks, Frank."

"Where have you been Sterling, to get home so late?" Frank asked.

"I was in Augusta today and I'm now a Maine Game Warden."

Frank heard the excitement in his voice and saw the expression on his face. "Congratulations, Sterling. Will you be staying here, or will you be shipped out somewhere else?"

"I have another detail to take care of first, and then I'll be back."

"It's good to have you home, Sterling."

There was no moon tonight and sometimes Sterling found it difficult to stay in the road. Half way up Lambert Hill he heard the clicking of teeth and knew he was close to a bear. By the sound of the clicking, he was probably in the ditch of the road. Then there was an awful commotion as the bear shot up the bank and into the pasture. He could hear horses running now. Sterling's heart was racing some and it slowly calmed by the time he reached the top of the first flateau.

At the Randall farm a doe deer blew and raced up the driveway still blowing. Sterling was glad when he reached home. And he had no problem falling asleep. The day had been eventful, to say the least.

* * * *

Before leaving the station, Sterling had some business to take care of in Merrill and Daggett's store. The First National Bank had an office and safe in one corner of the store and Sterling deposited $9,000 and then he talked with Fred Daggett, "What can I do for you today, Sterling?"

"I need a Colt .45 handgun and holster."

"Sure thing. I have two in. One with white pearl grips and one with brown wooden grips."

"I'll take the wooden grip, and a box of cartridges." He had a good knife. "How about a rain slicker? Do you have one?"

"Yes."

He bought a small spool of fish line and a small package of fish hooks, some leather gloves and an expensive pair of leather boots. "And these are guaranteed to be waterproof."

And lastly he bought a green felt crusher brim hat.

"You going on a trip, Sterling?" Fred asked.

"Oh, something like that."

After he had taken care of all the gear, on the living room floor, he walked up to see Mr. Allen. He was sitting on the front porch with a cup of coffee. "Hello, Sterling."

"Hello, Mr. Allen." Sterling told him all about him being a new game warden and how he would be gone from home a lot. "I'd like to offer you a deal, Mr. Allen."

"Go on, tell me about it."

"There is no way I could take care of my livestock. I'll give you the cattle and pig and grazing rights in the back pasture and you can have the hay. So long as I can have one cow to butcher each year, if I need the meat and when you butcher the pig, I would like for you to hang one ham and one side of bacon in the cold storage in the cellar. I'll keep my two horses and I'd like to pasture them with your own and you keep them during the winter. If you want me to pay some for boarding them, how much?"

"I'll take care of your horses for the hay and pasture land."

Mr. Allen thought on that for a minute before answering. "Do I have to butcher the cow too?"

"No, I can handle that."

"Okay, you have a deal."

"I'll be leaving here on July 15th and I have no idea when I'll return."

"What about your chickens?"

"I'm going to make the same deal with young Jimmy Randall."

That evening Sterling walked down to the Randall farm after supper and Jimmy was ecstatic about the idea. "You mean I can have your chickens and eggs too, and I can keep the egg money?"

"Yes Jimmy, but understand that when I'm home, if I need eggs I can have a dozen each month. If I need eggs. And I can have four chickens or roosters a year to eat. Do we have a deal, Jimmy?"

"A deal? Yes sir, Mr. Silvanus. When can I have the chickens?" He was already counting his egg money. "You have some good laying hens too, Mr. Silvanus."

"Why don't you come up in the morning after your chores are done and I'll help you crate them and haul them down here."

"Okay, Mr. Silvanus."

"Are you sure you want to do this, Sterling? You have 15 laying hens and several chicks?"

The next day, July 1st, after Sterling had hauled the chickens down for Jimmy, he put Duke in the barn corral and found the Title 12 book with all the laws he would be enforcing and he spent the rest of the afternoon on the porch reading and memorizing the laws.

After supper he went back out on the porch and finished

reading Title 12. *Two more weeks and I leave.* He made a mental list of everything he would have to do before then. He had already done most of it.

As he sat there in the warm summer air watching the fire flies, he began wondering to the extent of the problems that Wonnocka was having with the white trappers, other than trapping on Abenaki land. Not knowing who he would be after, he decided against advertising his presence as a game warden on his trek to Parmachenee Lake and Wonnocka's village.

He had packed and unpacked his knapsack a hundred times making sure he had the right equipment for the sojourn. And there again he didn't know how long he'd be gone.

He went to bed early on the eve of the 14th, happy that he was comfortable with all of his preparations. He would leave in the morning.

Chapter 3

He was up at day break on the 15th and after cleaning up after breakfast, he loaded his gear into his wagon and rode over to the Allen farm. Mr. Allen had agreed to bring the horse and wagon back and pasture him out with his own horses.

The train left the station on time. Sterling felt for his badge in his pocket. His handgun for now was in his knapsack. He wouldn't put that on until he was in the woods. He had been studying crude maps of the area and decided his best bet would be to go to Upton on the south end of Umbagog Lake. He would have to make three transfers to get to Rumford and from there he'd have to take a stagecoach to Newry Corner where he would trade coaches for Upton.

It was already dark by the time he arrived at the T-House at Newry Corner. Mr. Henderson said, "You can have one of the cabins out back."

Sterling showed him his pass for the lodging, meals and for the stage coach ride the next morning. "Mr. Henderson, this is just between us. I don't want it known that I'm a game warden. Not just yet, okay?"

"Sure enough. You had me fooled."

The next morning Sterling rode on top with the driver, Lewis Avery.

"How far you going, son?"

"To Upton."

"You ain't going fish'n. You got no equipment. What you going to Upton for?

"I'm vacationing. I'm going to hike around these mountains some." That seemed to satisfy Mr. Avery's curiosity.

Along the way, Lewis pointed out points of interest and what family lived at each farm.

"Use to be a saw mill there on top of the falls. Screw Auger it's called. Ice jammed up in the spring of '62 and washed the whole mill off the rocks."

A little further up the road Lewis slowed the coach and said, "Look over there, son. See that big hole in them rocks? That's 'The Jail'. The old timers around said that when someone got drunk and troublesome in Grafton, they would put them in that hole and leave 'em. They were free to climb out, but they usually couldn't do that until they sobered up. I don't think it is used much now."

"It is really beautiful up through here."

"It'll get prettier, a little further up." And indeed it did. Mountains that came right down the road.

"You see that dirt road there on the right?"

"Yeah."

"That's a driveway to Kirby and Rachel Morgan's house."

"He was the game warden, wasn't he?"

"Yeah, that's right. She used to go with him wherever he went. No matter the weather or time of year. They were both in their 60s when he had had enough. Then she died shortly after and the last that anyone ever saw of him was when he took his wife back to her people somewhere beyond Parmachenee Lake. She was Indian. Nobody ever see him after that."

Sterling looked up the road and saw someone coming towards them in another wagon. The other wagon pulled over to the side to let the stage pass by. Lewis slowed and said, "Morning, Joe. He back yet?"

"No, not yet. He will some day, though."

"Have a good day, Joe."

They continued on and Sterling asked, "Who was that, Lewis?"

"Joe Chapman, he's been taking care of Kirby's house ever since Kirby left with his dead wife. Joe is convinced Kirby will be back some day. He goes down every day, even in a storm or during the winter. He's been taking care of Kirby's chickens, too.

"Joe was only a kid when Kirby came into these mountains, and Joe and Kirby developed a real good friendship. Joe used to poach some and Kirby was always playing pranks on him. It's sad really, Joe misses his friend and his playmate. He's convinced Kirby will come home sometime."

"No one knows what happened to Kirby?" Sterling asked.

"Not a clue."

They rode on in silence and then Lewis said, "This is where Joe lives." That's all.

They rode on in silence again for a ways and then Lewis said, "Everybody around here liked Kirby and Rachel. She was so beautiful and she wore a vest made from some animal fur. I only saw her once. After she died and Kirby disappeared there were stories about that she was some kind of legend. I don't know what the legend was."

Sterling noticed some of the homes had been boarded up and asked, "Why are there so many empty houses?"

"When the timber was all cut over in this mountainous valley there wasn't enough work to keep people here, and the weather is too cold to grow cash crops, so people had to move out. Brown Paper Company has bought up each farm and burned many of the buildings. Some of the fields they planted to spruce trees."

As they traveled up across Grafton Flats, Sterling could feel the vibrations of this beautiful area touching his soul. Lewis pulled the team to a stop along side a farm house and said, "Throw that leather pouch there under the seat. This is the post office and that pouch is the mail."

Sterling pulled the pouch out. "Just throw it on the porch."

They proceeded on and came to another farm on top of

an incline and Lewis turned the stage to the right. "This is the Brown Farm. Captain Brown died in April of 1881. He and his wife Ruth founded this town. Ruth still lives here in the summer. During the cold months she goes out to live with a daughter. We're going across Popple Dam, two of the passengers are getting off at the hotel here. We'll only be a minute."

An hour and a half later they were finally at the Lake House Hotel in Upton. "You have a good hike, son, and be careful."

"Thanks for the ride, Mr. Avery."

Sterling climbed down and walked up the steps to the Lake House Hotel. He was met by the owner, Alpheus Ballard. "Can I help you? My name is Alpheus Ballard; I own this hotel."

"Mr. Ballard, I'm Sterling Silvanus and I'd like a room for a few days."

"Certainly, come inside."

"I'd like to take the room on a day to day basis, if I could."

"That won't be any problem at all. If you're hungry I'm sure my wife could fix up a sandwich in the kitchen. Supper will be at 6 p.m."

Sterling had a cup of black coffee with his ham sandwich and then went for a walk. He was looking for an old timer who might help him out on how best to get to Parmachenee Lake.

The old mill was closed but there was an active canoe building shop near the dam. An older man came out from the back working area. He walked with a limp. "Hello there, my name is Enoch Abbott. My grandfather, Enoch, built most of what you see here. Can I help you with something?"

"Yes, is there a place where we can talk?"

"You some kind of government man?"

"No."

"Okay, follow me." They went into his office and closed the door.

"Now what can I do for you?"

"I'm looking for the best way to get to Parmachenee Lake from here."

"You could canoe from here, but that's a lot of extra miles that wouldn't be necessary. You could put a canoe and your gear into a wagon and go out the Magalloway Trail to Wilson's Landing in Magalloway. Follow the Magalloway River up to Aziscohos Dam. There's a portage about a mile below the dam. Pull on the rope and a bell rings at the dam and someone will come down with a wagon to haul your gear up. Then keep canoeing upstream."

"Do you have ready made canoes here?"

"I have one that is supposed to be delivered to Wilson's Landing sometime this week. Are you looking for me to build you one?"

"Yes. How long would it take?"

"How long?"

"Eighteen feet, with seats front and back and two paddles," Sterling replied.

"I have the paddles. The crew just started on one eighteen footer today. Two days."

"That sounds good. Do you want your money now or when the job is done?"

"Why don't you wait until you see the canoe."

* * * *

For the next two days Sterling walked around the town exploring. He even went back up over the hill to the Fred Godwin Store on the corner next to the Abbott House. Sterling found a nice compass there. He had forgotten to get one. This looked like a wilderness trading post. There were many trapping supplies. "Hello there, is there much trapping that goes on around here?"

"During the fall season and winter there are quite a few trappers. I also buy hides. Most of the trappers are local men with time on their hands. We don't get many trappers up here in the winter from down below."

"Do you have any maps of this area and Parmachenee?"

"Yes I do. In fact they were just updated last year by the Farrar Company. Here's what you want, I think."

Sterling looked the map over and it was indeed what he was looking for. He also purchased a green wool jacket.

The canoe was finished at close of the next day and Sterling said, "This is exactly what I was looking for. How much Mr. Abbott?"

"That's $75 for the canoe and $10 for the paddles."

"Could I hire you to take me and my gear to Wilson's Landing?"

"I tell you what. I'm suppose to deliver this other canoe there and return Mr. Wilson's wagon and horse to him. If you will do that, I'll knock $5 off the paddles."

* * * *

After breakfast the next morning both canoes and Sterling's gear was loaded into the wagon and he headed out on the Magalloway Trail for Wilson's Landing. It was Sunday morning and promising to be a nice day.

He hadn't gone but maybe a mile and a half and heard voices off to his left. He decided this was part of his job to investigate. He tied the reins off and started out through the bushes. What he found was unbelievable. Out there in the middle of the woods was a golf course. With no roads leading to it.

When he got back to the wagon, he checked his map. The golf course was just east of Tyler Cove. Scratching his head, he untied the reins and continued on. After crossing the bridge below the Pond in the River he turned to the left. This would be the Carry Road which would go to Sunday Cove and the Magalloway Trail.

He pulled to a stop at Sunday Cove. He wanted to look at the lake. As he got closer, he saw something else that was unusual. A young man was crawling on his stomach towards the mouth of Sunday Brook, with a fish pole. He found a hidey hole from which to watch and see what this fellow was doing.

When this fellow reached the mouth of the brook he took something out of a glass jar and was tying his fish line to it. Then he took a small cedar shingle from his pack and placed whatever he had been tying on the shingle and set it adrift in the water. When the shingle was out there where he wanted it, this fellow gave the line a slight tug and whatever was on the shingle was now swimming on the lake surface. Then a big trout took whatever it was and this fellow backed up into the bushes and landed a four pound brook trout. "Well I'll be," Sterling said quietly to himself.

He had to see what this fellow was using for bait. It appeared all legal. He just needed to settle his curiosity. Sterling was standing behind this fellow before he knew anyone was around. "Good morning, I just had to see what you were using for bait."

"Little woods mice," and he showed Sterling his class jar with two more mice.

"I'm on my way to Wilson's Landing, my name is Sterling Silvanus."

"Hello, I'm Jack Gravlin."

"Well, good luck to you, Jack."

The rest of the trip was uneventful. Mr. Wilson met him at the landing and marveled at his new canoe. He helped Sterling unload his canoe and set it in the water. "Where are you going?"

"I'm exploring around Aziscohos. Looking for Indian artifacts." He seemed to accept that without question.

For the first three hours on the river he had to canoe through a long section of oxbows, like ribbon candy. About three hours later he found where a spring fed stream put into the river and figured this would be a good place to catch a nice fat trout for supper. First though, he found a place to set up camp and got a fire going. Then he tied his fish line and hook onto an alder pole and found a large white grub under the bark of a dead fir tree.

Almost as soon as the grub was in the water a big trout took the bait. One more and he'd have enough for breakfast, too. He wasn't long finding another grub and landed another trout about the same size.

While the fish was broiling over the fire, he pulled his canoe ashore and turned it over and propped one end up to use as a shelter to sleep under. As the fish was cooking, the smell of cooking fish was making him hungry.

The meat was pinkish orange and delicious. He ate everything except for the head and bones. Daylight was waning fast and he decided to get plenty of firewood now. He loved the smell of wood smoke. And it helped to keep the bugs away.

With the fire built up he laid down on his bed and felt very good about what he was doing and happy to be there in a comfortable wildwood bed listening to a loon call on the river.

The next morning after eating the remaining trout, he cleaned up and shaved and put the fire out and loaded his canoe and started up river on his excursion. The sky was dark with a thick layer of clouds and he wasn't looking forward to sleeping out that night. But he didn't have much of a choice either.

Shortly after noon he found the portage point and pulled the rope to ring the bell on the other end. An hour later a man driving a wagon showed. "That'll be $1.50 mister to tote you and all your gear. Payable up front."

Sterling gave him the money and helped to load the canoe. The trail up, that's all it was—a rough trail. After a short distance, he got off and walked behind the wagon.

It was feeling good to stretch his legs. Once they were above the dam the wind had come up. Sterling had not been aware of it on the river. "My name is Taylor Bodreau, what's yours?"

"Excuse me. Sterling Silvanus."

"Well Sterling, it's going to rain soon. The leaves have turned backwards. Yup, going to be a good one too. Unless you have shelter where you're going, I have an extra bedroom in my cabin. Once in a while folks get caught in foul weather. $1.00 for the room and $1.00 for feeding you."

It began to sprinkle and the wind was blowing stronger. This made up Sterling's mind. "Sure, but if we don't get moving we're going to get wet."

Sterling turned his canoe over first, then followed Taylor up the knoll to his cabin. Your room is over there. Been simmering a chicken, cabbage, squash and potato stew all afternoon." Taylor tasted it and said, "Won't be long now."

Sterling hadn't eaten since he had the brook trout for breakfast and the stew was smelling very appetizing.

"How about a drink? All I have is my own whisky."

"I'll have a little."

Taylor poured two glasses and Sterling watched as Taylor drank half of his without stopping. He sipped at his and his eyes began to water and the liquid burned all the way down.

The rain was beating on the roof much harder now and the tree tops were swaying back and forth.

"That stew smells so good, Mr. Bodreau."

"It does, doesn't it?" Then on another note, Taylor inquired, "I didn't see any fishing rods or tackle, so you aren't going to do any fishing. You government man or something?"

"No, I'm not a government man or anything. I'm doing some Indian archeological work. The connection with the Abenaki Indians and migrating caribou." He hoped Taylor would leave it at that. He didn't want to reveal his real purpose for being here or who he was. Everybody who came into this area had to come through here and he surely didn't want Taylor talking.

"Why don't you set the table while I take this off the stove. Dishes in that cupboard there," and he pointed with his spoon.

Taylor took some second-hand biscuits out of the oven that had been warming and then filled two bowls with stew. "No butter for the biscuits."

Sterling took a spoonful and was surprised with the taste. But he didn't want to hurt Taylor's feelings. Taylor ate spoon after spoonful, and then refilled his bowl. "Come on Sterling, it ain't that bad. A little gamey, that's all. Yes sir, this is pretty good chicken hawk stew."

Sterling coughed and almost choked. "Taylor, there aren't really any chicken hawks."

"Well he killed two of my good laying hens. And he was a hawk alright. Big fella, too. Rusty colored tail feathers."

"That sounds like a Red Tail Hawk."

"Well maybe, but he sure liked them chickens. Come on boy, eat up. It ain't that bad. A little gamey that's all. Least wise it's better'n that big owl I shot and ate last year. That one was so gamey, I like choked on the broth. Couldn't chew the meat none. I always says they come after my chickens, they're taking food right out of my mouth. So I, if I can, shoot them and eat 'em. Only have to do it about once a year."

"There was this one time, it was in the spring and I looked out the window and this yearling moose had his head over the chicken fencing and was smelling of them chickens. I get my shotgun out. He would have made some pretty good eating, too. Just before I pulled the trigger I noticed movement on the deadwater and I turned to see what it was and wouldn't you know it, it was that game warden Kirby Morgan. I hid my shotgun and scared the moose off then. Yeah, ole Kirby almost had me that time. He'd taken me for sure for shooting a moose when it ain't in season."

It was still raining when they went to bed, but the wind had stopped blowing.

For breakfast the next morning there was biscuits, eggs and black coffee. "Deadwater is full behind the dam. I'll have to pull a board or two and drop the water before it washes out around the ends."

"Do you need any help with that?" Sterling asked.

"I'll be fine. Ain't no job at all."

"Okay, I'll be on my way. And thanks for the food and lodging."

"When you coming back this way?"

"Not sure. Maybe I won't."

Sterling shoved off and waved goodbye with his paddle. It was a long haul up the length of Aziscohos Deadwater. The water had backed up into the tall weed grass on both shores. When he finally came to the end of the deadwater, according to his map he had to go up the right hand branch, and Parmachenee Lake was another two miles from Aziscohos.

The rain and wind had cooled the air and blew the humidity out. In fact, it was a bit cool on the shady river. Sterling slipped on a long sleeved green shirt. About half way up the river Sterling found a spring freshet and decided a broiled brooktrout would be good.

It didn't take him long to catch one corker of a trout. He built a small fire and put the trout on a spicket to cook. While the fish was cooking, he laid back on some moss and took a nap.

When he awoke, the fish was cooked and he ate his fill. The sun was overhead and any sports fishermen at the sporting camps on the upper lake, all should be inside and eating. This would be an ideal time to quietly canoe past the camps and on up the inlet. He thought it strange how the cabins were all on the islands. He could hear voices from within and there was no one outside to see him pass by.

He knew that he must be nearing the Abenaki village, so he stopped and pinned his badge to the pocket of his inside shirt but left the long sleeve shirt on. He also strapped on his gun belt. He continued on, paddling slowly and looking at each feeder stream, memorizing how each looked and where they were. He found many that he supposed would lead to excellent beaver trapping. He saw beaver, otter and mink on the stream banks and one lone bear swim across the stream just in front of the canoe. There was one narrow feeder stream on the left almost blocked completely with alders. The water was colder in this narrow stream and was probably good fishing. Not wanting to take the time today to explore it, he moved on. But when he had a chance he would come back to it.

The main stream was beginning to narrow in places and he could smell smoke in the air. Maybe he was getting close to the village. Or those who were illegally trapping on Abenaki territory. He slowed his canoe so not to make any noise and he was careful not to hit the gunnel.

As he eased his canoe around the last bend, Wonnocka was standing near the stream and he watched as the canoe slowly made an appearance around the bend in the stream. Wonnocka stood motionless even after the canoe and Sterling were now in midstream.

Sterling had seen Wonnocka and had turned the canoe in his direction. Still Wonnocka stood motionless. He thought he was seeing a ghost. He knew Kirby had died a few years back. But this stranger in the canoe reminded him so much of Kirby. Then Wonnocka saw the badge pinned to the inside shirt, and he understood then that this stranger was here because of the illegal activities of the white trappers. His voice had been heard. He beckoned for this stranger to come ashore. Sterling eased the bow of the canoe to shore and while Wonnocka held it steady he climbed out and then pulled it up on shore. He noticed there were many other canoes there, all turned over.

Sterling stood in front of Wonnocka. "I, Wonnocka, Chief of my village," and he waved his hand to indicate all the wikitups.

"I am Sterling Silvanus, Maine Game Warden." Sterling was surprised that Wonnocka was speaking English.

"Good, you come before trouble gets bad. Come, we eat. You had long journey."

As Sterling followed Wonnocka, the other villagers ran back to their own wikitups and when they all were near the cooking fires Sterling realized they all were wearing a green felt hat like his. He started laughing and removed his hat and held it in his hand. There was one beautiful woman who did not have a hat.

"Kirby Morgan and wife Rachel brought hats for all the people." That answered that question.

"Food all ready; we eat now." A woman, probably Wonnocka's wife, handed him a wooden bowl with food. Other women were handing their husbands bowls filled with food. And then the children were fed.

This beautiful woman handed a bowl of food to Sterling. "Thank you, ma'am."

"You are welcomed."

This surprised him. She walked over and got a bowl for herself. The bowl contained smoked fish, probably brooktrout, cooked mushrooms, onions and squash. There were no utensils, everyone was using their hands. So Sterling did also. The food was delicious. Particularly the smoked fish.

Everybody was watching Sterling as he ate. He hadn't realized he was this hungry. One thing for sure, this meal was by far better than Taylor's chicken hawk stew. Sterling saw that when all the men had finished eating, the same woman picked up their bowl. Sterling walked over and handed his to the beautiful woman. She smiled and said, "Thank you."

"You're welcomed."

Wonnocka put his hand on Sterling's shoulder to get his attention and said, "Come with me, Sterling Silvanus. We must talk in my wikitup."

Wonnocka's wikitup was on a high knoll that looked over the others. And it was also larger. They went inside and Wonnocka motioned for Sterling to sit.

Wonnocka brought out a pipe and filled it with tobacco and when it was going, he took a long puff and exhaled the smoke and passed the pipe to Sterling. He did the same. They passed the pipe back and forth until the tobacco was gone. Then Wonnocka said, "It is good that you have come. I was afraid my words fell on deaf ears and no one would come. If I let my young braves handle this, there would be trouble with the whites. I do not want trouble. I want my people to live in peace." Sterling noticed that Wonnocka's English was better now that they were alone.

"Wonnocka, why don't you tell me what has been happening on your land."

"My sons, Moskuos and Noison, last season were scouting for moose for winter food along other branch to the west of Magalloway Stream. They found remains where beaver and other animals had been skun. They also found dead moose and much of the moose was wasted. White man is not to be on our land trapping and hunting."

"Did your sons ever see who was trapping or who shot the moose?"

"No, only find the remains. No Indian people would leave so much."

"Do your sons have any idea how they came into your land?"

"No. Don't think they come through Parmachenee. They may come 'round Rump Mountain. We used to have a trail through there."

"I would like your sons to take me where they found the remains of the fur animals and where the moose was killed and where this trail is at Rump Mountain."

"Moskuos will take you tomorrow. Now is time to sleep. Come, follow me."

Sterling followed Wonnocka to an empty wikitup close to his own. "This will be yours to come or go as you work."

* * * *

The next morning Sterling and Moskuos set out in Sterling's canoe. Since Sterling didn't know where to go, Moskuos sat in the stern to guide the canoe. As they progressed, Sterling was memorizing land marks and occasionally checked their course with his compass. They stayed to the main channel until they came to the west branch of the Magalloway River.

At noon, the sun over head, they came to a small pond that set off the river and Moskuos turned the canoe into the pond. "Rump Pond," he said. He guided the canoe to the west shore and they got out and pulled the canoe on shore.

"This where found animal remains last year." Sterling looked around and found where they had had a fire and behind that in the fir thicket was a crudely made lean-to, the boughs now all rust colored.

"Trail here," Moskuos said and pointed.

"Let's follow it and see where it goes." It had been well used in the past but now not so much. This was probably how the Abenakis traveled back and forth from the Connecticut and Androscoggin River valleys. But since the influx of the white settlers, this trail had probably been abandoned.

They had not traveled far when Moskuos found where he and his brother had found the moose carcass. There were only a few rib bones left now. They continued following the Rump Mountain Trail and Moskuos found a cubby that would have been used for trapping, maybe a bobcat or lynx. And Sterling found a cubby also. He knew he was on the right track. *But when would they return again?* "Moskuos, do you know how many white men were here last year?"

"Two, maybe another. I didn't see."

They followed the Rump Trail all the way to the New Hampshire State Line. The border had recently been painted red. Sterling had seen enough to start and put things together. For now they would return to the village, but he knew he would have to make several more trips back to Rump Mountain before he fully understood the terrain and the trapper's routine. They weren't long hiking back to the canoe.

* * * *

Again that evening as the villagers gathered to eat, this same beautiful woman handed Sterling a bowl of food. This time her gaze at Sterling lasted a little longer as he looked in her eyes. She smiled and Sterling said, "Thank you."

"You're welcome." Then she filled a bowl for herself. There was little conversation while they ate. When Sterling had finished eating this beautiful woman came over to take away his bowl. When she looked at him he asked, "What is your name?"

"I am called Wynola Paul, which means gracious one." She took his bowl and left.

Wonnocka put his hand on Sterling's shoulder and said, "Come, we smoke the pipe and talk."

When there was nothing but ashes left in the pipe bowl, Monnocka said, "Tell about what you found today."

"Moskuos and I found a trail…"

Wonnocka interrupted, "Yes, the Rump Trail. We in earlier days—passed now—used to use this trail. Not so much now."

"We followed the Rump Trail to the New Hampshire State Line. I think the trappers are coming through that trail from the Connecticut River Valley. Either from Pittsburg, New Hampshire or coming down from Canada. It will take me many visits to Rump Mountain to see everything and understand their routine."

Wonnocka was silent then, thinking about how to say what was in his head. Sterling knew there was something Wonnocka wanted to say, so he waited patiently for him to continue.

"It is a great honor to have you here at our village."

"Thank you."

Wonnocka saw the confusion on Sterling's face and continued. "I have known about you for many years now. That Apache boy, whose life you saved."

Now Sterling was astonished to learn Wonnocka had known about that. "Yes, I have known that boy you saved; his father was Apache Chief. You did him a great honor when you bandaged his wounds and instead of taking him away from his people, you set him free. We have runners, as does all the tribes in all this country, and each brings news to each tribe and each tribe will then send out runners to tell others. I have now sent out runners to St. Francis and the Mohawk country to tell them you are here. You have brought great honor to our people. You can travel all across this country to all the tribes and you will be honored."

"Thank you, Wonnocka. I am honored to be here with your people. The beautiful woman, Wonnocka, that gives me food, does she have a man? I do not see her with any man and she gives food, as does your wife."

"Wynola has no man. She came here from St. Francis to

49

teach our women about your ways—keeping the body good. She is a medicine woman. She will be leaving before the leaves turn color. She is a good woman."

During the day while he was away, someone had brought fresh fir boughs for his bed. And his wikitup had a fresh aroma. As he laid on his bed thinking about what he had seen that day, he realized the rest of the village was quiet. But he lay awake with too many thoughts in his head. He got up to sit by the fire and noticed Wynola was already there. "Hello, Wynola." He sat on the log beside her.

"Hello, Sterling. What are you doing still up? I would have thought you would have had enough exercise today so you would be sleepy."

"Yeah, me too. But there are too many things going through my head. What are you doing still up?"

"I wasn't sleepy and it is such a beautiful night."

"Excuse me for prying, but your English is very good."

"Well, it should be, I attended college in Quebec and we had to learn English. I already knew French."

"What did you study in college?"

"I'm a nurse now."

"Okay, that explains what Wonnocka said about you being a medicine woman.

"You are not of this tribe? Wonnocka's people?"

"No, I am an Abenaki, the same as these people, but I am a St. Francis Abenaki. I came here to help teach these people how to better take care of themselves. I'll leave probably in the middle of September or sooner.

"What about you, Sterling Silvanus? Where will you go when your job here is finished?"

"I will go back to my home in Strong and work in North Franklin County."

Sterling put another piece of wood on the fire and watched the fiery cinders float up in the darkened sky and burn out.

"Are you married, Sterling?"

"No. Wonnocka has said you do not have a man?" More question than statement.

"No, I don't." She stood up and grasped Sterling's hand and he stood also. "Come, let's walk by the river."

There was a gentle breeze coming off the water which helped to ward off the biting insects. "These people are very happy here. They have lived here many years without being heckled by other roving bands or harried by the white settlers and they, so far, have not been affected by the plagues that have killed so many. You will stop these illegal trappers, but behind them, there'll be others. Maybe not trappers. They may only be inquisitive explorers who will tell friends who will tell others until more people from the outside will come here. And when that happens, and it will, Wonnocka's only refuge will be in St. Francis. Wonnocka knows this and he worries about the future of these people every day."

They sat by the river for a long time into the night, talking about many things. And neither one wanting the night to end. Finally, it was Sterling who stood and said, "Come, it is time we too get some sleep." And they walked back to the fire and said goodnight.

* * * *

While Sterling was shaving the next morning a throng of young children had gathered to watch. They were amazed when Sterling lathered a brush with soap and then put the soap on his face. They had never seen anything like this before. Sterling saw the throng of children in his mirror and turned around and smiled. Some took off running while two little girls and one little boy, so puzzled, they stayed to watch.

When Sterling started scraping the soap off his face the children could not understand why put the soap on and then take it off. But when Sterling had finished, he took one little girl's hand and rubbed his face with it, so the little girl could feel how smooth his face was now. Then the other two wanted to feel his face also. Then all three ran off laughing.

Wynola was watching and she felt a gladness in her heart.

When Wynola came to retrieve Sterling's bowl he said, "What I would give for a cup of black coffee."

"Sorry no coffee, but I can fix you a cup of hot tamarack tea."

"Thanks, but no."

Sterling was alone today. Scouting where the most beaver colonies were and looking for signs of last year's trapping. He was checking out everything from the intersection of the east and west branch towards the Rump Mountain Trail. The afternoon was getting late and he had one more spot he wanted to check out on the east branch where the alder strewn stream put in.

He eased his canoe through the alders to a small pond. Brooktrout were breaking the surface for a hatch of bugs on the water. Before leaving the pond, Sterling wanted to catch a few trout to take back to the village to help with the food supply. He found a natural sandy cove to beach his canoe and walk around to explore. He left the canoe in the water, but tied it off. When he turned around, he saw a wikitup that had not been used for a few years. Mold was growing along the bottom and the fireplace stones were cleaned of soot and ash. But he noticed some bones lying next to a tall pine tree. He knelt down to examine them and realized they were human bones. And not just one person. There were two complete skeletons. And it looked liked their hands were clasped together.

"This must be a sacred burial ground or something. I better leave and not disturb anything." He pushed off in his canoe and back through the alder bushes. He decided to fish at the mouth of the little stream. He wasn't long before he had six nice brook trout, all weighing between three and four pounds. "This will make a good contribution."

That night after eating, Sterling walked off to stand in front of Wonnocka and said, "Let's smoke the pipe. I need to talk."

Since it was Sterling who wanted to talk, he filled the pipe with tobacco and when it was going, he took the first puff and handed it to Wonnocka. When the tobacco was gone Sterling said, "I saw something today, Wonnocka, that has nothing to do with my being here. I think I, by accident, stumbled into a sacred burial ground." And he told Wonnocka about what he had seen.

Wonnocka sat in silence for several minutes before he answered. He was trying to find the correct words. Tears filled his eyes and this confused Sterling. Wonnocka had not known about the little hideaway pond where Kirby and Rachel made their camp.

"It was years ago that I last saw my friend and brother Kirby Morgan. His wife Rachel had died and he brought her back here so her spirit could be free forever. I never knew where he took her. This is the way of our people. But I knew from the sadness in his eyes that I would never see my friend again. And I never knew what happened to him.

"You say there were two skeletons and they were holding hands?"

"Yes, sitting under a pine tree. It is a beautiful place."

"I can not say enough about the goodness of Kirby and Rachel. I do not think one could live without the other. That morning when Kirby paddled his canoe here and Rachel was sitting up in the bow, I knew Kirby's spirit had already left his body and he was with Rachel. He left his body with Rachel's; he had no more need for it, as he was already with her." There were still tears in his eyes. "You make me think of Kirby often. I am glad to know finally what became of Kirby."

"Thank you, Wonnocka, for sharing Kirby's story with me."

* * * *

Some of the young men and Wynola took a trip to St. Francis for supplies and the latest news. Wynola wanted some special medicine only she could get.

Sterling went back to Rump Mountain every day and he had

found more cubby sets and old snares. And close to the New Hampshire border south of the trail, he found a makeshift camp and knew it must belong to the illegal trappers. He poked around the camp and out back he found a bone pile and then he knew the poachers were using this camp.

A little more snooping and he found a bubbling spring and close to that a wooden box, set in the cool ground for cold storage for food. He had everything drawn out on a sheet of paper.

He went to Rump Pond, the outlet put into the west branch. Here he made a place to conceal his canoe and he mapped out a trail from the pond to Rump Mountain. From now on he would not use the Rump Trail so he would not leave any evidence of his presence. He knew it would still be a while before the poachers arrived, as it was still too warm.

Each day when he returned to the village in late afternoon he would bring back some brook trout. He was beginning to enjoy life here with the people, but he also understood he was here for a purpose and then he would have to move on.

Four days after the small group had traveled to St. Francis, the group returned. Each was carrying a pack on their back, even Wynola. she carried some tobacco for Wonnocka, medicine and some real coffee for Sterling. The others carried staples for the winter. Salt was one of the staples, to preserve food stores.

That evening along with his food bowl, Wynola gave Sterling a cup of coffee. Hot and black. He smiled and said, "Thank you."

She smiled back, enjoying, knowing he had appreciated the gift. "You are welcomed." They both laughed. Wonnocka was observing those two and he knew they would make a good mate for each other. Then maybe Sterling would stay. He had adapted so well to living there.

Then it started to rain. Small hail first and then it poured. There were flashes of lightening way to the east but the thunder was still loud. It rained all that night and the next day. When it stopped, blue sky and sunshine returned and the air was cool and clear.

One day in early September while Sterling was at Rump

Mountain, Wynola said to Wonnocka, "Wonnocka, I need to talk with you."

He led the way to his wikitup and held the flap while Wynola entered. They sat down and Wynola said, "Wonnocka, I must leave now."

"This is sad news. Why now?"

"I have seen a vision. I must go to the land where my great-grandfather once lived."

This was unheard of. Woman openly saying they had had a vision. "Men have visions to help guide them and their people, not women."

"I understand this, Wonnocka. But I still had this vision, telling me to go. It will be a long journey."

"What does this vision say why you are to travel to where your great-grandfather once lived?"

"I did not see this. Only that I must go. Maybe once I am there I will know."

"Tell me the name of this great-grandfather."

"Pierre Paul."

"I know of this name. My father Falling Bear said Pierre Paul and Matelok were great friends."

"I understand now. My father said Pierre Paul was a good man."

Wonnocka stood and Wynola stood also thinking their talk was over. "Sit, Wynola. There is something that I must give to you before you leave."

He came back and resumed sitting and unfolded a beautiful fur. He held it out to Wynola and she said, "This is so beautiful. It is too much for a gift, Wonnocka."

"Hear me out, Wynola," he said sternly. "This is the wolverine fur that *Carcajou*, the Great Peacemaker, wore. His daughter, my father Falling Bear brought to our people when she was only little girl. She lived with our people and when she left, my father gave this fur to her to wear when she traveled, to protect her. When Rachel left her body behind and it died, her husband Kirby brought this fur back and said I would know what to do with it. I know now what I must do. Stand."

Wynola did and Wonnocka put the wolverine fur over her shoulders. "I will always wear this, Wonnocka, when I travel. I have heard stories about *Carcajou*, the Great Peacemaker."

"Sit and I will tell you everything my father has told me."

When Wonnocka had finished talking, there were tears in Wynola's eyes. "Thank you Wonnocka for sharing that story with me. Now I must go."

"What about Sterling Silvanus, he will miss you. Maybe you should stay and tell him yourself."

"If I stay, Wonnocka, I would never leave. And leave I must."

"I know you had a vision."

When Wynola left Wonnocka's wikitup wearing the fur vest of wolverine, everybody stopped what they were doing to look. Many thought that Rachel had come back.

* * * *

When Sterling returned that day and Wonnocka told him Wynola had left, he saw the sadness in Sterling's face. That night one of the small girls that watched him shave gave Sterling his food. "Thank you." She only smiled.

The days were long for Sterling. He really missed Wynola, especially in the evening when they could talk. Then one day while he was at Rump Mountain he had found food stores that had been left and some trapping and skinning tools.

That night back at the village and after they had eaten Sterling said, "Wonnocka, the trappers are back. I found where they have brought in food supplies and trapping gear. It looks like they left for another trip and will probably be back tomorrow or the next day. When I leave in the morning, I won't be back until I have caught them."

"Moskuos go with you to help."

"No, Wonnocka. Your people should stay out of this. I'll be

okay." Wonnocka had no doubt that Sterling was very capable of taking care of himself.

As he laid down to sleep he tried not to think about Wynola. Instead he started to plan how to catch the poachers. He was soon asleep.

The next morning after eating, Sterling was about to ask Wonnocka for food to take with him when his wife Azeban (Little Raccoon) handed Sterling a leather pouch of food. She nodded towards the food and said, "Take with you. Food."

"Thank you, Azeban," she smiled and left.

"You come back before you leave?"

"Yes, Wonnocka."

Sterling climbed into his canoe and Wonnocka pushed him out into the river. He stood there watching as Sterling disappeared around the bend and wondering what it was that drove him to do it alone.

Sterling left his canoe beached in the usual spot and proceeded towards the makeshift camp. Always listening for a noise that shouldn't be there. When he was on the Rump Trail he was careful not to leave any tracks and always watchful for new tracks. Instead of following the poachers trail to their camp, Sterling circled low and came in behind it. The camp was in view and there was no activity yet. He waited to make sure. When he was satisfied they had not returned, he checked the camp and the food supplies. Nothing had changed. He found a better place to hide and where he could watch the camp.

He was hungry so he opened the food pouch Azeban had given him and he snacked on dried smoked fish, some nuts and dried cranberries. He waited all day and then finally about an hour before sunset, two men arrived carrying more supplies. One had a double-barrel shotgun and the other a Winchester rifle, and both had handguns that looked like small caliber.

They busied themselves with storing the additional supplies and they were speaking English, so they probably were not Canadians. The tallest of the two, still not of Sterling's height, was called Fletcher and the other shorter, heavyset fellow, Sterling thought he had heard him called Isaac.

"That's a long hike in here, Isaac. I don't know how many more years I can keep doing this."

"Well, we made more than a year's wage from the hides we took out of here last year and the price of fur is better this year than it has ever been. I'll keep coming back as long as my legs will allow me."

"I just hope those damned Indians don't catch us," Fletcher added.

"Why should they? There ain't a damned soul who knows we're in here," Isaac said.

Shortly after the sun had gone and the forest was black, the light went out inside the camp.

Sterling pulled his wool blanket from his pack and laid back, and he, too, like those inside, was soon asleep.

The next morning after some coffee Fletcher said, "We'd better go get us some meat and take care of it before we start trapping. You want moose or deer?" he asked jokingly.

"I'd like a nice black cow. The meat last year from the bull was too tough."

Fletcher had his shotgun and Isaac was carrying his Winchester and when they left camp they headed down hill, or north towards the finger brooks.

All Sterling had to do now was be patient and wait for the shot. He ate more of his food until he was full, and then he checked the camp to see if there might be some hot coffee left. There was and he helped himself.

Satisfied, he went back to wait. And just like he had figured, about 8 a.m. he checked his pocket watch, there was one rifle shot and not a shotgun report. His first instinct was to go down and catch them on the spot. But he decided to wait and let them bring the moose meat to the camp.

Apparently these two knew what they were doing, because Sterling didn't have long to wait when he heard them coming up the hill towards camp. They each were carrying a hindquarter of the moose strapped to backboards that were on their backs. "This has got to be too good," he said to himself. With the weight on their backs, they surely won't have anything left in them for a fight.

He removed the shirt-jacket so his uniform and badge would be visible. Just as they were about to remove their backboards, Sterling stepped out and said, "Hold it right there and don't remove those packs."

"Just who in hell are you?" Fletcher asked.

"My name is Sterling Silvanus and I am a Maine Game Warden and you both are under arrest for killing a moose on Indian Territory."

"We didn't know this here land belonged to the Indians," Isaac said.

"Well, Isaac, that's not what you said yesterday."

The game was over then. They realized Sterling had been there and had heard everything they had said. "Now what, Warden?" Fletcher asked.

"Now we walk back to my canoe. But first you give me your shotgun and rifle."

When Isaac passed him his rifle, Sterling took one look at it and said, "Hum, .45-70, nice caliber. Probably a good caliber for moose."

"Where are you going to take us?" Isaac asked.

"The nearest lock up is in Rumford and that's a two or three day trip. Now let's get moving."

It was down hill most of the way, then it leveled off about 400 feet before the pond. The two were wanting to stop and rest, but Sterling figured it would be best to keep them moving and tired. But their progress was slower.

When they finally reached the pond, Sterling uncovered the canoe and pushed it into the water and told Fletcher to get in first and up at the bow. Then Isaac in the middle and he laid the firearms on the bottom between his feet. "Can we take these off now, Warden?" Isaac asked.

"No. As long as the meat is on your backs you probably won't try to do something stupid, and I won't have to break this fine paddle over your heads. So just sit and enjoy the trip." They were silent then.

The canoe was loaded heavy and sitting low in the water. He was glad it was an eighteen footer and not smaller.

Sometime around 2 p.m., Sterling guided the canoe around the last bend before the village. "What the hell are you doing? I thought you were taking us to Rumford," Fletcher said.

"What's the problem, Fletcher? You afraid to face these people?"

People were shouting excitedly and soon Wonnocka was walking towards the river. He steadied the canoe while all three got out. "Chief Wonnocka, this is Fletcher and Isaac and they are the poachers who have been hunting and trapping on your land."

"You leave them here, no?"

"No, Wonnocka. I have to take them to jail in Rumford. It is too late to leave today. I would like to stay here tonight and leave in the morning."

"Why they still carry moose on backs?"

"Less trouble that way," and Wonnocka nodded his head that he understood.

"We take meat now and prepare feast." He signaled some young men to take the meat and then Sterling put Fletcher and Isaac in handcuffs and took them up near the fire and had them sit down. They looked worried and uncomfortable.

Sterling took the firearms to Wonnocka's wikitup and said, "Here, Wonnocka, I'll leave these for you. There is also some ammunition for each. I need to talk with Moskuos also."

"You sit down and I'll get Moskuos."

When they were back Sterling said, "Moskuos, do you remember where the Rump Trail went along the north side of the mountain?"

"I know this trail."

"Their camp was off to the right. I broke some branches

60

where you will need to leave the Rump Trail. There are many trapping supplies and some food supplies. All this belongs to your people now. They had not had time to do any trapping. The moose carcass is down near the finger brooks. If I were you, I would burn the camp."

"I will take two with me and do this thing. It is good. It is good that you have them."

It was dark before the moose meat was cooked and Fletcher and Isaac were given food first. "Why, Warden? Why do they feed us first?"

"This is to honor the one who brought food for these people. You are being honored," Sterling said.

"Honored, in spite of what we did? I do not understand," Fletcher said.

"I'm afraid there are many whites who do not understand their ways."

When the feasting was over they were handcuffed again, Isaac asked, "Aren't you afraid we might run off?"

They were only handcuffed and not restrained. "Well you could, but I wouldn't recommend you do anything but lay right here all night. Because if you were to run off, these people would hunt you down before you could leave their land and they probably would kill you.

"Have a good night, gentlemen."

Sterling went to his wikitup and laid down on his sleeping mat. He laid on his back not really wanting to sleep. He kept thinking of Wynola and wishing she was still there. He would always remember her.

* * * *

The next morning, early, after they had had something to eat, Sterling said, "We must leave now, Wonnocka. I have a long journey ahead of me."

"I can send two men to go with you."

"Thanks, Wonnocka, but you should keep your people out of this. I think it would be best.

"I have enjoyed my stay, Wonnocka. I really hate to leave, but I must."

"I understand, Sterling Silvanus. Do not forget us."

"I will always remember you. And thank you."

"I thank you, Sterling, for all my people."

Sterling helped the two handcuffed poachers into the canoe and then he seated himself and Wonnocka pushed the canoe out into the river. He stood there watching until they were out of sight. He was also thinking that if the white settlers were like Kirby and Sterling maybe it was time to join their way of life. He didn't know, but he was afraid of losing his way of life.

* * * *

He canoed by the sporting camps on Parmachenee and no one paid them any attention. The wind was at their back and they made fast time down Aziscohos Deadwater to the dam. Taylor was fishing off his wharf and he didn't recognize Sterling at first. "Taylor, any more of that chicken hawk stew left?"

Taylor knew who he was now and he recognized the uniform and badge. "Well I'll be to go to hell! You're a game warden. No chicken hawk stew," he began to laugh, "but I have some fish head soup."

"Are you going to charge me to feed all of us?"

"Not if you forget about that chicken hawk stew."

"Done," Sterling replied.

When Taylor saw that Fletcher and Isaac were in handcuffs, he turned to look at Sterling with a new sense of respect. "I see the new warden is in town."

After they had eaten, Taylor hauled the canoe down the portage to the river. Sterling and his two prisoners walked behind the wagon. "I don't know why you wouldn't spend the night. Now you'll have to camp in the woods somewhere."

Sterling looked at his prisoners and then back at Taylor. Taylor nodded his head that he understood. "Good luck to you, young fella."

Sterling paddled until about an hour before sunset. He put ashore and while Fletcher and Isaac sat in the canoe, he started a fire and brought in enough firewood to last the night. They ate the last of the food Azeban had given him. "This will have to do until we are out of here."

The next day Sterling had to paddle against a headwind. It was blowing terribly hard, and it made it more tiresome, and it was late in the afternoon when they arrived at Wilson's Landing.

Captain Wilson had seen them coming downriver and had walked down to see what was about. And he was surprised when he recognized Sterling, but in a warden's uniform. "Well I'll be."

"What have you here, Sterling?" he inquired.

"They were hunting and trapping on Indian land."

"Where you going with them?"

"To Rumford. Is that a stage I see over there?"

"Yes, it is. The driver, Bill, said he had to be back in Upton tonight and leave first thing in the morning."

Sterling talked with Bill and he didn't have any passengers. "Only have to pick up the mail in Upton and then in Grafton."

"What about your canoe, Sterling? You can't take that on the stage," Captain Wilson asked.

"That does present a problem. I was only here for this detail."

"I've been needing another canoe. I'll pay you what it cost you new and the paddles."

Fletcher and Isaac were still in handcuffs, so Sterling had to help them climb into the stage. And since they were the only passengers, Sterling rode on top with Bill.

* * * *

A night's rest with hot food and hot coffee with breakfast, Sterling was feeling like a new man. Already everybody in

63

Upton and at Wilson's Landing were talking about the new game warden and how he had fooled everybody earlier.

The stage only stopped long enough in Grafton to pick up the mail. They had to make one more stop at Kilgore Station in Newry to change teams and then they were on the road again. They arrived at the T-House at Newry Corner at noon. The stage continued towards Bethel, and Sterling and his two prisoners had a light lunch while they waited for the stage from Bethel to Rumford. Before sunset, everybody in the area had heard the story of the new game warden and his two prisoners in handcuffs.

When they arrived at the county jail in Rumford, they were all exhausted from the trip from Rump Mountain. Sterling sent a brief telegram to Chief Perry in Augusta telling him the task had been completed and he was now on his way home and would soon forward a complete detailed report.

Fletcher and Isaac weren't liking it much, shut up in a steel cage, and they had no money to make bail and would have to stay in jail until they could see the judge. Sterling stopped to see them before leaving. "Let me give you some advice. Stay off Indian land. And tell that to your friends, if you have any."

It was too late to think about trying to get home, so he slept in a back room at the county jail and the next morning he boarded a train for Strong. Of course, he would have to change trains twice.

At the Strong station, Sterling shouldered his now heavy pack and started walking home. But he stopped first at the post office for his mail. He stopped at the Depot Street intersection with Main Street and took a long look at the town. He didn't know why he had never thought of it before, or why he was thinking it now. But the stores and buildings along Main Street looked exactly like a western town, with wooden sidewalks and all.

He left his pack on the kitchen floor, took off his boots, had a cool drink of water and then sat out on his porch for a long time. He would write out a report tomorrow. All he wanted now was to rest and think of Wynola, who he was probably never going to see again.

Chapter 4

Sterling wrote a very thorough report about the detail at Parmachenee. It was now September 15th, and it had taken him two and half months to complete. It would have been longer if he had waited for them to trap.

In his mail was a detailed synopsis of his next assignment. This would be in his own district, but in country he was not at all familiar with. He unfolded the letter and began to read:

Sterling.

Have received information that illegal hides and sometimes moose and or caribou meat is being shipped out of Barnjum Station to someone in Portland. The complainant who wishes to remain anonymous said most of the hides looked like summer fur. The lack of any guard hair. Also beaver and large cats had been shot. Not sure who is doing the shipping, or who is receiving the hides and meat. Frank Barnjum is an honorable man. I don't believe he is involved. He has too much to lose. Not sure about his men. So go in carefully, like you said you were going to at Parmachenee. Take care of this before moving on throughout your district. Remember, no one at any of the lumbering communities have ever seen a game warden in those areas. All lumber contractors have

*been sent a copy of the laws regarding using moose,
deer and caribou meat to feed the crews. So proceed
accordingly. Be careful out there, Sterling.*

Chief Warden Don Perry

Sterling reread the letter again. He decided he would take a few days to rest before starting out on another long task. He checked the wood in the shed to make sure there would be enough for winter. Then he made a mental note to make sure he didn't leave anything to freeze when he left, since he had no idea how long he would be. There was a pile of tree-length firewood behind the barn and for exercise and to use up some anxiety he began working on it, sawing it into stovewood lengths. He split and piled it against the barn wall and under the eaves.

When he wasn't working on the firewood, he put together some dried food to take with him and some warmer clothes for this trip. His pack was heavy, but in the army he had had to carry heavier packs. He had about everything he thought he would need. He wanted to take his father's favorite rifle, a Winchester .38-55, but decided against it. He would be carrying enough weight as it was without the rifle.

A week later on September 22, Sterling sent a telegram to the Chief Warden that he was leaving for Barnjum that day.

"Where you off to this time, Sterling?" Pansy Newell asked.

"Train to Barnjum," Sterling replied. "And Pansy, if possible, I'd like to ride up front with the engineer."

"That's okay with me, Sterling, but you'd better ask Dana Aldrich. He'll be the engineer all the way to Skunk Brook Camp today. He's having coffee at Daggett's Store right now."

"I'll wait until he is in the yard. Thanks Pansy."

Pansy went back to work, and wondering about Sterling's request. He was up to something. *What?*

"I'm alone today Sterling. You can ride up here as long as you don't mind setting the tracks for me at Perham Junction."

Sterling jumped at the chance. He had always been fascinated with the steam engines. "Dana, I've ridden on bigger engines than this Lilliput engine; I don't understand why the railroad isn't using the standard rails so they could use the bigger engines."

"Matter of economics really. It was easier, faster and cheaper to build a narrow-gauge rail, especially up through the mountains. Those little engines will pull quite a load. And they're no way as dangerous as the bigger ones. They hang to the rails real good.

"Because of the narrow-gauge railroad, the lumber contractors have opened a lot of timber land to harvest, which otherwise wouldn't happen. In the next couple of decades, the narrow-gauge will make a lot of people wealthy. Not to say anything about the owners of the narrow-gauge railroad. Old Josiah Maxcy and Herbert Wing.

"We're coming into the Phillips Station now. We'll fill up with water and there'll be a change of passengers. Most will be going to Rangeley.

"Coming back we'll be hauling railcars freighted with pulpwood, and sawn lumber. It'll be a heavy train and a second engine will have to hook on at Redington to help hold the train back coming down over the sluice. Without the second engine, we wouldn't keep the train upright. A few have tried but failed. Sluice Hill drops 4%, or 400 feet from Redington to Perham Junction."

They were leaving the Phillips Station and Dana added, "It's an easy run up to Perham from here. The line rises 400 feet here also but it's a longer grade. It's an easy grade."

At Perham Junction Sterling got off and set the rails for Barnjum and then he jumped back on.

"What you going to do in Barnjum?"

"I'd like you to keep it to yourself that I'm even around. And I can't say what I'm working on." Dana nodded his head that he understood.

Shortly after leaving Perham Junction they crossed a good gravel road. "Where does this road go?" Sterling asked.

"The left will take you up Mecham Hill and then into Barnjum. There are a few farms up there also, Mecham's, Wing's, Rodrick's, Fred and George Toothaker. To the right is the largest farm, the Wheeler Farm. Big set of fields it is. Good view of the Mt. Abraham Range also. The first mill in this whole area was on Perham Brook. Then there was a shingle mill where the Barnjum mill now sits. All those buildings had to have cedar shingles or shakes for the roofs."

"Where's this Barnjum from, Dana?"

"Frank J.D. Barnjum. Don't know what the J.D. is. He was a business man from Massachusetts who saw the possibilities of becoming a wealthy man. He obtained a lumber contract, then he petitioned the state and the Sandy River and Rangeley Lakes Railroad to build a spur line from Perham Junction.

"The shingle mill was a paddle wheel operation, but Barnjum built a steam-powered band saw. It works good, too. At least that's what his men all say. Leastwise we haul a lot of his lumber out of here."

"What kind of a man is he, Dana?"

"He's a hard worker that's for sure and doesn't like a lazy man or a dishonest man. I guess if you're up front with him, he is with you.

"You can see smoke now from the chimneys at the mill," Dana said.

"Do people live in here?"

"Yes, you'll see the cabins as we slide through the station. There's a big boarding house with a good dining room."

"All those farms I told you about supply the operations in here with food for the crews and grain and hay for the work horses. Takes a lot of hay and grain to feed horses that work as hard as these do every day. Course the men eat a lot also. I know I'd hate to have to buy groceries for them," he laughed and Sterling laughed with him.

Sterling was beginning to understand that Dana was a living encyclopedia when it came to this area of the state.

Dana started to slow the train before he came to the last bend. He gave a blast on the steam whistle to let everyone know he was coming that might be on the tracks. They were switched to a side rail and the engine was disconnected. "Now would be a good time for you to leave if you don't want to be seen."

"Thanks, Dana," and Sterling stepped to the ground and disappeared in some bushes before anyone was on that side of the train. With the engine now disconnected, Dana pulled it ahead to the turntable and two men swung the table around and now the engine was pointing in the other direction.

Sterling's first objective was to get away from the village and mill and find a place to set up a temporary camp. He needed some place where there were not any workers or not likely to be. He decided to follow up along the brook that was closest to the tracks. His pack was heavy and he stopped often to catch his breath, so he wouldn't work up a sweat.

About a half mile north of Barnjum, he found what he was looking for. A couple of two-year-old beaver had built a new dam on the brook forming a nice pond. Sterling knew there would be trout in this and he also found a spring freshet which ran into the pond. Now he had fresh water to drink.

He set his pack down and stretched his shoulders and then looked for a likely spot to build a lean-to shelter. He found two huge spruce trees growing about eight feet apart with a thick canopy overhead. Here he built a lean-to, lacing fir boughs tightly together to keep out rain. He closed in both sides to block the wind.

Next, he dug out a hole in the sandy soil close to the spring to keep his food cool. When he had his camp site set up with fir boughs for his bed, he went fishing. The small beaver pond was well stocked with brook trout between 8 and 10 inches. He caught four for supper. He gathered snapping dry wood for his fire, so it would not smoke too much.

He was still hungry after he had eaten all four fish so he had a hand full of nuts and raisins. Feeling better, it was time to put the fire out and go to sleep.

* * * *

Sterling was awake the next morning before the sun was up. He kindled a small fire and boiled some water for coffee. He ate a piece of hardtack. His own recipe of flour, water, bacon fat and strawberry preserves. There was enough nourishment in one biscuit to last him all day. As soon as there was enough daylight to see, he put the fire out. Then he put everything in the lean-to and started to reconnoiter the area looking for anything that looked out of place. He was methodical and he started to work his way east towards Farmer Mountain. When the terrain on the slope of Farmer became too steep, he went a little to the north and traversed the slope back to the brook where he had set up camp.

With each pass he drew in grid lines on his map. He did this traversing back and forth all day without finding anything interesting or out of character.

He'd had enough for one day and while working his way down the brook he was camped on, he spotted two partridges. Not wanting to shoot his gun and alert those he was after, he picked up four one-inch stones. He waited until they were close together and he threw the handful of stones at them and to his astonishment he had hit both birds. One was dead and the other was flapping its broken wing.

Once he was at camp he cleaned both birds and then went to see if he could find some mushrooms to go with them. He soon found what he was looking for, a hardwood grove. And in particular, he was looking for beechnut trees that were partly rotten. He found a beech that had fallen and there were mushrooms growing all over it. He was looking for mushrooms he was familiar with and near the top of the tree he found it. A big bear's head tooth mushroom. He cut it away from the trunk and said, "This will go great with partridge."

As he laid in bed that night thinking about the day, his thoughts kept wandering back to Wynola and wondering where she had gone.

The next day was almost a repeat of the first. He had gone up into the valley between Farmer Mountain and the base of Mt. Abraham. He did find a lot of cat tracks in mud. But no traps or human tracks. It was getting late to stay out much longer so he checked his compass and started back for camp. He hadn't gone far when he found an old trail. There were no foot tracks, human that is, but up hill he found many moose tracks. Thinking this may only be a game trail, he left it and headed for camp.

But as he laid in bed that night he kept thinking about that game trail. What better way to camouflage your own tracks, than to use a game trail. In the morning he would go back and start his day there.

Along towards midnight, Sterling was awakened by what he thought was a gunshot. He lay still waiting for another. He was sure he had heard a rifle shot. If it was, it had to be a long ways off. And it seemed to come from up in the high country. He waited and waited for another that didn't come.

When daylight came, Sterling made a cup of coffee and ate a good breakfast of hardtack and some dried meat. He washed it down with coffee. He knew this might be a long day. He put the fire out and he had a feeling he'd find who he was looking for today, so he put his warden shirt and badge on. He also wore another shirt for a wind breaker. The morning air in the mountains was cold. It would probably warm up. He hoped.

He went directly to the game trail he had found and started following that up into the mountains. He had only gone a short distance when he found a light covering of snow on the ground. This would make it easier to see tracks and follow them, but his tracks would also be visible.

He could smell smoke in the air. Was it coming from some hidden camp or the mill? The higher he hiked the more snow he found. It was impossible not to leave tracks in this. There was an inch of snow. He stopped and looked at the sky. "If I wait, it won't be long and this snow will be gone." So he found a place to sit and wait.

71

The sun was rising higher in the sky and the air was getting warm and Sterling could almost watch as the snow began to melt. When it was all gone he resumed his search. He found fresh moose tracks in the game trail. He was on the top of a flateau now and he could look down on Caribou Pond.

He circled off the flateau towards the west and the brook that would take him back to his campsite. He kept working back and forth and then he found what he had been looking for. A well used human trail that was heading towards Caribou Pond. The afternoon was waning so he decided to follow the trail westerly, towards the brook. There were boot tracks in the mud in places.

But the trail was getting narrower and looking more like an older trail. He kept following it only because it was bringing him closer to his camp site and the sun was getting late.

* * * *

"Hartley, I told you didn't I, we should forget about this side of the mountain. Over the last couple of years we've taken a lot of hides out of here," Saul said.

Hartley Griswold and Saul Montague were cousins. Saul's parents left him in the house when they moved out of East Madrid and Hartley's family had adopted him and raised him as their own. They were the same age and both had been permanently expelled from school while in the sixth grade for fighting. Not with each other, but with other students.

Hartley stood about 5'-11" and weighed 200 lbs. and Saul stood 5'-10" and 195 lbs. and both were built like a beer barrel and extremely strong. They were good natured, but they loved to fight. Amos Griswold had said, "Since you boys are expelled from school forever you have no choice but to work with me in the woods. You're going to have to support yourselves now. And you'll pay your mother for room and board, also."

When they were 18 they left home and their father's employment and went to live in the wood camps. Only thing was, they were kicked out of every camp because of fighting with other workers. They were good workers, they simply liked fighting more.

So being kicked out of every woods camp, they went to poaching fur animals and moose and caribou meat. They had a friend, believe it or not, at Barnjum who would ship out their bounty to a friend of his in Portland. Heywood Lax lived by himself in a dingy cabin, far from the others. He was clean up man at the mill. And he loved to carve and whittle wood. He was very clever with wood and made some nice ornaments.

Hartley and Saul used him to ship their bounty. That's all. They didn't even like Heywood, but he had agreed to ship their hides and meat under threat of receiving a brutal beating.

Hartley was ahead of Saul as they were on their way back to their camp when Hartley saw Sterling following their trail and coming towards them. Without a word he signaled Saul that someone was coming and he stepped off the trail behind some jackfirs and Saul back-stepped down the trail.

Sterling saw Saul, but he hadn't seen Hartley duck behind the jack fir trees. When he walked by, Hartley stepped out quietly and hit Sterling behind his head with the butt of his rifle and Sterling fell to the ground.

"Look at this Saul!" Hartley said excitedly. "He's one of these new game wardens. Just look at that uniform and badge!" Then he kicked Sterling in the ribs and Saul kicked him in the ribs on the other side.

"What'll we do with him now, Hartley?" Saul wanted to know. "Is he dead?"

"Nah, he ain't dead. But he is hurting. We'll leave him. After this beating he won't be back."

They left Sterling there laying on the ground and they went back to their camp. Sterling could hear them talking and walking away, but he couldn't move. His ribs felt like they were on fire and his head was bleeding and it hurt. He knew if he succumbed and went to sleep, he'd never wake up. He started talking to himself, trying to stay awake.

His head was a little clearer and he tried to stand. It was an aggravating feat to get to his feet. He just stood there trying to catch his breath. It hurt to take a big breath. He was in a fix and he knew it. And he also knew he had to get moving while he could. He found two dead sticks he could use as canes.

His head was hurting and his vision was blurry. He didn't know how far he had come or how far he had to go. He had to get to Barnjum for help. He kept going one painful step at a time. He was thirsty but he didn't try to bend down.

The sun was going down but the full moon was already up. Finally he could hear activity at Barnjum and he could see the engine on the turn table. He stepped out into the opening close to the turn table and he fell forward. The engineer in the cab saw him go down and stopped the turn table and he hollered to the men.

"He needs a doctor," Dana Aldrich said. "He can't wait. He has a head injury. You men carry him into the front passenger car and make up a bed for him on the floor. As soon as I get this engine turned around I'll hook on, only to the passenger cars. We'll have to forget the freight tonight. This is an emergency. Move it!" Dana was used to giving orders.

When Frank Barnjum heard there was an injured man, he came out to inquire, "He's a game warden. Forget the freight cars."

"Already done Mr. Barnjum."

"Alright, get him to Dr. Bell in Strong. I'll send a telegram that he has a head injury and will be coming in on the 9 p.m. train.

"Make good speed Dana."

"Yes sir."

It had been a fast run, alright. One that Dana would not want to repeat. There was a wagon waiting at the station when the train pulled in and four men carried him to the wagon and two rode with him in back to steady him.

Dr. Bell had been informed and he and his staff were prepared and waiting.

As Sterling was laying on the emergency room table he

started to regain consciousness and then he collapsed again. But in that brief moment he thought he had seen Wynola standing over him. He tried to say her name but his lips wouldn't move.

"Oh my God!" Wynola said. "I know him. This is Sterling Silvanus."

"Yes it is," Dr. Bell said, "we all know who he is, but how do you? You have only been here for two days?"

While the doctor worked on Sterling, bandaging his ribs and stitching the gash in his head, Wynola explained how she had come to know Sterling.

Tears dropped onto Sterling's chest and Dr. Bell looked at Wynola and said, "I think you know Sterling better than you are letting on."

* * * *

Sterling regained consciousness two days later and slowly opened his eyes. He didn't know where he was and he couldn't move his head. But he was feeling better. He closed his eyes again and took a deep breath. His sides still hurt but not as bad. He concluded that he must be in a hospital. He remembered then, he thought he had seen Wynola for a brief moment before everything went all dark.

He reached up with his arms. They were working. He tried his legs next and they were okay. It was only his head he couldn't move. Had he broken his neck? He couldn't remember. He couldn't remember much of anything.

A nurse came over then. He could tell by her uniform. That means he was in a hospital. "And how are you today, Mr. Silvanus?"

"I'm lucid, but I hurt all over."

"It's no wonder. Can you remember what happened to you?"

Sterling was thinking. No, he couldn't. "Sorry, I can't remember."

"It'll come back to you. You rest now."

"Excuse me, who are you?"

"I'm sorry. I'm a nurse working with Dr. Bell. He will be here shortly. My name is Alberta Probert."

Sterling tried to take a deep breath, but he couldn't. "Last night when I was brought here, I opened my eyes for only a moment and I thought I saw someone I knew."

"Well, it was two days ago when you were brought in and you probably know most of the people who live here. At least everyone knows you."

Nurse Alberta left then and Sterling tried to relax and he was trying to remember what had happened to him.

Dr. Bell came to see him, "How are you, Sterling?"

"I hurt, Doc. But I can't remember what happened."

"That's understandable. You have had a concussion and there is still swelling on the brain. When the swelling reduces you will likely regain your memory. You have a serious gash in the back of your head. I had to stitch it up. And that's why you can't move your head. I had the nurse immobilize your head so the wound would heal faster. Now you get some rest. You're healing just fine."

In the afternoon another nurse came to check on Sterling. "Hello, Sterling, do you know who I am?"

"Yes. You are my neighbor Minnie Allen."

"That's good. I wouldn't worry much about remembering what happened to you. It'll come. Now rest."

He was tired of being told to rest. He was tired of laying on his back. He needed to get up and walk around.

"Mrs. Allen?"

"Yes, what is it, Sterling?"

"I'm hungry and I'd like a cup of coffee please."

"Well, that is a good sign. I'll go see what we have."

Minnie came back as soon as she could with a tray of food. She set the tray down and said, "Let's see if we can get you into a sitting position, Sterling."

It hurt to move, but with Minnie's help he was sitting up.

She set the tray on his lap and said, "I found some nice chicken broth in the kitchen and a slice of bread with butter. But I think for now you'd probably better stick with tea."

Sterling was able to feed himself, so Minnie left to attend to other patients. The broth was good, he only wished there had been some chicken and potatoes in it. The bread was warm and tasted like it had just come out of the oven. When he had finished eating he put the tray on the side stand. This movement hurt his ribs but he did it. He was feeling sleepy now and not wanting to slide back under the covers, he fell asleep sitting up in bed.

Minnie kept checking on him to make sure he was still sitting up and had not slumped to one side. At 8 p.m. as she walked by his bed, he opened his eyes. "My, you had a good nap, Sterling. How are you feeling now?"

"You know, Mrs. Allen, I'm feeling much better. My head is not hurting so much now. My sides are okay until I move."

"You see just the broth from chicken soup will do wonders."

Sterling started laughing then and Minnie looked confused. "What do you find so funny, Sterling?"

"When you mentioned chicken broth, it reminded me of another chicken soup some one had given me. Only it wasn't chicken soup, it was chicken hawk soup." And he laughed some more. To him it was funny but Minnie didn't see the humor in it.

"Just can't remember who gave me the chicken hawk soup."

"If you remembered eating a chicken hawk soup, then as your head heals you'll probably remember who gave it to you and more."

"Mrs. Allen?"

"Yes, Sterling?"

"What time does your shift end?"

"Twelve midnight. Why?"

"Who comes in then? Mrs. Probert is on the day shift, there has to be some one else after you leave."

Minnie could see his mind was beginning to respond more now. That was good.

"Wynola," Sterling interrupted her then. "I knew it! I knew I saw her, even if it was only a flash. I knew I had seen her and I wasn't imagining it." He was smiling and Minnie left him since he was in such a good mood.

In a few minutes, as much as he wanted to stay awake until Wynola came to work, he was sound asleep and Minnie was able to slide him down back under the covers.

When Wynola came in, before her shift started, the first thing she asked, "How is Mr. Silvanus? Is he healing?"

Minnie was smiling and said, "It's none of my business, but somewhere, somehow you spent some time together. Now back to your question, Wynola, Mr. Silvanus was awake off and on today. This evening he was able to sit up in bed and have some chicken broth and bread and then he went back to sleep. He did say though that he was feeling better. Oh, I almost forgot. He remembers you, Wynola."

Wynola breathed a sigh of relief. "I was so worried when he was brought in, Minnie. He looked so awful."

"I think he'll be just fine. How about you, Wynola? I'm only guessing, but I'd say you haven't had much sleep since he came in."

Wynola didn't respond to that. She simply said, "Good night, Minnie."

During her shift, when she wasn't busy, she would sit by Sterling's bedside, like she had done every night since he was brought in. There were times when his whole body seemed to be racked with spasms and he would turn his head from side to side and sweat would run down his face. Wynola would wash his face with a cool damp cloth and hold his hand and talk to him softly. This would calm whatever battle was going on in his mind. She had no idea what had happened to him or where he had been.

When Alberta Probert relieved Wynola in the morning she asked, "How is our patient this morning, Wynola?"

"Minnie said he sat up and ate some chicken broth and bread

and talked rationally with her. He has been asleep ever since. I wish I could talk with him," she was almost pleading.

"You will, Wynola, you will," Alberta assured her.

Five minutes after Wynola left the room, Sterling woke up. Alberta rushed after Wynola, but she had already left the building.

After Sterling had had a good breakfast and he had shaved and Alberta had helped him to wash up, he was feeling much better and stronger and his memory had completely returned. "Let's see if you can get out of bed and stand on your own, Sterling."

Alberta and Dr. Bell stood by, in case he started to fall. With some effort Sterling swung his leg around and off the bed and standing was actually easier than swinging his legs around. "Good, Sterling, now can you walk?"

"Maybe if I had a walking stick," Sterling said.

Alberta went after a cane and then Sterling was able to walk. However slowly, but he was walking.

"Good. You have healed faster than I first thought you would. You get back in bed now and after you have had your lunch and dressed, I'll discharge you. I'll send someone up to the livery for a driver to take you home."

Alberta had already sent an orderly to get Wynola at the hotel. "I don't care if she is asleep. You wake her and tell her about Sterling. Now!" Alberta said.

When Wynola was told Sterling was awake and up, she dressed and ran to the hospital. It was close by.

Alberta saw her come in and said, "He's been asking for you."

"Thank you, Alberta," and she went directly to Sterling's bedside.

"Hello, Sterling."

"Wynola. Hi. It was you that I saw when I came in." Then he started to grin and she was smiling too.

"My God, it's good to see you. Seeing you is worth a trip to the hospital."

She bent down and hugged him and then looked into his eyes. "I have been so worried about you and what happened."

Alberta stayed in the hall to give them some privacy. They were in love, she was sure of that.

Dr. Bell came into Sterling's room and said, "Sterling, the telegraph office sent over a telegram from Chief Warden Don Perry. I think you should answer it as soon as you can."

Sterling read it and said, "Yeah, I think I should. Wynola can you get me a piece of paper and pencil?"

Chief Perry wanted to know what Sterling's condition was and had he improved any. And he wanted Sterling to write out a report of the incident; whatever had happened.

Sterling wrote a short message that he was feeling much better and would be going home that afternoon, and would send a full report soon. "Is there anybody who can take this over for me?"

"Dr. Bell, don't let him leave the hospital until I get back. He can't be left alone with no one to help him. I will go with him and take care of him," Wynola said. "Or at least help him."

No one wanted to argue with that. "You heard her, Doc. I'll be in good hands."

* * * *

Sterling had regained more of his strength than even he had thought. Dr. Bell had asked Wynola to remove the stitches in another day, "And make sure he is not immobile for too long. But don't let him overdo it either."

Sterling decided to use the cane for a while. It did help to steady him. Stairs were going to be a problem for a few days.

"Don't hurry, Ray. He has two broken ribs." Ray drove the horse slowly, so not to jar Sterling's broken ribs.

"Yes, ma'am."

Sterling couldn't help but notice how Wynola had taken charge. He wasn't complaining.

They came to a stop beside the side door at Sterling's house. "Do you want any help, ma'am, getting him inside?"

"Maybe if you'd help us off the wagon."

It was a slow walk to inside the house. "Burr, it's cold in here, Sterling. You sit here, right here, and I'll start the woodstove." There was plenty of cedar kindling split and piled up in the shed and along with plenty of seasoned hardwood. Wynola wasn't long getting a fire going and she went downstairs in the cellar and started the wood furnace. And it wasn't long before the house was comfortable.

"Are you going in to work tonight, Wynola?"

"No, Dr. Bell said I should stay with you and take care of you tonight. I'll have to go in tomorrow night.

"What do you have for food here, Sterling?"

"There's plenty of food. Except it's all down in the cellar in cold storage."

Wynola found enough food to make a very hearty supper. "You have been up all day, Sterling, wouldn't you like to lie down."

"Yes, I have been feeling tired." Sterling leaned on Wynola's shoulder as they walked to his bedroom on the east end of the house.

Wynola turned the blankets back and Sterling sat down and she pulled his boots off and then took his clothes off. At first he was hesitant about letting her undress him and then he gave in. When he was in bed and the covers pulled up around him Wynola stoked the fires and turned the gas light off.

The light in Sterling's room was still on as she undressed and crawled into bed beside him and then she reached up and turned the light off.

He started to say something and she put her fingers over his mouth and said, "Shhh, not tonight. We'll talk in the morning. We both need sleep."

Sterling tried to put his arm up and around Wynola and hold her close, but he just couldn't do it. It was causing too much pain in his ribs. So she turned over on her stomach and laid her head on his chest. "Does this hurt you?"

"No. You feel good Wynola. I know we said we would talk in the morning. I just wanted to say how nice it is to see you and to have you lying beside me."

But Wynola had already gone to sleep. And Sterling was shortly.

* * * *

Sterling slept good all night. He only wished he could turn over. Wynola apparently had slept good also. She never stirred all night. He awoke first and he didn't want to spoil the moment. He was relishing in happiness about Wynola being there with him. He inhaled the scent of her hair and caressed her face with his finger tips. She stirred and put one leg over on top of his. "I could get used to liking this," he said softly.

She surprised him when she turned and looked at him.

"How long would it take for you to get used to it?"

"A lifetime.

"Why did you leave the village?" he asked.

"I had had a vision which was telling me to come here to my Great Grandfather's land."

"How do you mean?"

"All this land around here at one time belonged to my Great Grandfather."

"Who was he?"

"His Christian name was Pierre Paul. His native name was Pierpole."

"Yes, I know this name. He was a great man. Kind and always helped the white settlers. And there's a legend about a lead mine on Day Mountain. The legend says that whenever he needed money he would go to his mine and get some lead and canoe down the Sandy River to Farmington Falls to sell it."

"Yes, he was a great man. But only partly true. He used to

hunt for moose on what you call Day Mountain, on the north slope. It is an easy incline. On one hunt after he had killed a moose and was cleaning it and quartering it he stuck his hatchet in a rock. This made him curious, as you aren't supposed to be able to cut rock with a hatchet. He cut away some of the rock and he thought it might be lead and he later took it to a white trading post in what he called Lower Town, Farmington. He was paid for the price of lead, but he always thought that it was silver or silver mixed with lead. But he didn't want any problems with the white settlers so he never said anything. He said the lead was always in a white hard rock."

"Quartz," Sterling said.

"How do you know about all this?" Sterling asked.

"My people have never and still don't keep a written (words) history of their life. But it is always told and retold to family members and the entire tribe. That way we always remember and don't forget our ways or the old ones."

"History here says that when he left, no one knew why or where he went. Do you?" Sterling asked.

"As I said he was a kind and generous man. He was originally from the St. Francis tribe and in the spring many people from St. Francis would travel to summer at the coast. Food there was always plentiful. This was an old route through here. And when the people came to his house, it is our custom to not turn them away, but to provide food and shelter. So many were coming and at times staying too long. He didn't have enough food left for his family and to see them through the winter.

"Then he lost two children, first was little Hannah Oppalunski. He buried her on his land. Then his son Iganoose died. And this was more than he could bear. He wanted to take him back to Canada for a proper burial. But he would have to wait until winter and there was snow on the ground. So he put the body of young Iganoose in his chimney and smoked the body to preserve it. Then when the new year came, 1812, he loaded the body on a sled and left here and never returned."

"That's quite a story. What happened to his land?"

"Before he left, he petitioned the Commonwealth of Massachusetts to sell his land. This always bothered him. Why should he have to ask the Commonwealth of Massachusetts to sell his property? He surely did not understand the ways of these white settlers. His wife Hannah was more than happy to leave. She had never liked living amongst the settlers.

"Day Mountain as it is known now, back then it was called Pierpole's Mountain, because his lot went up and over the top."

"That is fascinating, but what did all this have to do with you coming here and leaving Wonnocka's village so suddenly?"

Wynola hesitated before answering and then she looked into Sterling's eyes and said, "I knew if I waited for you to return, you would talk me out of it. Then when you left...well I didn't think you'd ask me to travel with you."

"I missed you, you know."

"I really wanted to stay and be with you, but that vision had showed me I was to come here. My spirit was guiding me. At the time I didn't understand why, but visions are supposed to be followed. So I came and now I understand why. To find you again. Even if you are all beat up," they both laughed.

Then seriously, she looked into his eyes again and said, "I love you."

He took her in his arms and said, "I love you too, Wynola. That's why I was so hurt when you left without saying anything."

"How are you feeling this morning?"

"My head is fine and my sides don't hurt as much."

"This is good. Let me look at your stitches. Um...um, they can come out today."

She got out of bed and walked around to his side, Sterling was absorbed in looking at her nude body. She was so beautiful. Playfully he pulled her down to him and kissed her passionately and she responded. He whispered in her, "Oh, I would love to make love to you, but I'm afraid that would only aggravate my ribs."

"You're right there." She stood up and said, "Come on, it was time you were up. I'll fill your bathtub with hot water and you bathe and soak in the hot water while I fix us something to eat. The heat will do your body a lot of good."

After they had eaten and everything was cleaned up, Wynola walked out to the back pasture to get old Duke. Then Sterling helped her to hook him to the wagon. "We'll go up to the Allen's first and get some milk." He put the milk can in back and Wynola helped him into the wagon seat. Then she drove.

Minnie was out front when they drove in. "Well, hello you two. This is a surprise."

"Hello, Minnie, we need some milk." Wynola stepped off the wagon and said, "You stay right there, Sterling, I'll get this," and she carried the milk can and followed Minnie into the barn.

Sterling gave her 50 cents. "Thank you, Minnie. Tell Freemont and Harry I said hello." June came out of the house then. "Hello, June. This is Wynola. I don't know if you have ever met her or not."

"Hello, Wynola. Minnie has talked about you."

Their next stop was at the Randall farm for eggs. "Hello, Mr. Randall. I know Jimmy is in school, but we need a dozen eggs," and he handed Dean an egg basket.

While Dean was getting the eggs, Sterling told Wynola about the arrangement he had made with young Jimmy.

"We'll take these back to the house and call it a day. I have a report to write for the Chief Warden, too."

While Sterling was writing, Wynola started to clean the house. She soon discovered that it had been a few months since the house was last cleaned. As she worked, she kept marveling at the structural beauty of the house and how simplistic it had been built. Everything was right where it was needed, and wide pine boards for the floor.

That night all Sterling could do again was lay on his back and Wynola laid her head on his chest. But tonight he forced himself to bring his arm up and around her. This was fine, as long as he didn't move. The stitches removed, his wound was healing nicely. "I think tomorrow you should go into work with me and have Dr. Bell check your ribs. He may take the bandage wrap off."

"I think you should move in, so you can keep an eye on my wounds."

"Okay. Actually that would make more sense than me living in the hotel."

"Maybe I should stay with the wagon so you won't have to walk home."

"I don't mind walking. I probably have had to walk a great deal more than you. In my culture we were more adept to walking or travel by canoe. We never had much use for a horse.

* * * *

The next day, early in the morning, Freemont and Harry brought down a side of beef for Sterling and Wynola. "This was part of the bargain, wasn't it, Sterling?"

"Yes sir, but I didn't expect any this soon."

"Well, I feel a little guilty of taking advantage of your generosity. Last week your Holstein cow gave birth to twins. One male, one female. I say you have a long ways to go before we're even."

When they had left, Sterling explained what Freemont had said. "Now we must can as much of this beef as we have jars for."

While Sterling was busy cutting up meat, Wynola built up the fire in the kitchen stove and then found all the Mason jars and lids and washed them.

"There is a big copper canning kettle hanging up in the shed."

They worked until 4 p.m. and Wynola put the last Mason jar in the copper kettle. "There now, I must go to work. You will have to come back...or why do you need to go to town anyway? Maybe you should stay here and finish canning. I can mail your report to the Chief Warden. Is there anything else you need?" Wynola asked.

"Yeah, before you leave town in the morning would you pick up a newspaper?"

Sterling watched as the kettle boiled away almost all afternoon. That evening he sat out on the porch and for the first time since his encounter with the poachers at Barnjum, he began to think about what he had done wrong. First off, he had been careless and probably a little tired since he had been hiking all day. He was angry, not so much for what they had done to him, but because of his own carelessness. It wouldn't happen a second time, he allowed.

As he crawled into bed that night, and that's what it was without Wynola's help, he was missing her. He had felt very comfortable with her sleeping beside him. He liked having her in his life. He decided to think about making it permanent once he had finished with the Barnjum affair. Yes, he was going back.

He was already up the next morning when Wynola got home from work and he had breakfast and hot coffee waiting for her.

Because they had been so busy with the beef the day before, they had forgotten about seeing Dr. Bell. "I talked with him this morning and he said I could unwrap the bandages around your ribs. But he also said to still be very careful. The ribs are still mending. Not to do any twisting or heavy lifting. He said as a rule of thumb, when you could split fire wood with an axe, you were okay to go back to work. And he said you probably would have a scar on the back of your head where you were hit with the rifle butt."

So after they had eaten, Wynola gently unwrapped his ribs and he was feeling a lot better. "It is easier to breathe without being wrapped up.

"Are you tired?"

"Some, but I don't think I could sleep just yet. Maybe this afternoon I'll lie down. I brought all of my belongings from the hotel."

While Wynola was taking care of her belongings, Sterling unharnessed Duke and put him in the corral with feed, water and some oats.

He leaned against the corral watching Duke eat and thinking how good life was being to him and Wynola.

As far as he was concerned, life couldn't be better. And he was thinking that Wynola was probably feeling about the same. Their life together was surely filling a deep void for them both.

* * * *

With each passing day, Sterling was regaining his strength, but he had not tried splitting a block of firewood yet. He could reach above his head, but not his toes. That would come.

Then one night while Sterling and Wynola were lying in bed—it was her night off—he managed to roll over and he was looking into her eyes. "I have never seen such beauty in all my life. When I watch you, it is like watching a meadow of beautiful flowers all swaying in a gentle breeze. There is a natural perfume emanating from your very sense that is sweeter, and more alluring and desirable than anything I can imagine. You seem to know me better than my parents ever did and I loved them both. And you carry with you always a high sense of virtue and honor. You have come into my life shining as bright as the morning sun to guide me."

He kissed her very tenderly at first and when she eagerly responded, he kissed with a hot passion. He cupped her firm breasts and softly caressed them. He kissed her throat and she began to moan. He kissed each nipple and then between her breasts and down her stomach and she spread her legs and he was engulfed with her beauty and essence and nothing in the whole world mattered at that moment. Only fulfilling her desire and need and his own. This simple beautiful and graceful woman had managed to conquer him and he had succumbed willingly.

* * * *

They awoke the next morning still wrapped in each other's bliss and arms. When he opened his eyes to look at her, Wynola was already looking at him.

"I think I'm ready to split the wood."

She grinned and began to laugh. "Yes, after last night I think you should split a lot of wood."

For some reason breakfast and coffee this morning was more enjoyable for them both. Wynola couldn't stop smiling and Sterling had a renewed spirit about him. Yes, life was being good.

When Sterling grabbed the axe and headed out to the woodpile, Wynola went along with him. "I want to watch."

He started off with an easy piece. A straight grain white maple. He swung the axe and it was like going through butter. He tried a piece of yellow birch next and that too split like butter. Then he chose a piece of gnarly beech. There was no definitive grain. He placed the block on the chopping block and swung. The axe bit deep, but the wood didn't split. He brought the axe up over his head and turned it so the hammer head would impact the chopping block with the beech block still wedged to the axe. Sterling swung with all he had and the block split in two pieces. He put the axe down and turned to look at Wynola. "You know what this means?"

"Yes, I'm afraid I do. And I know you are going back to Barnjum to get those who did this to you."

"How did you know? I haven't been thinking about going back until the other day."

"I knew long before you did. You are not the kind of man who would not go back. I only ask you to be careful. When will you leave?"

"Tomorrow morning."

* * * *

Wynola seemed to know before he did what he would need to take with him. She made some good hearty food stuff and packed extra clothing and a piece of canvas she had found in the barn. "So you can build a small wikitup. Much warmer than a lean-to." She could understand what he was thinking.

As they were in each other's arms in bed that night, Wynola said, "When you have made your wikitup and your camp is all set and that night when you lie down to sleep, before you go to sleep, relax your body, close your eyes and focus your attention here," and she gently touched his forehead and between the eyes, "and look into your mind of what you wish to find the next day. And then go to sleep. The following day let the Spirit of the Great Creator guide you and you will find that which you look for."

"I will do this."

* * * *

Wynola drove him to the train station in the morning and instead of waiting until the train left she said, "I go home now Sterling. Do not stay away for long. I love you."

He kissed her and said, "I will return as soon as I can. And I love you."

She drove off and Sterling asked the telegrapher to send this message to:

Chief Warden Don Perry.
Have returned to work. Taking train to Barnjum.
Sterling Silvanus.

Then he walked up to the ticket window and said, "Train to Barnjum, please," and he showed Pansy Newell his pass.

"Yes, Mr. Silvanus. See you are going in uniform this time."

"Yes sir, I am."

People were boarding the train and before Sterling could

step on, the engineer Dana Aldrich asked, "Don't you think it's a little stupid to go back there? I mean after what happened last time."

"I know what you mean, Dana, and that's exactly why I'm going back."

The conductor announced, "All aboard, Train to Barnjum."

Sterling sat alone and next to a window. When he entered the railcar, everybody had stopped talking to look at the man wearing the game warden uniform. Some knew of his troubles and some didn't.

Sterling decided that on this trip, he was not going to hide. He wanted people to see who he was, where he was going, and for most they could speculate why.

The train stopped in Phillips to pick up more passengers for Redington and Langtown and then stopped at Reed's Station so two could disembark. The switch was made at Perham and it wouldn't be long now and he would be back at Barnjum.

It was in the middle of October and nights in these mountains would be cold, and maybe even permanent snow by now at higher altitudes. The train stopped and the conductor announced, "Barnjum Station. All off for Barnjum."

This was Sterling's cue to get off. He stood on the loading platform outside and everyone stopped to look at him. The mill was running, and lumber was being sawn. As he was walking across the mill yard, Frank Barnjum came out of his office and walked over to greet Sterling. "Mr. Silvanus, I see you have recovered nicely. But aren't you taking an awful chance coming back here?"

"Mr. Barnjum, I suspect there is one individual here, maybe two, who is assisting those who I am after. Until I return, no one is to leave here." When Mr. Barnjum started to object, Sterling said, "No one, Mr. Barnjum."

"Yes sir, as you say."

He walked up across the mill yard and log piles and into the woods and followed the brook towards Lone Mountain. He decided to camp away from where he had before. He would stay totally away from there, in case the two had found it.

He found a sheltered spot near the brook and began to build his wikitup. It didn't take long to have the frame poles up and then he wrapped the canvas around it and fashioned a flap for the door. Then he made a small fire place inside and brought in fir boughs for his bed and gathered dry firewood.

He checked the brook and there were some deep pools with a few brooktrout. The season was closed but this was different. It was survival. He caught three and ate them along with some special survival food Wynola had put together for him.

It was still daylight and the temperature was dropping, so he made a small fire inside the wikitup to warm it up. Then he boiled some water and made some coffee. As he sat next to the fire, he wasn't worried or anxious. Instead he had a feeling of complete confidence and he was looking forward to the morrow.

* * * *

It was warm inside the wikitup and he had plenty of dry wood for the night. He laid back on his bed of fir boughs and relaxed. Draining his mind of all worries and then he placed his attention on the spot where Wynola had said and he began to see in his mind of that which he needed to do and find tomorrow. Then he gently went off to sleep.

When he awoke in the morning there were only a few embers left to the fire, and he added some dry kindling and he soon had a nice fire. He boiled water for coffee and warmed up some food Wynola had prepared for his trip. He was feeling good about the day ahead and was not anxiously pondering on what had to be done. The air outside was cold and water had frozen to some of the rocks along the brook bank.

When he had finished eating and his second cup of coffee, he put the fire out, shouldered his pack and started up and over Lone Mountain. He figured going this way, he might come in behind them. He didn't go over the top of the mountain, but around it on the east side. His sides were only giving him enough sharp pains for him to remember why he was there.

He walked around on the north slope and sat down on a ledge precipice. From there he could look down on Caribou Pond and the flateau above the pond. And then he saw them. He dug out his binoculars for a better look. It was them alright, he recognized the second man following the first. It had to be the man in front who had hit him with the rifle butt. He was wearing a red and black wool jacket. The other man was wearing a dark green jacket.

He decided to sit there and watch to see what they were up to. After a few minutes, he lost sight of them as they were in some thick cover. Still Sterling was not overly excited or anxious. He was just doing what came naturally to him.

A half hour went by and then he heard a rifle shot and then two more. "They must have shot a moose or caribou. Now would be a good time to go down and wait for them to come up their own trail carrying what they had shot. He moved through the forest with the stealth of a lynx. He was so quiet, he walked up on a grazing deer before the deer knew he was there.

He wasn't too particular now whether he left any boot tracks or not. He found the trail the two had used and he walked along it away from the flateau until he found a perfect spot to wait. The ground was carpeted with moss and there was a clump of low growing cedar trees to hide behind. There was nothing to sit on so he had to stand. And then he had to pee.

After what did seem like a long time he could hear faint voices coming towards him. And then he saw them. Good, the one he wanted first was now following the other. He waited without hardly breathing. They stopped not far from him to catch their breath. He could see now what they were carrying. It wasn't moose or caribou meat, but two big cats slung over their shoulders.

As the first one walked by, Sterling drew his handgun out

and when the second one went by, he waited two steps and then like a lynx he stepped in behind him. He was right behind Hartley, the taller of the two. The cat was over the left shoulder and Sterling swung his gun as hard as he could and hit Hartley's collarbone sending him to the ground, howling and in a great deal of pain.

Saul turned to see what had happened and all he saw was Sterling charging at him. Saul dropped the cat and brought his rifle up to his hip to shoot at Sterling. Sterling saw what he was doing and took the rifle under his left arm. Securing it momentarily, then he brought his gun down on Saul's nose, breaking that and blood spurting everywhere.

Saul let go of his rifle, but he was still on his feet. Sterling swung the rifle and hit Saul beside the head, sending him to the ground. Hartley saw what was happening and managed to get to his knees and was reaching for his rifle when Sterling swung Saul's rifle at him and hit him square on the right wrist, breaking the bone. Sterling heard it snap. Hartley howled in pain again. Saul was trying to get to his knees and Sterling said, "How much more of this do you want?"

"Okay, okay mister, we've had enough," Saul said. "Just who in hell are you?"

"I'm Sterling Silvanus, Maine Game Warden and you two are under arrest. And I'm the guy who you kicked when I was down."

He figured Hartley could do nothing with a broken wrist and collar bone, but Saul on the other hand, only had head injuries. "You," and he pointed to Saul, "lay on your stomach and put your hands behind you." He did and Sterling handcuffed him. He looked at Hartley then and said "If you give me any trouble, I'll break the other arm. Now sit up if you can and I'll bandage your wounds so you can walk out of here."

Sterling tore strips from his blanket and made a splint for Hartley's wrist and then a sling and tied another strip around his shoulders to stabilize the collar bone. Saul's wounds had stopped bleeding, but to make him feel better he tied a bandage around his head.

He had to help each man up, "You will take me to your cabin." Then, "What are your names?"

"Hartley Griswold."

"And I'm Saul Montague."

"Let's go. Move it," Sterling commanded, but he had yet to raise his voice.

Their cabin, about 14 feet by 14 feet, from fir logs and a sloping roof, wasn't far away. "You two sit out here on that wood pile."

He waited until they were seated and Sterling opened the door and looked in. There were animal hides hung from all the walls. "Well boys, when I have you two safely in jail, I guess I'm going to have to make another trip up here and haul all this stuff out. Who is your partner at the mill? The one who ships all these furs to Portland."

When neither of them said anything, Sterling acted as if he was going to swing the rifle at them again. Saul blurted out, "His name is Heywood Lax."

"Okay boys, we'll head out of here."

Walking with two injured men wasn't easy. They had to go slow. Sterling overheard them talking. "We have never lost a fight in our life, Hartley. And this guy took us both and look what he did to us."

"Just shut up, Saul, and stop your whining."

The sun was overhead by the time they came to a twitch trail. This would lead right to the mill and it was easier walking. They met horse teams and drivers and they all pulled over to the edge to let them pass. It was lunch break at the mill and it seemed everyone in the village had come out to see what the excitement was. Frank Barnjum came out of his office and walked over to see Sterling. "Are these the two that worked you over?"

"They are. There is a third man that I want and he works here at the mill."

Frank looked surprised.

"I want Heywood Lax. He has been sending the hides for these two to Portland. I want him also, Mr. Barnjum.," Sterling said on an even tone without raising his voice.

"Heywood cleans up the mill. He is cleaning the band saw and deck now. I'll walk over with you."

When Heywood saw them come towards him, he dropped his tools and said softly to himself, "Oh my God, look what he did to those two." He climbed down off the deck and put his hands up and said, "I won't give you any trouble, mister."

Sterling let his guard down just long enough to put the handcuffs on Heywood. "Now, Mr. Lax, take me to your cabin."

He hesitated and Frank Barnjum said, "You'd better do as he asked, Heywood."

In Heywood's cabin Sterling found two wooden crates all made and pieces for a third. And on the two boxes was stenciled a Portland address. "Mr. Barnjum, I'd like you to put a lock on this cabin until I can come back and inventory everything here."

"Sure thing, Mr. Silvanus." From his gentle tone Frank knew Sterling was nobody to fool with. He commanded compliance without raising his voice.

"Thank you. I may be a few days before I can come back."

"Where will you take these three?"

"To the county jail in Farmington."

"There won't be another train leaving now until late tonight."

That wasn't good news. Sterling marched them down to the train station and inquired from the station agent when another train will be in.

"Not scheduled until this evening. Is there a problem?"

"Sort of. I have three people under arrest and two of them need medical attention."

"I tell you what I'll do, I'll send a telegram to the Phillips Station and see if they can help."

"Thank you."

Sterling and the three sat on benches at the station, while

Sterling waited for a reply.

"Mr. Silvanus, I got an answer already. Orris Vose, the company superintendent is bringing a special engine and one car up to get you."

Sterling breathed a sigh of relief. But he still had an hour to wait.

Saul had dried blood all over his face and looked worse off that he actually was. Hartley was the one who was hurting the most. With a broken collar bone there was no position he could sit without it hurting. Heywood was like a timid mouse who was caught in a corner by a cat. Before lunch break was over every living soul in Barnjum had heard the story about the game warden bringing in two dastardly fellows all beat up.

Mr. Vose finally arrived with a special train from Phillips and one look at Saul and Hartley, he said, "The doctor is out of town in Phillips. I'll have to take you to Strong."

"That'll be even better, Mr. Vose."

"Come on boys, let's get in the passenger car." For the first time all day Sterling was beginning to feel relief. Saul, Hartley and Heywood were apprehensive about their future. And there was no doubt in his mind that if Saul was not in handcuffs he would have attacked Sterling before now. He had that hateful look about him. Hartley on the other hand was in too much pain to be thinking about revenge.

The train made the change in direction at Perham Junction and Orris had opened the throttle a little more. For a little engine they were moving right along, about 30 mph.

They slowed as they went through Phillips without stopping and people were scratching their heads wondering why. Sterling had his window down and he could smell the sweet aroma of Cook's dairy farm before he could see it. Percy was walking up the field road leading a stray cow.

And then Orris started backing off on the steam slowing the train before entering Strong. He stopped so Sterling and company could get off at the platform. As he walked by the engine, Orris was leaning out the window. "Mr. Vose, if there is an extra charge for this, send the bill to the Chief Warden, Don Perry in Augusta. I'm sure we'll get enough fine added on to pay for the trip."

This made Hartley snarl. As Sterling marched the three towards the hospital, Orris was smiling to himself, and happy to be of service. He was acquainted with Saul and Hartley and to be honest, he was surprised that Sterling or any one man could have gotten the best of them. And this time Sterling didn't have a scratch on him. Now Orris was laughing out loud and went into the station house to talk with Pansy Newell. He could do that; he was the boss of the Sandy River and Rangeley Lakes Railroad.

"Now boys, before we go inside I want you three to be on your very best behavior. If not, I'm afraid that come time for court, you'll have to be carried in. Do we have an understanding?" He looked at each one and one by one they all said, "Yes."

When they went inside, Alberta Probert was standing at the front desk. "Oh my word." She looked at each one and then at Sterling. "What about you, Sterling, are you okay?"

"I'm fine Alberta. Is Dr. Bell busy?"

"No, you can bring them down to the emergency room."

Once in the emergency room, "Can you sit on this examining table?" Alberta asked.

Sterling had to help Hartley sit on the table. Dr. Bell came into the room then and was shocked at what he saw.

"Mr. Griswold, let me give you a word of caution. These people are here to help you. If you give them any trouble or me, I will break your other arm."

"Mr. Montague, something tells me all of the fight isn't out of you yet. Let me remind you, this is neither the time or place. If I have to, I will bring my gun down on top of your head this time and lay you out cold."

Sterling looked at Heywood and said, "Mr. Lax, I'll squash you like a bug."

Alberta didn't know what to think as she looked at Dr. Bell. They each were surprised how Sterling commanded such compliance and respect and talked to them almost like a gentlemen.

"You did a remarkable job, Sterling, stabilizing his arm, wrist and shoulders. I couldn't have done better myself. I'll just put a more permanent restraint on the wrist and forearm. The collarbone will heal nicely as is. I'll just put on a clean wrapping around your shoulders."

While Dr. Bell worked on him, Hartley knew he had been bested by this man and he wasn't about to try anything.

Dr. Bell had to set Saul's nose and stitch the wound on the side of his head. "What did you hit him with Sterling?"

"His rifle."

"What about this one?" and he pointed at Lax. "Does he have any injuries?"

"No, he's okay."

Minnie Allen came in to relieve Alberta. "My, what do we have here? Does Wynola know you are back already?"

"No Minnie, and I can't wait around either. I need to get these three to the county jail in Farmington. Would you tell her if I don't get back tonight, that I'll see her in the morning?"

"Sure thing, Sterling."

Sterling marched his three arrestees over to the station house. "When will the next train for Farmington be leaving?"

"There's a south bound from Kingfield that was due here at 4 p.m. It's late, so it'll be along soon."

"Okay boys. Sit down. The train is a little late."

Ten minutes later they heard the train's whistle as it neared the station house.

* * * *

At the Farmington Station there wasn't a driver and a carriage available to take all four of them up to the county jail just a few blocks up the road, so they walked. Sterling had no doubt that these three would welcome a cot in one of the cells.

They were unhandcuffed and put into separate holding cells and the deputy asked, "What are the charges?"

"For now, on Mr. Montague and Mr. Griswold, assault and battery on an officer. Mr. Lax, for now, shipping illegal hides and contraband. Once I have a chance to go back to Barnjum and search their cabins there'll be more charges to follow."

"What about bail?"

"If they were able to make bail, I don't believe any one of them would show for court.

"There isn't a train out of here until 6 a.m., do you supposed I could sleep in one of the cells?"

"Sure thing, take your pick."

* * * *

The next morning, at 6:45 a.m., Sterling sent a telegram to Chief Perry:

> *Have successfully completed task at Barnjum.*
> *Subjects in county jail. I'll send a full report*
> *tomorrow. Will have to return to Barnjum to search*
> *cabins and haul all contraband out.*
> *Game Warden Sterling Silvanus*

That done, he walked over to the hospital. He sat down in the waiting room and the girl at the front desk went to find Wynola.

"My, you need a shave," and she rubbed his face with her hands.

"How did it go?"

"Just like clock work. Just like you said."

"Do you mind waiting here until my shift ends?"

Before the shift ended, another younger woman and Minnie walked into the hospital together. "Hello, Minnie."

"Hello, Sterling."

Wynola came out and asked, "Are you ready? Let's go home.

I'm tired."

"Who was that with Minnie?"

"A new girl, Suzann. She will be taking my place."

When Sterling looked surprised she continued, "I'm not staying home alone, worrying about you or where you are. I'm going to go with you." She had expected Sterling to object but when he said, "I can get used to that," she was shocked. On the way home Sterling told her all about the trip. "Only thing is, I'll have to go back and search the two cabins and bring whatever I find back here."

"You mean we. I'm going with you."

"Okay. I'm hungry. I haven't eaten since daybreak this morning and I'm tired."

That night they reveled in each other's love and desire for one another. Each trying to fulfill their own needs. Wynola won out when Sterling laying from exhaustion went to sleep.

* * * *

Early the next morning Sterling wrote out a full report, including everything. "Wynola, I have to go to town and mail this report and then I have some errands to do."

"Okay. I'll stay here and put up some food for us to take. Do you have another knapsack?"

"I'll have to get one for you at Daggett's Store. Anything else you can think of?"

"No, I guess not."

Sterling hooked ole Duke to the wagon and headed for town. His first stop was at the Post Office. Then he went to Daggett's Store. "Hello, Mr. Daggett."

"Good morning, Sterling. What can I do for you this morning?"

"Well Albert, I need a few things. First I need two gold wedding bands. And I must have your promise to keep this to yourself."

"Sure, sure thing. Let's see, you should have about a size 10. Here, try it on."

"It fits fine."

"Wynola would probably be a size 6, she is a slender woman. What else do you need?"

"A colt revolver like mine."

"A .45?"

"I thought about a smaller caliber, but then we would always be having to carry two different caliber ammunition with us. Yes, a .45."

"I only have one left. A holster and ammo belt?"

"Yes."

"What else?"

"Two pair of snowshoes. The Alaskan type. A shorter pair for Wynola of course. And harnesses."

"Anything else?"

"Yes. A pair of warm leather boots like mine, and two pairs of wool socks for her and a pair for me. She'll be needing a warmer coat than she has now also. A knit hat for both of us. Mittens for both. Oh yeah, a knapsack. And that probably will have to do it for now. How much Albert?" Sterling could see the sparkle in his eyes as he was mentally counting.

"$375. Do you have that much Sterling or do you need some credit?"

"It'll probably break the bank, but I have it."

Albert Daggett helped Sterling load everything into his wagon. Sterling put the rings in his pocket.

"Come again Sterling. Sure do like doing business with you."

All the way home, Sterling was smiling, thinking about how he would surprise Wynola. Then it came to him. Instead of going directly to Barnjum, they would get off at the Reed Station. There was a little church across the stream, almost hidden from view.

Wynola was surprised with all Sterling had bought for her. "Don't want you getting cold on the trail."

"I have never shot a gun before, Sterling."

"Well, when we have time I'll teach you."

"When do you think you'll have to go back to Barnjum?"

"Tomorrow, before we get any snow that could cover everything up."

"Then we have a lot of work to do today," she said.

Sterling cleaned out his knapsack and repacked it with warm clothes and food. "Where will we stay, Sterling?"

"The first night in the wikitup I built. And then if we have to stay another night we'll use their cabin."

* * * *

They were up early the next morning and after a good hearty breakfast, while Wynola was cleaning the kitchen, Sterling was making sure the house was okay for cold weather. Then Wynola came out of their bedroom wearing her wolverine vest. Sterling stopped to stare. "While we walk to the train station, I'll tell you all about this vest."

After Wynola had finished her story, Sterling said, "I read an article in the New York Times newspaper about someone called *Carcajou* Woman. Now I guess you are *Carcajou* Woman. I'm in good company." She squeezed his hand.

* * * *

There was plenty of food in cold storage in the cellar, besides some water Wynola had set aside for their return, whenever that might be. There was kindling and dry wood beside the kitchen woodstove and the wood furnace in the cellar. "I'm ready if you are," Wynola said.

Wynola pulled on her wolverine vest and shouldered her backpack. Sterling already had his on. "Hope you don't mind walking to the train station?"

"As I said before, I am well accustomed to walking."

"I sure hope so, because we're going to be doing a lot of it."

When they walked by the Randall Farm, young Jimmy was chasing chickens near the road. He asked, "Are you *Carcajou* Woman, Wynola? My teacher has been reading to us articles in the old newspapers."

Wynola didn't know how to answer and she looked at Sterling for help. He nodded his head. "Yes, Jimmy. But the story in the newspaper was not about me. Her name was Rachel Morgan."

"Where you going this time, Mr. Silvanus?"

"We're taking a train to Barnjum. We will be back in a few days. When we do, we'll need some more eggs, Jimmy, and maybe a rooster or an old hen to eat."

"Okay, Mr. Silvanus," and Jimmy ran off chasing his chicken.

When they walked upon the loading platform, the conductor announced, "Train to Phillips, Barnjum and beyond, all aboard."

Sterling boarded the first passenger car and every one was looking at Wynola with her vest. They sat down and the train bumped ahead. "Excuse me, Wynola, I need to speak to the conductor."

He stood up and found the conductor in the next car. "Excuse me, Bob, Wynola and I will be getting off at Reed's Station, but I would like our backpacks to go on to Barnjum and taken off the train there," and Sterling handed him a silver dollar piece.

"Sure thing, Mr. Silvanus."

Sterling went back to his seat. "What was that all about?"

"Oh, just a surprise," he said.

"What surprise?"

"Well, if I told you, it wouldn't be a surprise, would it," that's all he would say.

The train stopped at the Phillips Station and two people got off and several sport hunters boarded for the Greene Farm in Coplin Plantation.

"Where's Coplin Plantation?"

"It's between Rangeley and Flagstaff. We'll go there eventually. Just not this trip."

It was an easy pull to the Reed Station. The elevation only

rose a little under 100 feet. When the train stopped, Sterling said, "This is where we get off, Wynola."

Bob, the conductor, met them at the door and said, "You folks can leave your backpacks right here. I'll see that they are put inside the station house at Barnjum."

"Thank you, Bob."

"Where are we going, Sterling?"

"We have to cross Orbeton Stream."

"Okay," she said, wondering what in the world was going on, and why was Sterling acting so secretive. "Are you sure you know where we are going?"

"Oh yes, I'm sure of this."

They walked across the bridge over the stream and started up the hill and then Sterling turned to the left. "A church. Way out here in the woods…" She stopped talking and turned to look at Sterling. He was smiling so radiantly her heart began to beat faster.

"A church in the woods, a surprise for me. Does this mean what I think it does?" She was so excited now she could hardly stand still and Sterling had never seen her so happy and so beautiful.

"If you'll have me?"

"Of course I'll marry you!" And she kissed him with a fiery glow all through her being. And he could feel the warmth in her soft lips.

"How long have you been planning this?"

"Only a few days actually. Come, let's go inside and see if any one is here." The church was new and not quite complete yet.

From the far corner came a low, kind voice. "I'm Morrell Wing. One of the deacons here at the church." A woman entered from a side door and then Deacon Morrell said, "This is my wife, Elvira."

"My husband laid the cornerstone for this church and then all the people in the community helped to put it up. We're almost done. We have been working on it since 1898. Our son Chester

Wing and his wife Netty were the first couple to get married here," Elvira said.

"Would you like for me to marry you two now or are you looking for a time to wed?"

"Actually, we would like to be married now," Sterling said.

Elvira was admiring Wynola's vest. "My word, this is pretty. What is it?"

"It's wolverine, ma'am," Wynola replied.

"I can do that," Deacon Morrell said. "My wife and I can be your witnesses. Shall we get started?"

* * * *

They walked out of the little church hand in hand. They were now man and wife and they each could feel a warming glow that was surrounding them. "Where to now, my husband?"

"Barnjum, only we have to walk. There probably is enough daylight left for us to reach the wikitup." It was a good day for a walk. The colorful foliage was still bright although it was a little past peak. The air was cool and easy to breathe.

"It isn't as easy walking this track as it is in the woods," Wynola said.

"No, but if we left the tracks, we'd have it up hill all the way and some of it rather steep."

There was a crew working at Perham Junction and they all stopped to watch them pass. Everyone had by now heard about the new warden and how he had gotten the best of Saul and Hartley, two people that no one liked. But now they were as interested in the woman who wore the wolverine vest. Who was she?

Frank Barnjum was in the station house when Sterling and Wynola arrived. "I heard you two got off at Reed Junction. That was quite a walk. Why did you get off?"

"We got married, sir. This is my wife, Wynola. Wynola, Mr. Barnjum."

"So what would you like now, Sterling?"

"We're going up into the mountains and bring back all of the illegal contraband we find. It might take us a couple of days. When we have everything down, I want to look inside of Lax's cabin."

"Just let me know when you want to enter his cabin and I'll unlock it. You really created quite a buzz around here when you brought Griswold and Montague down. They worked here for a day before I fired them. Nobody would work with them. I haven't found anyone who has anything good to say about those two. But how does Heywood Lax figure with those two?"

"He was sending their hides and meat out by rail to someone in Portland. I hope to learn more when we look at his cabin."

"Well, you know where to find me when you're ready."

Sterling and Wynola shouldered their backpacks and walked across the mill yard to a new twitch trail heading up Lone Mountain. The trail didn't go very far after leaving the yard. The crews had just started cutting the spruce here. "Look at the sky, Sterling," Wynola said. "It'll snow tonight."

"It'll cover a lot we need to look at."

The climb up the southern slope of Lone Mountain was steep, so they stayed close to the brook like Sterling had done before.

By the time they reached the little flateau where Sterling had made camp, they both needed to sit down and rest. Wynola was looking around at the surroundings. She got up and inspected the wikitup. There was dry wood inside and fir boughs for a bed, next to water, and situated out of the wind. "For a white man you picked a good location and built a nice wikitup." She laughed then and Sterling laughed, too.

While Wynola kindled a fire in the wikitup Sterling went after more dry wood. He had accumulated quite a pile. Then he went after more fir boughs to make their bed wider. All they had were two blankets, but inside the wikitup that would probably be enough.

"You heat up some water and I'll warm up some food." She

had brought plenty. She took a roll of aluminum foil from her pack to wrap the food in and heat it over the fire.

Sterling saw the roll and asked, "What is that, Wynola? It looks like metal." She handed him the roll. "It is metal, but so thin."

"It's called aluminum foil."

"Where did you get it? I have never heard of it before."

"I bought it at a trading post near St. Francis. My people have been using it for a few years now. I don't think you can buy it yet in this country. It was produced in Schaffhausen, Switzerland in 1907. We began using it my last year in nursing school. I brought two rolls with me from St. Francis."

"This is remarkable. I have never seen anything like it."

"It works well for wrapping food and cooking over an open fire like this."

When they had finished eating and everything was picked up, Wynola took her clothes off and washed up with the warm water. "When I am done you will have to heat more water, if you don't want to wash up with cold water."

Sterling laid back on the bed and watched Wynola as she washed her body and then dried off standing by the fire. There wasn't enough room in the packs to bring towels.

"Your turn."

He filled the can and while the water was warming he took his clothes off and stood close to the fire. The heat felt good against his skin.

"Are your ribs painful at all?"

"Not unless I slip or turn too quick to one side. Hiking, even up this mountain, didn't seem to bother too much."

The water was warm and Sterling washed up while Wynola lay on the blankets watching. Then he too dried off next to the fire.

"Come here, Sterling, and lie down next to me." He was all dry so he lay down next to her and held her in his arms. "My husband, there is something about me that I must tell you.

During my first year of nursing school, I was sick and had to have my stomach operated on." She took his hand and held it to her belly just above the pubic hair. "There was a cyst growing on my ovaries and the doctor had to remove the ovaries. I can never have babies." She was looking into his eyes.

"That doesn't prevent me from loving you. Besides, the life that you and I will be living together…well, there wouldn't be any place for raising a family. But thank you for sharing this with me."

She reached over and pulled him over on top of her. "Let's not talk anymore, this is our wedding night. I'm going to keep you up all night making love to you."

* * * *

The wind had blown for a while during the night and the temperature dropped and now at daylight there was two inches of fluffy snow. Sterling and Wynola were still wrapped in each other's arms and very warm and comfortable. "Come on, wife, time to get up."

"Instead of wearing you out last night, I think I wore out myself. My muscles are stiff and sore," she said while laughing.

"Better put on warmer clothing today in case that wind comes up again."

They had a good breakfast and washed it down with hot coffee. "What do we take with us?" Wynola asked.

"Everything, except the canvas. I hate to leave it here, but we don't have room to take it."

"Do you have more at the farm?"

"Yes."

"Then we leave it."

In spite of the snow, the walking conditions were good and they were at the poacher's cabin in less time than it had taken Sterling a week ago.

"What are you expecting to find?"

109

"Well, they each had a mountain lion over their shoulders when I encountered them. Those I had to leave. There probably won't be much left. I'm pretty sure other animals would have eaten them by now. I saw where they each had been shot and I can testify to that. I expect to find similar hides inside the cabin."

He pushed the door open and entered; Wynola behind him. There were two lynx pelts nailed to the wall drying. One bobcat, four huge beaver and one otter. He checked each hide and discovered that they all had been shot and not trapped. There were no trap jaw marks on any of the hides and there wasn't any trapping paraphernalia. "Looks like they were shooting the animals and not trapping. They must have had a bait pile or several. And they probably used the carcasses of the animals they skinned for bait. We need to look around outside."

"What are you looking for out here?"

"Any place where they have meat stored. Let's split up. Look for disturbed moss, a wooden box set in the ground, anything that doesn't look right."

The new snow cover was making it more difficult. Sterling found a small stream and followed that in both directions and found nothing.

He caught up with Wynola, "Find anything?"

"No, nothing."

"The information Chief Perry had was that they were shipping moose and/or caribou meat. They must have something somewhere for their own use. Let's keep looking."

The cabin floor was dirt so it couldn't be under the cabin. Maybe if it hadn't snowed.

"Sterling?"

"Yeah, over here."

"I think I found something that shouldn't be here." Sterling came over to her and she pointed to a mound under the snow. "This isn't a rock, but a pile of freshly dug sand."

Sterling walked around the area trying to feel something with his feet. Everything seemed normal. But there had to be an answer about the sand. It was left there for a reason. He and Wynola got down on their hands and knees. They crawled around the ground feeling with their hands and Sterling noticed some cedar trees three or four inches in diameter had been cut down. This had to be for a box under ground. They kept looking and finally Wynola pulled up some loose moss and saw dry sand under it. This wasn't right either. They both started scooping out the sand with their hands and found a tightly made cover to a nicely made cedar log box about three by four feet. And inside were three moose hind quarters and three strips of tenderloin. "They probably only took the hind quarters and tenderloins and left the rest."

The quarters were heavy and Wynola had to help Sterling carry them back to the cabin. When they had all three quarters outside the cabin, they stopped while Sterling wiped the sweat from his face. "They must have had something to haul all this down to the station in, or on." They went inside and Sterling had not seen it before but in the rafters was a hand made toboggan. "This must be it," and they pulled it down.

"We have two choices; we can eat a lunch now and plan to stay the night here or skip lunch and get to Barnjum for the night."

"I don't want to stay in this pig pen."

"Okay, we go now, but first I want to look around. I'd hate to think we missed anything."

While Sterling was searching the cabin, Wynola was loading everything onto the toboggan and securing the load with rope found in the cabin.

Sterling found a black account book of their past kills and sales and name and address in Portland. Leman Griswold. "I'm glad I found this. It'll be good evidence in court. Are you all ready?"

"Yeah, let's go," she replied.

It was a downhill drag all the way to Barnjum and there were several times when it took both of them to hold the toboggan back. It was getting dark and the 4 o'clock steam whistle blasted the silence. They came out to the log yard just as all the workers were going home. Mr. Barnjum was walking towards the boarding house for supper and he noticed Sterling and Wynola, and he walked up to greet them.

"I wasn't sure if you'd be back tonight or not. You have quite a load there." He stepped to the front door of Lax's cabin and unlocked it.

"Mr. Barnjum, while I search I would like you to stay to be a witness in case I find anything," Sterling said.

"What are we looking for here, Sterling?" Wynola asked.

"Heywood might have some of the moose meat here. Hides and I'd like to find an account book like we did at the other cabin."

Wynola found seven mason jars containing meat and assumed it would be moose. She set those on the table and Sterling found a small notebook under Heywood's mattress with dates of shipment and what was shipped.

"This is what I wanted. I'm going to write a report about what we found here and I'd like you to sign it as witness, Mr. Barnjum."

"Sure enough. If you don't have paper, I'll get some from my office," Frank said.

"I think you'll have to."

While he was gone, Sterling kept looking and what looked like a window box was actually a newly made shipping box. "Look at this, Wynola. Lax was going to use this to ship everything. It looks like he made it here."

"Are we going to take all this home with us?" she asked.

"I was thinking about shipping this to Portland to their handler there and send a telegram to the Chief Warden and ask that someone be there in Portland and arrest whoever picks the box up."

"Okay…but how is that person to know to pick up the shipment."

"Yeah, you're right. They probably would send a telegram. And if they were real smart the telegram would be sent to a third person. Maybe I'll send it to Augusta."

Frank Barnjum returned with the paper and Sterling wrote out a brief report and inventory of what was found and then signed by Sterling Silvanus, Wynola Silvanus and Frank Barnjum.

"The last train has already left and the next one won't leave until 10:30 a.m. Passenger train from Rangeley. You're free to use this cabin for the night if you wish and why don't you two have supper with me at the boarding house?"

While they waited sitting at a corner table, Frank said, "You really have people here stirred up…in a good way though. I don't think you'll ever have any problems with anyone here. People here didn't like Griswold and Montague much, and they were happy to watch you march them through the mill yard to the station house. I didn't know Heywood Lax had any business with them. They must have come and gone at night with the cover of darkness. I never supposed Lax would be involved in any business like this. I can guarantee you this, he'll never be allowed back here."

"Mr. Barnjum, we really hate the idea of having to haul those three hind quarters with us. You'd do us a big favor if you'd take them off our hands and you can use the meat to feed your crews."

"That's an offer I can't refuse. If you ever need a place to stay when you two are back in the area, I'll keep Lax's cabin available for you."

"Thank you, Mr. Barnjum."

"Not at all; that's the least I can do."

* * * *

Sterling and Wynola slept in Heywood's bed, but used their own blankets. It was only a three-quarter bed, but that was okay, too. They slept wrapped in each other's warmth and comfort.

The mill whistle went off at 5 a.m. to get everybody up and to work by 6 a.m. They were awake, so they got dressed and walked down to the boarding house for breakfast. When they opened the door and walked in, the conversations stopped and everybody was looking. "What are they looking at, Sterling?"

"It sure isn't me. They probably have never seen such a beautiful woman." This made Wynola blush and she smiled.

They sat down at an empty table and it was still so quiet. "Come on boys, don't let us spoil your conversations." The tension was broken.

The mill whistle blew its usual fifteen minute warning and suddenly everybody got up and left the boarding house for work.

The train arrived and Sterling loaded their shipping crate on the freight/passenger car bound for Augusta. Sterling and Wynola took a seat and people were staring at Wynola and her wolverine vest.

The train lurched forward and people stopped staring. The switch was already made at Perham Junction and the Lilliput Train increased speed towards Phillips.

There was a brief stop at Phillips and then on to Strong.

Before leaving the station house, Sterling sent a telegram to the Chief Warden advising him of the crate that was being shipped by rail and that on the morrow he would forward a written report.

"Oh, Mr. Silvanus, I almost forgot. I have a telegram for you from Augusta. Do you still want me to send yours?"

"Yes."

"What does it say?" Wynola asked.

"We have to be in court in Farmington on November 11th. Pansy? What day is this?"

Pansy laughed out loud before answering. "This is Friday the 8th."

"Whoa, I never would have guessed. Looks like we have the weekend to ourselves, wife."

Wynola squeezed his arm and smiled. This wasn't such a

bad life. Exciting really. When the train had continued on for Farmington, Sterling asked one of the porters if he would give them a ride home. "We're tired of walking, and these backpacks are heavy."

"Sure thing, Mr. Silvanus."

At home Sterling gave Tim the last dollar he had. "Gee, thanks, Mr. Silvanus."

The house was cold. While Wynola kindled the kitchen stove, Sterling went downstairs to start the wood furnace. Then he came back upstairs and before changing his clothes, he began to write a complete report. He decided that this job was requiring a lot more report writing than he liked.

"You know what I'd like for breakfast tomorrow?"

"No what?"

"Thick slices of bacon and flapjacks."

"What's a flapjack?"

"Pancake."

"Oh. I have never heard them called flapjacks. Is there any syrup?"

"There should be, I'll go and see."

* * * *

They had two marvelous days together. They took Duke and the wagon out to the woods and cut fir and spruce boughs to put up against the house to help keep the winter cold out. They worked together on the wood pile behind the barn. And everything they did, they did with laughter and a good time.

Then on Monday morning, they boarded the early train to Farmington and left Duke tied up at the station house. Sterling and Wynola were already sitting in the courtroom when the sheriff brought Griswold, Montague and Lax over, in handcuffs. Hartley's shoulder and wrist were still bandaged, but Saul's nose and head had healed.

When Saul walked by where Sterling and Wynola were

seated he sneered at Sterling. Judge Butler entered the courtroom and all had to stand until he was seated. He looked squarely at Sterling and asked, "Are these two your respondents?"

"Yes, Your Honor, they are."

"What are you charging them with?"

"There are several counts, Your Honor. First, Mr. Griswold and Mr. Montague, assault and battery."

The judge interrupted, "Who did they assault, Mr. Silvanus?"

"They assaulted me, Your Honor. I was hit behind the head with a rifle butt and I was on the ground. They each kicked me in the ribs and broke two. I was four weeks recovering. The second charge would be illegally killing two moose. The third charge would be the illegal killing of two lynx, one bobcat, four beaver, one otter and two mountain lions. The fourth charge would be the marketing of illegal contraband. Against Heywood Lax, would be one count of illegal marketing of illegal contraband."

"Mr. Griswold and Mr. Montague, did Warden Silvanus provoke you in any way before you attacked him?"

"We didn't give him a chance to provoke us. Just him being there was cause enough," Hartley said.

"And what about the illegal killing and selling of these animals and meat?"

"We can't get no work, no where. This job pays pretty good. We has to do something to live," Hartley replied.

Wynola tugged on Sterling's pants and handed him the two books he had confiscated.

"Your Honor, I have two ledgers that I confiscated from Saul and Hartley's cabin and one from Heywood Lax's cabin and a signed affidavit and witnessed by Mr. Frank Barnjum of what was found at Lax's cabin." The judge motioned for Sterling to bring the two ledgers up to the bench.

"We'll take a short recess while I review these."

Fifteen minutes later Judge Butler returned to the courtroom. "Mr. Griswold, how many years have you been in this business?"

"This would have been our third."

"Well, you didn't lie about that. But I find Mr. Griswold and Mr. Montague and Mr. Lax guilty on all charges. Mr. Griswold and Mr. Montague, for the charge of assault and battery, I sentence you to two years in the state prison. And for all the other charges, another additional year. So that's a total of three years. Mr. Lax, even though you didn't participate in the killing of the animals, you still are just as guilty. You'll have one year to spend with your friends."

Saul turned around and glared at Sterling and said, "I'll get you for this."

"Mr. Montague! Do you want me to give you another year on top of the three for threatening? You'll have three years to think about what Warden Silvanus did to you. You two attacked him unprovoked, then when he came after you, he beat the living hell out of both of you. Take my advice, Mr. Montague and Mr. Griswold, when you get out of prison, stay as far away from Warden Silvanus as you can, for your own good."

Judge Butler left the courtroom and Sterling was smiling as he looked at his wife and winked.

Sterling sent Chief Perry a telegram from the Farmington Station House before returning to Strong, informing him of the outcome of the Griswold, Montague and Lax cases.

Sterling and Wynola took the next few days off to rest and enjoy each other, before going out on another mission. It was now the middle of November and there was about ten inches of snow on the ground. "Where do we go next, my husband?"

"Well, let's work our way along the railroad. Next stop and point of interest would be Redington. There's a huge saw mill there and a nice community I've been told. It's only a little ways beyond the Perham Junction. From Perham to Redington it's a steep grade all the way and a second engine is used to pull trains up over the top of Sluice Hill."

"Have you had any complaints about Redington?"

"No. I understand the woods boss is a big Swede who expects a lot from his crews and they don't have time for any foolishness."

"What is the Swede's name?"

"I don't know. One of the engineers, Dana Aldrich, told me about him. He just called him the big Swede. I guess most of his men call him that also."

"Have you ever been to Redington?"

"No. This will be a new experience for both of us."

Two days later they were both eager to be on the move again and agreed to leave the next day, November 18th.

Before leaving the station house, Sterling sent Chief Perry a telegram telling him where he was off to now.

This trip, they boarded the train with their snowshoes and each were bundled as if expecting cold weather. The train lurched forward as they left the Strong terminal for Phillips. As they were passing the Cook farm, Percy was driving a team of work horses down from the barn. Maybe after some firewood.

As they were entering Phillips and the train was slowing down, Wynola asked, "What is that huge building there, Sterling?"

"That's the International Clothespin Factory."

"Clothespin? What's a clothespin?"

"You do know what a clothes line is?"

"Of course."

"Well, clothespins hold the clothes on the line."

"Oh."

Phillips was behind them now and they began the gentle rise in elevation towards Toothaker Pond and Perham Junction. The train was stopped at Perham Junction so the tracks could be switched. And while there the northbound tracks for Redington were also switched so they would not have to stop again.

They stayed on board at the Barnjum stop. No one got off, but two people boarded for the Greene Farm in Coplin Plt.

They hadn't gone far beyond the Perham Junction and there was an engine waiting to help push the train over Sluice Hill to Redington. It was a slow climb up the steep grade, but the view was pretty good. "First time up here?" an elderly woman asked.

"Yes, it is for us both. Hi, I'm Wynola Silvanus and this is my husband, Sterling."

"Hello, I'm Bernice. I'm cook at the boarding house. You can eat any time for 50 cents a meal."

They walked onto the station house loading platform and dry fluffy snow was blowing in the air. They picked up their gear and were walking inside and overheard a disgruntled worker talking to the station agent. It was clear he was upset. He was French, and he was wanting to leave.

As they were about to walk past this person, he saw them and said, "Mon, wish you luck, mon ami." Sterling's uniform shirt was under his coat and this fellow had no idea who he was talking to.

Sterling asked, "My friend, what is your name?"

"Pierre Lebeau. You come here! Good luck to you, mon ami. I have had too much and go home. Back to Megantic. You want place to live? I give you my cabin and all my things inside. You give me $40. That will get me home."

"Why do you want to leave, Pierre?"

He was almost hollering now, "D'Swede! All he do is push, push. Swede, he a big man. Bigger than me. Expect me to work as hard as he. He push, push all time, every day. When too cold to piss outside, he push, push. He knows only to push and work and push. I go home! You want my cabin?"

"Let me talk with my wife for a minute."

Sterling walked away from Pierre and Sterling asked, "What do you think?"

"It will give us a place to stay whenever we are here. Do you have that much money?"

"I have the money and I like the idea.

"Okay, Pierre we will buy your cabin and all things inside right?"

"Right! $40.! All yours!"

Sterling gave him the money and asked, "Which cabin is it, Pierre?"

"Last one, that way," and he pointed. "Good luck you and you."

A woman walked over towards Pierre then and Sterling and Wynola assumed it was probably Pierre's wife.

"Well, shall we go see our new home?" Wynola asked.

Outside in the mill yard everybody was busy. There was no lollygagging. "It is colder up here in the mountains, that's for sure." Men were busy loading railcars with sawn lumber and other cars with four foot pulpwood. The mill was operating and the saw was making a lot of noise.

"Everybody is working hard maybe to stay warm," Wynola said.

They found their cabin and it was the last one on the far end of the village. It was small, but it had a porch and smoke was coming from the chimney. "At least it'll be warm," Wynola said.

Sterling opened the door for Wynola and they both stepped inside. "It is warm in here. It is small, but neat. There's clothes here they couldn't take with them, boots."

"And look at these Wynola. Crosscountry skis. Two pair. Have you ever crosscountry skied?"

"No."

"I use to when I was at home with the folks."

"There's blankets, sheet, pillows, dishes. This is unbelievable, Sterling. We really lucked out here. But what's this?" and she touched a bright globe hanging from a wire.

"I wouldn't have believed it, but they have electricity here. They must generate electricity at the mill." Then Sterling had to explain to Wynola what electricity was.

"How does it get here from the mill? How does it make this globe shine so bright and why is it hot to touch?"

Sterling was smiling and almost laughing. And he was having a difficult time explaining to his wife, because he knew very little about electricity.

They stored their snowshoes against the wall and unpacked their backpacks. There were enough shelves to hold their clothing and personals. "Hey, there's even towels. I'm really surprised he sold everything so cheap," Sterling said.

"Well, I'm hungry. Want to try the food at the boarding house?" Wynola asked.

"Sure, let's go."

Even as cold as it was and now snowing heavily, there were small children playing on a rock in the yard in front of the boarding house. Wynola had taken her vest off but still, as they entered the boarding house, everyone there all stopped what they were doing to look at them and wonder. They had heard the stories from Barnjum about the new warden and what he had done to Griswold and Montague. As curious as they were about Sterling they were as equally curious about the pretty woman with him.

They sat down and had beef stew and biscuits and apple pie. The noon mill whistle blew and shortly after some of the mill crew came in to eat. And then a tall man covered with pitch, snow and sweat, and he walked over to Sterling and Wynola. "You must be the new game warden that we have been hearing so much about from Barnjum. I am woods boss here. Carl Haggan, but most people just call me the Swede," he extended his hand to shake Sterlings.

Sterling stood up and shook hands. "Mr. Haggan, this is my wife, Wynola." Wynola stood and shook Carl's hand.

"Nobody round here ever calls me Mr. Haggan. It's Swede. You looking to help out in the woods some? I lost a no account, good for nothing man."

"No thanks, Swede. We bought his cabin and he left."

"You don't have to worry none about my men shooting illegal game. I make sure they work enough to be too tired for any of that foolishness. Anytime you need anything you just ask the Swede. This boarding house is also depot. You can buy food, clothing here or boots.

"This is pretty good place to work and live. On Sunday some folks take the train to Marble Station in Rangeley and go to church. It gets cold here though. Cold like you never see before and snow, sometimes there so much snow that when a chopper fells a tree it comes down so hard and is buried in the snow and then it has to be dug out before it can be limbed or sawed into log length."

The mill whistle blew its five minute warning and everybody got up and left. And then the last whistle to start work again. It was still snowing and Sterling and Wynola went back to their cabin. "I think I'd better take stock how much food the Lebeau's left."

"While you are doing that, I'm going to strap on my snowshoes and have a look around here," Sterling said.

"Don't get lost," they both laughed.

Sterling followed the main skid trail up from the mill and it soon branched out towards different crews. The spruce trees were big and straight and he decided that the owners Putnam, Goodwin and Closson were making a lot of money from the mill. And not only from sawn lumber, but also from the many railcars shipped out daily loaded with pulpwood for the paper mill. The mill had started up in 1891 and still there was a lot of timber left to cut. He could see reforestation already in the old harvest areas.

When he came to the last crew he strapped on his snowshoes and began making a wide arc up beyond the workers and back towards the rail line going towards the Eustis Junction. Much to his surprise he was not seeing any moose or deer sign. He thought that this would have been a perfect place to winterout in fresh choppings.

The only signs of animal life he saw were partridge, fisher and squirrel tracks. The snow was still coming down hard and he checked his compass and headed down the mountain back towards the tracks. He could hear a train coming up from the Eustis Junction and he figured he must be close now to the tracks.

He snowshoed out to the right of way and waited for the train to pass. Except the train was the engine and tender plowing the tracks. He was too close and was covered by the snow being thrown back from the V-plow on front of the engine. He dug the snow out of his jacket and from around his neck and then dusted himself off.

Before going into the cabin he kicked the snow off his boots and opened the door. When Wynola saw him she began to laugh. "What have you, been playing in the snow with the children?"

"The snow plow got me."

That night the wind began to blow and when it had subsided some it began to snow again. "Boy!" Wynola exclaimed, "This is some brutal weather up here in the mountains. And speaking of the cold, we need more wood for the stoves. I have brought in everything that was piled up against the cabin."

"In the morning I'll go over to the mill and see what they have."

There was another eight inches of new snow in the morning and the wind had stopped blowing but during the night the wind had blown the snow into drifts in many places throughout the village and mill yard.

Sterling talked with the mill foreman, Bruce Wilkins. "Good morning Mr. Wilkins, I'm about out of firewood and what Lebeau left was scrap slabs from the logs. Do you have any more I can have?"

"Sure thing. I'll show you where they are. Everybody in the village uses these slab ends for heat and cooking. There is such a demand for wood I have a man that that's all he does is saw the slabs into stove length fire wood. We set up a special saw just for that. Over here. See that pile? Take all you need and use that hand sled leaning against the wall there to haul them.

When Sterling figured he had plenty of wood piled up against the cabin walls, he went inside to see Wynola, "I'm going down to the mill and see if I can help the boys shovel snow and clear out the mill. The wood was given to us, but I'd like to repay them."

Sterling was helping to clean off the deck and the logs that were already piled on the deck. When he finished that he started shoveling paths from the mill to stacks of sawn lumber and to the boarding house. When he had finished that he threw snow up against their cabin for insulation against the cold and then he did the same for all the cabins.

He took a break at noon and ate lunch with Wynola at the boarding house. The Swede sat down at their table and said, "Boy you must like shoveling snow. The boys said you shoveled snow and banked all the cabins, helped the crews at the mill clean out and cleared the paths. You know, I could sure use a big strong fella like you in the woods."

"Oh, that's okay, Swede. Thanks but no. I wouldn't have any time then to do what I'm supposed to be doing."

Sterling had left an indelible mark on everyone at Redington Village about what they thought of the new game warden now.

"I'm going to help Bernice clean up in the kitchen to help pay for our meals," Wynola said.

"Okay I'm going down to the station house and send an update to the Chief."

The mill whistle signaled there was only five minutes left before everyone had to be back at their work sites.

"Mr. Wilson, I wonder if you would send a telegram for me to the Chief in Augusta?"

"I would but the system is down. Somewhere during the night trees must have blown across the lines. Trains can't run until the lines are back up either."

"I was wondering why there hadn't been any trains through this morning."

* * * *

Wynola picked up a tray of dirty dishes and carried it into the kitchen. Bernice was leaning over the big sink and moaning and holding her stomach. Wynola set the tray down and went over to Bernice. She put her arm around her shoulders, "Bernice, what is it? What's wrong?"

"My stomach…hurts so much."

"I'll help you to your bed, Bernice." Wynola helped to steady her as they walked over to the side room where her bed was. "Sit down on the edge of the bed first, Bernice." When she had done that, "Okay Bernice now lay down." Wynola picked her legs up and helped Bernice to swing around and lay back.

"Bernice, I'm a nurse. Can you show me where it hurts?"

She put her hand down to the right side of her stomach. Wynola very softly started to probe the area with her finger tips. Bernice winced in pain and said, "There! It hurts there."

"Okay, Bernice. I'm going to open your blouse. I need to look at your stomach."

"Okay," she said between clenched teeth.

Wynola pulled her blouse open and saw that the skin around the affected area was red, warm and slightly protruding from swelling on the inside.

Sterling opened the door and entered the boarding house. When he didn't see Wynola he called out to her. "Wynola?"

"In here, Sterling."

Sterling went to the bedroom, "What is wrong, Wynola?"

"Her stomach hurts. I'm sure it's appendicitis. It has advanced and she needs an operation. We need to get her to a doctor as soon as we can."

"We can't. The trains are not running."

Wynola motioned towards the next room and they left the bedroom. "I didn't want Bernice to hear this. If she doesn't have an operation soon she may not survive until morning."

"I have an idea, but first I must go back down to the station house. If you don't see me, it is because I have left for help."

He ran back to the station house, "Mr. Wilson, is the telegraph system working yet?"

"No, no change."

"I need to get a doctor or Bernice may die before morning. Is there a doctor in Rangeley? It is closer."

"There is, but he has left and won't be back for another week. The only doctor would be Dr. Bell in Strong."

"Then I must go there, or perhaps only as far as Phillips. Maybe they can send a telegram to Strong for me."

"How do you intend to do this? It is eight miles to Phillips."

"I have cross country skis in my cabin. I will ski."

"It is downhill, Sterling, from here all the way to Toothaker Pond. Then from there to Phillips it is almost level. There will be one slight incline after you leave Reeds. The switches are all ready set for a direct run to Phillips, so you will not have to worry about that. Just be careful."

"I will, and tell my wife where I have gone."

Sterling ran to his cabin and took his skis, knit hat, mittens and poles and strapped the skis on out front and skied down to the tracks and got in between the rails and started towards the top of Sluice Hill. Once there he pushed off and he discovered he hadn't gone far down the hill and the last snow storm had only been in the higher elevation and here the snow between the rails was packed hard and his speed increased and he kept going faster and faster.

He didn't know how far down Sluice Hill he had come but he was still gaining speed. The rails were so narrow there was no way to slow down. He couldn't put his skis into a snowplow position and he couldn't turn. He didn't know how fast he was going, only he knew he had never skied so fast in his life. He knew if he fell now he would never get to Dr. Bell in time.

He was going so fast now he began to think he would probably coast over the slight incline beyond Perham Junction. But then he remembered the dangerously tight curves just before Perham Junction. As he went through the first curve his left ski kept hitting the rail and then he straightened it out as he was coming into the next. When he was clear of the last curve, he bent his knees into a tuck position, now trying to gain more speed for the run into Toothacker Pond.

He went by Perham and there were steep rocky cliffs on his

left. He didn't dare to take his eyes off the rails and look up. He was no longer gaining speed but he was going incredibly fast. He went by Reeds Station, around the bend and started up the slight incline. He knew he was going to make it. He was at the top and now going down towards Toothaker Pond.

He knew his fast pace would soon be over and he would have to cross country ski from there to Phillips. He had coasted further than he had expected and now he was on the flats. He started using his poles to help with the forward motion. He wasn't sure how far it was now to the station house in Phillips. He was tired but he couldn't stop.

He was close enough now to town and he could hear voices. What he didn't know was they were shouting at him. Finally, he reached the station house, unstrapped the bindings and stumbled inside exhausted.

Mr. Orris Vose met him at the door and asked, "My word, Sterling, what's happened? Why are you so exhausted and why were you skiing between the rails and from where?"

"There's a sick woman at Redington who needs an operation or she may not make it until morning."

"The telegraph system is still down. I tell you what, Number 14 is all warmed up, we'll hook a tender to it and take a flying trip to Strong and get Dr. Bell." They rushed out to the big engine and Vose backed it up and connected a tender.

"Jump on, Sterling. You'll have to be my tender. This is a bigger engine than we usually use and I'll have to keep my attention on her. You start feeding her some coal and I'll tell you when to stop."

As they rolled out of the Phillips Terminal, Sterling was beginning to sweat. "That should be good for a few minutes, Sterling. Who's sick?"

"Bernice, the cook at the boarding house. My wife says it is appendicitis and she's staying with her. She's a nurse."

As they flew past Cecil Voter's farm, Vose said, "More coal." Sterling began shoveling.

When he wasn't shoveling coal he noticed that down in the river valley there was very little snow. "You know, Mr. Vose, in Redington we have had some terrible snow storms. There must be twenty inches on the ground now."

"It's a different world, Sterling, up in those mountains. The folks who live and work up there are full of grit and fortitude.

* * * *

Wynola had put cold compresses on Bernice's stomach, trying to slow the swelling and she had a cool compress on her forehead also. She was beginning to show signs of a fever, which was not good. She had not seen Sterling for quite a while now and had assumed he had gone for help.

Just then there was a knock on the door jam and Wynola turned to see who was there. "Mr. Haggan. Any word from my husband yet?"

"No, he had to go to Phillips."

"He'll never get back in time, if he had to walk."

"He didn't walk ma'am; he skied with those cross country skis Lebeau made." Carl didn't want to say it, but he was thinking he wouldn't want to ski down Sluice Hill. He hoped he made it okay.

"I'm sure he'll be back soon. How is she?"

"A fever is beginning to show and that isn't good."

* * * *

"Sterling, as we cross Main Street, jump off and get Dr. Bell at the hospital and I'll turn 14 around and meet you right on Main Street. Hurry!"

Sterling jumped off and ran for the hospital.

"Mrs. Probert, is Dr. Bell here? I have an emergency."

"You wait here, Sterling, and I'll go get him." Alberta ran down the corridor and before she came to the room where Dr.

Bell was she began calling his name, "Dr. Bell! Dr. Bell!"

"Yes, what is it, Alberta?" he asked as he came to the door.

"Sterling is here without Wynola and he says he has an emergency."

Dr. Bell ran down the long corridor to see Sterling. "Dr. Bell, there's an emergency at the Redington Pond village. My wife says Bernice, the cook, has an inflamed appendix and she may not last through the night."

"I'll get my bag and some medicines and I'll be right back."

"Sterling, you said your wife?"

"Yes, Alberta, we were married at Reed's a few days ago."

"Oh, I'm so happy. You two make a splendid couple."

On the way to meet Number 14, Dr. Bell asked, "How did you get here from Redington? The telegraph is down and the trains won't run when it's down."

"I skied to Phillips and Mr. Vose brought me here in Number 14 and a tender. He'll take us to Redington."

"You mean to tell me, you skied all the way to Phillips from Redington?"

"Yeah, and believe me it was a fast trip. The fastest I have ever traveled on anything."

"Umh."

"Here comes Mr. Vose now."

The engine stopped briefly while Dr. Bell climbed aboard. It was already moving for Sterling and he had to run and jump on.

"Okay tender, we need a lot of coal now. You might want to take your jacket off, or you'll sweat in that. Hang on, Dr. Bell, this is going to be a fast trip. Sterling, you did say all the switches were set for a straight run to Redington?"

"Yes sir."

They were traveling at 40 mph as they went by the Cook Farm, and then were able to maintain that speed until they crossed the Sandy River just below town. Orris slowed the speed a lot going through town. Don't want to run over anybody while they are on their way home. Then as soon as they were clear of town, Orris opened the steam throttle valve and ole Number 14 came back to life. They were able to maintain 40 mph all the way to the slight rise just beyond Toothaker Pond. From there up, because of the steep increase in elevation and the tight curves, Orris kept or tried to keep their speed about 20 mph. Ole 14 was really working hard and Sterling couldn't stop shoveling coal.

"There's more snow here than in Phillips," Orris said.

"Wait until we clear Sluice Hill," Sterling said in between shovelfuls.

"Is this your first trip to Redington, Doc?" Orris asked.

"First time in the engine, but I have had to make two other trips because of accidents in the woods."

The sun had set now and everything was dark on either side of the engine. The headlight was shining bright though. And this helped to make an eerie scene with the new snow and shadows from the headlight.

They were beyond Reeds now and the grade was getting steeper with every 100 yards or so. Ole 14 slowed slightly to about 15 mph as it was climbing the approach to Perham Junction.

"The climb gets tougher from here all the way to the top."

Sterling didn't have any time to enjoy the ride. He was too busy, shoveling coal. They began the climb up Sluice Hill and much to Sterling's and Dr. Bell's surprise, Ole 14 had only slowed a little. "Makes a big difference whether you are hauling a full train of railcars or just the tender. I see what you mean, Sterling, about the snow. There's a little snow covering the rails, but we should be okay. If not we'll take a ride backwards down this hill."

That made Sterling and Dr. Bell feel better. Once in a while one of the drive wheels would slip, only a little. Ole 14 never missed a beat on its way to the top of Sluice Hill. But as they came near the peak, Orris had to back off the throttle so the train would not shoot forward and maybe derail. He pulled to a stop at the station house and blew the steam whistle one long blast. In part to celebrate a really fast ride from Strong and to let people know Dr. Bell had arrived.

The electric lights were on and as Dr. Bell stepped from the platform he said, "This is a completely different world up here."

They hurried over to the boarding house and it was empty except for Bernice, Wynola, the Swede and Bernice's kitchen helper. The Swede had laid down the law, "Bernice isn't feeling good, have your wife prepare supper tonight."

Dr. Bell went directly to see Bernice and Wynola. "Cold packs. That's good, Wynola, and cool body washes for the fever."

He examined Bernice's stomach and almost instantly said, "Oh my word, we need to get that out now. We need her on one of those tables."

"Sterling and Swede, come here please," Wynola said.

"We need Bernice on one of those tables in the dining room. Lift her in the blanket and put her on the table and then you leave. Dr. Bell doesn't need an audience and we have to keep this room as sterile and germ free as we can. Please," and she smiled at them.

"Dr. Bell, I have hot water already and I'll help you wash up. I also have new linen and towels ready."

"Wow, are you ever efficient, Wynola, I'm sorry to have lost you."

Wynola helped Dr. Bell wash up and then dry his hands. His surgical gloves were in his case. "Would you get my gloves and instruments from my carry case?"

Wynola helped him into his gloves and Dr. Bell went to work. All while he was cutting and cleaning and suturing, he kept talking to himself. "Oh yes, she would not have lasted much longer. This little bugger is almost ready to rupture. Then poison would have flowed all through her body, and she would have died probably by 10 p.m. tonight. It was fortunate for her, Wynola, you were here. Can you sew her up while I get rid of this?"

"Yes, Dr. Bell."

While Wynola was stitching up Bernice's stomach, Dr. Bell threw the appendix in the stove and along with his gloves and then he washed.

* * * *

"Are you hungry, Sterling?" Carl asked.

"Yes. I'm starving."

"Come on over to my cabin, maybe my wife Manette can fix us something. She good cook when she wants to. Sometimes helps out Bernice in boarding house. Looks like now she will have to step up, until Bernice is back on her feet."

While Manette was fixing supper, Carl and Sterling sat by the wood stove talking. "How you ski down Sluice and all way to Phillips?"

"Real fast down the Sluice. The tracks are too narrow to slow down. I was going so fast I coasted half way to Phillips from Toothaker Pond."

"You ski much?"

"I did when I was a kid on the farm. That was fifteen years ago though."

"Even so, I still find it hard to understand how soon you made it back."

"Well, Mr. Vose really knows how to drive that engine when he has to. He said we were doing 40 mph until we reached the bends below Reeds."

A knock came on the door. "Come in!" Carl hollered.

"I need to get this engine back to Phillips before the normal runs start and I'll need a tender," he looked at Sterling. "You up for another ride? You can come back with the morning train or perhaps the plow."

"I'll get one of the other men, Sterling. You've done your share. And you must be tired."

"Yes, but the men all have to go to work in the morning. I'll make the trip, Mr. Vose."

Orris joined them for supper and then he and Sterling left. "Tell my wife, will you, Swede."

"Sure thing."

There was snow blowing in the air. Probably just coming off the trees, but it was looking ominous.

Chapter 5

Sterling boarded the first train out of Phillips. It was going first to Barnjum and then to Redington. The night train left the Greene Farm at 6 a.m. and coupled the loaded freight cars waiting at the Eustis Junction and stopped at Redington. Dr. Bell was the only passenger getting on that morning. The train picked up two railcars loaded with lumber and then headed down the sluice with No. 10 hooked on to help brake the train.

Dr. Bell had stayed up all night with Bernice while Wynola had a chance to sleep. Now that Dr. Bell was gone, she was back at Bernice's bedside. She had come to, and her fever was gone. Wynola gave her two pills for pain that Dr. Bell had left with her.

Sterling arrived back at Redington at 10 a.m. and he needed sleep. He stopped at the boarding house first to see his wife and find out how Bernice was doing. Then he went to his cabin and fell asleep as soon as he stretched out on the bed.

* * * *

It was a tough few days for everyone and each day Bernice got stronger and the pain from the surgery was much better. She was feeling so good, that she was feeling guilty while Manette had to do her job. On the third day Wynola allowed her to get up and wash a few dishes and walk around the dining room and then back to bed.

On the fifth day she was out of bed and preparing breakfast when Wynola woke up. "Not one word, young lady. I feel fine and I'm not going to stay in bed any longer."

There was such determination in her voice, Wynola started laughing and then Bernice laughed also. "I'm going home, Bernice."

Sterling was still in bed and she removed her clothes and crawled in beside him. "I don't want to fool around. I want to sleep," she said.

* * * *

Thanksgiving was in two days and the mill crew and the woods crews were allowed to leave a day early to spend Thanksgiving with their families. But they would have to work Saturday and Sunday to make it up. Besides Sterling and Wynola, there were three families who would be staying at Redington. Wynola volunteered to help out it the kitchen. Sterling helped the Swede kill the turkey and pluck all the feathers out. When the turkey was all de-feathered, Sterling told Wynola. "I'm going to ski down to the Marble Station in Rangeley and look the country over between here and there. I'll come back on the evening train."

"Okay. Just make sure you're back tonight. Thanksgiving is tomorrow." She understood his need to get out and do his job, even if it was to familiarize himself with the countryside.

Sterling strapped on his skis and started down the slight grade towards the Eustis Junction. About a mile below Redington, the tracks ran through a swamp and marshy area. At the further end of the marsh he saw blood in between the rails. There was also moose tracks and hair. "Probably hit by the train."

The moose was dragging a hind leg, leaving obvious signs in the snow. He didn't want the moose to suffer with a broken leg, so he started to follow this trail through the snow. To his surprise the moose was laying down at the edge of the marsh and looking back at him. He took careful aim with his Colt .45 and took a fine bead just behind the head. He squeezed the trigger and the moose stopped struggling. He gutted it out and hiked back to the village for help to bring the meat back.

"We can take a hand car down and load the meat on that and bring it back," the Swede said.

Swede hollered to someone Sterling had not seen before, "Hey Pearley! We need some help!"

Pearley walked over where Sterling and the Swede were standing next to the handcar on the tracks. "Pearley, this is Sterling Silvanus, the game warden, and this is Pearley LaBlanc. Pearley, we need some help bringing a moose back. It was hit recently by the train and Sterling had to shoot it."

"Why sure, I'll gladly help," Pearley said. "Is it stove up bad?"

"One hind leg was broken at the knee and I had to shoot it. I'll have to have help to roll it over so I can cut the legs off and strip out the saddles."

"Uh um, I can smell and almost taste the gravy now. I'm kinda fond of moose meat," Pearley said.

The three boarded the handcar and rode it down to the marsh. By the time they had the four legs, the heart and liver and tenderloins on the hand car, they all were covered with blood and hair. Wallowing in snow didn't help matters any.

Back at the village, they cut off about twenty pounds of steaks from one hind quarter and this was given to Pearley. "I'd like the heart," Sterling said.

"We'll hang the rest up in the cold food storage room and we'll use it to feed the crews. There ain't no law against that is there, Sterling, since you gave us the meat?"

"None at all!"

The next morning Wynola sliced the heart into thin slices and fried it along with a few onions and eggs. "This is really good Wynola. I have eaten a lot of beef heart but never for breakfast."

Jokingly she said, "You'll be surprised with what you can learn from an Indian," they laughed.

Bernice, Manette and Wynola worked all day the day before and on Thanksgiving Day and as usual there was a lot of food left. "Before everybody leaves," Bernice said, "I want to thank Wynola and Sterling. If it had not been for you two, I would not be here now. You are family now, here at Redington, and you'll never have to pay for another meal eaten at the boarding house." They all clapped their agreement.

* * * *

That night while lying in bed Sterling said, "In the morning we must leave for a few days. I do have a job to do."

"Where do we go?"

"We need to work our way along the railroad to the end at the Berlin Mills in Coplin Plt."

"Will we go by train or walk?" she asked.

"We'll probably either walk or snowshoe most of the way over and then ride the train back."

The next morning before leaving, Sterling walked down to the station house to send a telegram to the Chief.

Have purchased cabin at Redington. Staying here at times. Working my way to the Berlin Mills in Coplin. Will send report when finished. Stopping at Langtown first.

"Send this please, Mr. Wilson." Ed Wilson read the telegram and then said, "You sure you want to go to Langtown? Those are some very strange people, Mr. Silvanus. You be careful."

"Thank you, Mr. Wilson."

While Sterling was at the station house, Wynola was saying goodbye to the Swede, Manette and Bernice. "Sterling wants to stop first at Langtown."

Wynola noticed facial changes of all three when she said Langtown.

"You and Sterling be mighty careful around those folks at Langtown. They don't cotton much to outsiders and probably even less of the law. I know you two are quite capable, but be careful," Swede said.

"We will. I promise."

"Mr. Silvanus," Ed Wilson said, "if you wait only a few minutes, the morning train will be leaving for the Marble Station in Rangeley and when it stops at the Eustis Junction you could get off there. It would save you some walking."

"Okay. That sounds good." He waited for Wynola to come down before boarding the railcar.

It was a short ride to the junction and they jumped off while the tracks were being switched. They had light packs each and carrying their snowshoes. Wynola was wearing her wolverine vest and each was carrying their handgun, strapped around their waist. Wynola made quite a picture, dressed as she was with a backpack, snowshoes and wearing her vest and handgun. Dana Aldrich watched as they began walking up the tracks. "Langtown won't ever be the same again. Those folks have no idea what is coming towards them."

"They make quite a pair don't they," his tender said.

The train lurched forward and Sterling and Wynola turned to look. Soon it was out of sight and the snowy wilderness was silent. The air was cold, but not unbearable. Cold enough to have frozen the packed snow between the rails, which made for easier walking.

"What do you think we'll find at Langtown?"

"I'm not sure. Strange acting people, that's all I know."

Before they reached Quill Hill, they began to see a lot of deer tracks in the snow. Along the tracks as well as deep trails going to and from the woods which were mostly low growing cedar trees and bushes. Ideal habitat for deer during the snowy cold months of winter.

Wynola stopped and touched Sterling's arm. When he turned she pointed towards several deer standing in the bushes watching them.

Once they started up Quill Hill there were no more deer or tracks. They were staying in the low cedar thickets. The sun was out bright and a really nice day. The air had even warmed a little. "It's so nice out here, away from everything. No noise and no people," Wynola said.

"Yeah, I agree."

They were back into thick spruce and fir trees and the only sign of life were squirrel tracks. At the Dyer water tank they turned left and followed the short spur line to Langtown. They could hear the saw mill now and axes biting into trees as the chopper made his notch.

The workers in the mill yard all stopped what they were doing and watched intently as those two walked past. They stopped first at the station house to get directions. There was someone standing in front of the door watching them through the window. He backed up when Sterling opened the door and he and Wynola walked in.

"Hello, I'm Sterling Silvanus and this is my wife, Wynola. I'm the game warden in this area."

The station agent just stood there for a few moments looking at the two. "And your name is…?" Sterling asked.

"Clemis, Amos Clemis."

"Whose in charge here?" Sterling asked.

"My brother, Doug Clemis."

"And where could I find him, Amos?"

"He's over in the mill."

"Thank you, Amos." They went outside and closed the door behind them.

As they were walking over to the mill, Wynola said, "What do you think of that?"

"That's about what we were warned about, I think."

The sawyer was standing on the deck with a cant dog in his hand when Sterling and Wynola walked up.

"Good morning. I'm Sterling Silvanus and this is my wife, Wynola. We're looking for Mr. Clemis."

The fellow spit out some tobacco juice and then said, "Which one? We're all pretty much Clemises in here. I'm Duke Clemis."

"I'm looking for Doug. The boss?"

"He's in talking with the filer. He's a Clemis also and he's sharpening the saw."

"Thank you."

There was a door next to the deck and Sterling opened it and walked in, Wynola behind him. Everyone inside the mill stopped to look at the two strangers. They walked over to the two men who were sharpening the saw. "Mr. Clemis?" Sterling asked.

"Which one do you want?"

"Doug Clemis."

"I'm him. Who are you?"

"I'm Sterling Silvanus and this is my wife, Wynola." Sterling raised his voice a bit so everyone there would hear. "I'm the new State Game Warden in this area and I would like to talk with you."

Doug climbed down from the carriage rails and said, "Let's go outside, so these men can get back to work."

They followed him out into the yard. "Now what is it you want?"

"I'm just making sure you have been notified from the Warden Service Department in Augusta that lumber camps can no longer kill caribou, moose or deer to feed the crews. This law was passed in 1880 and I understand there hasn't been a game warden in this area at all, and I just wanted to make sure you understood the law."

"I understand alright what the law says. Now is there anything else I should know?"

"Only that I will be around. And now we would like to go up to the dining hall and get a meal. We'll pay of course." Doug seemed to bristle up a little more.

They left the mill and walked up to the dining hall and took their backpacks and snowshoes inside, and set them against the wall.

"Can I help you?" a squat middle-aged woman asked.

"Yes ma'am. We would like to have lunch if that would be possible. I will pay for the food of course."

"The lunch is 50 cents each. Paid, before I serve you."

Sterling gave her a dollar with a smile. Another woman brought two bowls of beef stew and biscuits. She looked very much like the first woman, maybe somewhat younger. And she poured them some hot coffee and then left.

"This is really good stew," Wynola said.

"Yeah, but it isn't beef."

"What is it?"

"Well, there's a hair here that looks like moose."

"It seems odd she would give us moose stew. Well maybe she doesn't know you're a game warden. Take your jacket off and see how she reacts to your uniform."

Sterling took his jacket off and put it on the back of his chair, and then sat back down and continued eating while keeping a watchful eye on the kitchen.

When they had finished eating, Sterling walked over to the kitchen door and opened it and stuck his head in and said, "Thank you ma'am for the lunch. The stew was very good." Then he put his coat back on and they left the dining hall.

They shouldered their packs and Wynola asked, "Where do we go now?"

"Follow me. I think we'll give them something to think about."

"What are you talking about?" she asked as she followed him towards the wood line.

"We'll put our snowshoes on and snowshoe up through their choppings and then make a circle to the right back to the railroad."

"What good will that do?"

"It'll shake 'em up a little. Getting to thinking and worrying about that stew we ate."

They stopped at the edge of the mill yard and strapped on their showshoes. People were watching.

Sterling found a horse trail and they began following that until there was a team of horses twitching out a load of spruce logs. They stepped off the twitch trail and out of the way to allow the team, load and driver to pass. When the driver saw them he stopped the team for a short rest.

He hollered, "Hey you! What you doing up here?"

Sterling snowshoed over to him and said, "I'm a game warden. Sterling Silvanus and this is my wife. And who are you?"

"Tim Clemis. What you doing up here?"

"Just looking, that's all."

"Looking for what, Mr. Warden?"

"Oh…for anything that shouldn't be here."

Tim slapped the reins and the team took off.

"I think we have raised enough hackles here," and he began to laugh.

They were finding a lot of deer tracks in the woods and Sterling had decided that he would have to do some work here. They crossed Dead River and back to the tracks.

They found a lot of deer between the harvest area and Dead River. They found ice solid enough to cross on and then uphill to the tracks. "You've been awful quiet. What are you thinking about?" Wynola asked.

"I think some one back there is still killing deer and moose to feed the crews. I was thinking about how to prove it. It'll be hard on snow."

They took their snowshoes off once they were back on the tracks. They had about a mile to go to the Stratton Junction at the Greene Farm.

As they were leaving the station house walking towards the main house at the farm, they were met by a friendly man. "Hello. Can I help you?"

"Yes, is Mr. Greene here?" Sterling asked.

"Isaac Greene sold out to me a few years ago and moved to Rumford. I'm Ralph Reed. My friends call me Jim."

"Mr. Reed, I'm Sterling Silvanus, the game warden in this

area and this is my wife, Wynola. You have quite a set up here."

"Thank you, but I can't take all the credit. My predecessor Isaac Greene had already built up much of this. He was an amazing man with a big dream.

"Forgive me, where are my manners. Would you like to come in where it's warm, and have some coffee?"

"Thank you. That would be very nice," Wynola said. "My legs are tired."

Mr. Reed, (Jim) escorted them to the huge dining hall and pulled up three chairs close to the fireplace. Mrs. Reed brought in three cups and a pot of coffee. She filled each cup and then went back to work in the kitchen.

Wynola held her cup in her hands, warming her cold fingers. "Now tell me, what brings you all the way out here and on foot, dragging your beautiful wife along?"

"We left Redington this morning and stopped at Langtown and talked with Mr. Clemis and then we snowshoed through some of his choppings. Then we came here. I'm talking with each crew camp to make sure everyone understands the law about no longer being able to kill caribou, moose or deer to feed the crews. So far the only indication of any problems was at Langtown." Sterling told him about the beef stew that had moose meat instead of beef.

"You'll have your work cut out for you if you think you're going to change things at Langtown. They're an odd bunch. Be careful though with any dealings you have with Doug Clemis.

"Silvanus, that name rings a bell in my head. Are you the warden who cleaned out the poachers at Barnjum?"

"Yes sir."

"Well maybe I should be telling the Clemises they had better be careful. You won't have any trouble here, Sterling. I only do a little lumbering on my own land in early winter before the snow gets too deep. We farm here and supply the crew camps and villages with food, milk, and feed for their horses and we board a lot of the work horses here in the summer."

"How big is the farm Jim?"

"Five hundred acres and most of that is in agriculture or hay and grain fields. Last summer we put up over 10,000 square bales of hay. We raise poultry, pigs, sheep and cows. It takes a big crew to take care of all that."

"Did Isaac Greene build this farm?"

"He and his brother, John, bought the Kennebago farm in 1874. They were from Salem. In 1878, John and his entire family, except for one daughter died of diphtheria. In 1887, Isaac bought his brother John's share of the Kennebago farm and then sold it and bought this farm. It was called the Mann farm then.

"Isaac was en enterprising man. There was a stage line from Stratton to here, but in 1898, Isaac extended the line to Rangeley. Now tourists and sports people could come from Rangeley when the train isn't running. I now have two sport cabins for the tourists and hunters. Deer hunting here is excellent.

"I have a small grist mill on the property and a smoker to cure hams and bacon. To lure more summer tourists and sportsmen, Isaac dug two small ponds and stocked them with brook trout."

"This is really a beautiful setup you have here, Mr. Reed."

"Do you have a room for us, Mr. Reed?"

"Please, call me Jim, everyone else does. Our cabins are closed for the season, but we have plenty of rooms in the main house. We often have to put up train passengers."

Sterling gave his pass to Jim. "This will cover our room and meals. I'll sign the bill and all you have to do is send it to the Department in Augusta."

"Nonsense, you and your wife can put up here any time you want and no charge for your meals either. And you can stay here while you harangue a few of them at Langtown. Don't get me wrong, Sterling, you won't find any harder working men and women anywhere, but outsiders stay clear of there. The only people who do are the railroad people and they don't socialize none. I'd like to be there when you catch them red handed. From what I have heard about you, I think you'll find what you are looking for."

"Now, enough talk. I think supper is ready. Sterling, Wynola, this is my wife, Freda."

"Hello Freda, nice to meet you." It was odd, both Jim and Freda noticed how Sterling and Wynola both answered at the same time with the same words. They truly were in sync with each other.

During supper there was more conversation about the farm, the railroad and where Wynola was from. Jim and Freda were as interested with listening to Wynola as they were about Sterling.

After supper while Jim and Sterling moved their conversation to the other room in front of the fireplace, Wynola helped Freda clear the table and put away the food. "Where do all of your workers eat, Freda?" Wynola asked.

"They eat in the main dining hall. We usually eat with them unless we have guests and then we prefer to eat in here. The kitchen girls will do the dishes."

"What will I find for attitudes at the Skunk Brook Camp and the Berlin Mill at the end of the line?" Sterling asked.

"Most of the crews are down from Megantic, there are a few from Stratton and Flagstaff. They're all good workers. Good men too. And they work well together. Whether they are still serving wild meat at the table, I don't know. But you won't have any trouble talking to the manager and foremen."

That night as Sterling and Wynola laid in each other's arms Wynola asked, "I know you have been thinking all afternoon about Langtown. What are you going to do?"

"I'm not sure yet. But something has to be done. I'll bet that woman who gave us moose meat stew was probably beaten later. I think we stirred them up enough so they won't be killing anything for a while."

"Or," Wynola added, "they feel so brazen where they have gotten away with it for so long our presence may not deter them at all."

When Sterling went to sleep that night the last thing on his mind was how to stop the illegal hunting at Langtown.

* * * *

When they awoke in the morning Sterling had his arm around Wynola and she had her head against his chest and an arm across his stomach. Sterling was awake first and he laid there smelling the natural perfume of Wynola's hair and body. She slowly awoke and opened her eyes and looked at Sterling and smiled.

"Are you awake?"

"Just barely. Don't move. I'm so comfortable."

"I had quite a dream last night."

"Can you remember much about it?"

"I can remember everything in great detail. The last thing I was thinking about before going to sleep last night was Langtown. And in this dream, it was more like I was actually there. It wasn't just make-believe images. It was as if I was really there. I had a body that I could see and I could feel to touch things. I saw how to catch whoever is doing the illegal hunting."

"How?"

"We wait until the night of the full moon and we go in on foot, walking in the deer trails so not to disturb any snow and leave boot tracks. And then we wait.

"It's odd, I could smell the freshly cut wood and I could see everything in clear detail, even though it was night. I have never had a dream with such clarity and then to be able to remember it."

Wynola began to laugh and she said, "My husband, you have had a vision. The spirit of the Great Creator was showing you how to accomplish this. Are you sure you're not Indian? Sometimes you seem to be more Indian than me." She laughed again and kissed him.

They had a good breakfast of eggs, ham and pancakes and plenty of hot coffee. "Are you going to wait for the train to take you to the end of the line?" Jim asked.

"No, we'll walk and look the country over. I want to thank you for your hospitality," Sterling said.

"You are certainly welcome here any time," Freda said.

"Thank you. I'm sure we'll be back." Wynola got up then and pulled her wolverine vest over her head.

* * * *

Jim and Freda Reed stood in the doorway and watched until Sterling and Wynola had walked out of sight. "They'll go back to Langtown, won't they, Jim?"

"Yeah, maybe not today, but they will go back. He has that kind of determination.

"You know, Freda, he is so polite and well spoken, it's difficult to understand how he can handle people like the Clemis and not be concerned about it. He seems to be too much of a gentlemen for this job."

* * * *

At the Dago Junction, they took the line to the right, to the Skunk Brook Camp. From the tracks they could see the massive logging operations on the north slope of Black Nobble Mountain. And they could hear the saw mill.

There was a lot of activity around the mill and the yard and everybody stopped what they were doing and watched as the two strangers crossed the mill yard. There first stop was at the station house and the boss of the mill was there talking with Fred Amery, the agent.

Sterling introduced himself and Wynola the same as he had done at the previous stops. The atmosphere here was so much different than what they had seen at Langtown. The workers all went about their work happy and talking cheerfully among themselves.

He talked openly with John Phillips, the manager, about the new laws and Mr. Phillips said he had complied with them. "We are here to cut trees and saw out lumber. It would cost me more to take someone away from their job to hunt. No, Sterling, you don't have to worry any here."

"Where are your workers from?"

"It's about half and half, between Woburn, Quebec and Stratton. They're all good men. Would you like a lunch before you leave?"

* * * *

Instead of walking back to Dago Junction and following the tracks to the Berlin Mill north of Crocker Mountain, Sterling took a compass heading and they snowshoed through the woods to the north slope of Crocker. They saved some time and a mile or so of travel.

They came out to a new harvest area and there were deer everywhere feeding on the tree tops and browse. When they would be seen by a woods worker, the worker would wave. They waved back. There was no animosity here either.

They were met out in the mill yard by Jake Parsons. Here he was called the supervisor. "Are you the warden who finally took care of Griswold and Montague?"

"Yes."

"They were doing the same thing here, until I had the boys run them out of this country. But I'm surprised that you alone bested them. Those two lived to fight and sometimes I think they fought each other."

They talked for a long time with Mr. Parson about the goings on in and around the wood business. "I don't know if this is in your area, Sterling, but there's stuff going on at the Bigelow Station. Once in a while if the air is right we can hear rifle shots coming from there. And I don't know any more than that."

"Well, we'll have to spend some time on it, I guess."

They stayed for supper but when the evening train left, they were on it. There was one combination car and the rest were freight cars loaded with pulpwood and four cars with sawn lumber. At Dago Junction, the train picked up a few more cars and then at the Greene Farm the train spent most of the night parked behind the farm. It would leave just before daylight and pick up more loaded cars at either Langtown or Eustis Junction. Sterling and Wynola were back at Redington by 10 a.m. After the fires were going and the cabin warm, Sterling wrote out a report to Chief Perry and Wynola was preparing something for lunch. He took his report down to the station agent and put it with the outgoing mail and then he sent a brief telegram.

Have completed this circuit of the Sandy River Railroad and have talked with villages and lumber crew chiefs. Found work needing done in Langtown. Rest of loop was good. Staying in Redington until completed task at Langtown.

When they had finished eating a light lunch they lay on the bed and soon they were making passionate love. In spite of the mill noise. Then they slept until it was time for supper. They ate with the crew in the dining hall at the boarding house. All were glad to see them back.

When they had finished eating, some of the men sat near the fireplace, swapping stories of the day. Sterling asked Pearley, "Pearley, where's your wife? You stayed here for Thanksgiving, but you are married."

"Trying to get that ole hag to leave me and go back where she came from. When I came up here for the season I didn't leave her any money or food. She's probably gone by now. She's an awful woman, that one. When I'm home, I can't do anything but she's always jumping down my throat."

"Do you have any children?"

"My God no! I've been lucky there. With a kid or two, she surely wouldn't leave."

"What are you going to do if she is still here when you return in the spring?"

"I'll drop her off at your door step," he answered, and they all laughed about that.

Chapter 6

Sterling and Wynola took a few days to rest and spend some time together without worrying about game wardening. Sterling worked down at the planer and trimmer shop making a special rocking chair for his wife for Christmas, which was in two days.

Most of the crews were planning to go home for the holiday and the usual stay behinders started planning a special Christmas dinner. Instead of turkey, Bernice had ordered earlier a side of smoked ham. She also ordered sweet potatoes. Wynola helped her in the kitchen baking cinnamon rolls, bread, pies, and a frosted Christmas cake. And she had also ordered some apple cider.

Christmas morning Sterling and Wynola lay in bed for a long time. There was no noise from the mill, only the light wind that occasionally rattled a window. The sky was blue and the air temperature was only a little below freezing. She moved her leg over the top of his and felt the warmth of his body. He brought his arm up and around her back and kissed her softly and then he looked into her sparkling eyes. They seemed to be laughing. "I love you, Wynola. I can't imagine life without you. Before I met you at Wonnocka's village, I never dreamed that I would ever meet anyone like you. Thank you for coming into my life."

There were tears in her eyes. Because she was feeling the same emotions as her husband. With their desires, passions and emotions satisfied they got up and got dressed. This morning,

Sterling made breakfast, while Wynola kindled the fires. When she saw the rocking chair Sterling had made for her, she sat down in it and rocking back and forth, she began to cry. And then she started to laugh. "It is so beautiful, Sterling, and so comfortable."

She gave Sterling a wool vest that she had been knitting while he was at the planer shop. It was lined with cotton cloth and it fit him perfectly.

* * * *

With January and the new year, unbelievable cold settled in the mountains. For a week it was too cold to even take the work horses out of their stalls. The cutters shoveled out trees and brushed out twitch trails for the horses. Sterling and Wynola returned to Strong for a few days to check on their house. There was a full moon coming the last week of January and Sterling was hoping the cold weather would be over. If not he would still go to Langtown.

The cold temperature did break the day Sterling and Wynola returned to Redington and much to their surprise there was a dead animal lying on the porch. It looked like a deer, but the head and feet had been removed along with the tail. "What's going on, Sterling? Why did someone leave us a deer with no head or feet?"

"I don't know." He examined the animal closer and decided it wasn't a deer at all. The hair was wrong. It was close though. "Somebody playing a joke maybe. No need letting it go to waste, we might as well can the meat."

The cabin was cold and it took a long time to warm up even with both wood stoves going. The animal was frozen and had to be brought inside to thaw before they could take care of it.

The next day Sterling said, "Wynola, why don't you fix us some food we can take with us to Langtown. I'll look after the canning."

"How many days do you think it'll take?"

151

"Better plan on three."

When the canning was finished, Sterling set the Mason jars aside and said, "We'll keep these jars for a special occasion." He was thinking now that the animal was probably more goat than deer and this was probably someone's idea of a joke.

The full moon would be the next day, January 22nd, and for the rest of that day Sterling and Wynola lounged around their cabin and the boarding house conserving their energy. "We will leave in the morning Wynola, we'll board the morning train to the Berlin Mill and get off at the Dyer Tank when the train stops for water. Then go in by snowshoes from there."

The next morning they were up well before daylight and had a hearty breakfast and plenty of coffee. Then they dressed in warm wool clothing and waited for the train. The Swede suspected what they were going to do and he met them at the station house. "Remember this isn't any game. Those people up there have always had things their own way. They may not take too kindly to you and whatever it is you're going to do. Be careful, I'd hate to see anything happen to either of you."

"Thanks, Swede, we'll be okay." Swede watched as they boarded the train. Wynola with her wolverine vest, knit hat pulled down around her ears, Colt .45 strapped around her waist and dressed in wool head to toe. She looked like a miniature mountain man. He laughed to himself then and said, "She probably has as much of a bite as Sterling." But he still worried about them both.

An hour later the train stopped at the Dyer tank to take on water and Sterling and Wynola got off. Strapped on their snowshoes and left the tracks and crossed Dead River towards the outer perimeter of the harvest area, tree tops and slash. They had plenty of time and there was no need to hurry.

Sterling found an out of the way spot where the westerly breeze would blow wood smoke away from Langtown. He kindled a small fire with dry tree limbs and they took off their backpacks and melted snow to make some coffee. "Now what?"

"We wait and listen for shots. If we don't hear anything come dark we'll move down in the cuttings and wait. With the full moon I can't see how they could pass the opportunity to go out after supper when everything is quiet and the men are all out of the woods."

The fire was comforting even though it wasn't as cold as it had been. The mill whistle blew the noon time signal and the mill went silent and everyone was heading to the dining hall. Wynola was heating their lunch on a crotch stick. "I had thought earlier that the noon break might be a good time for someone to shoot a deer, but the boss Doug Clemis probably wouldn't allow the kill to interfere with anyone's working. Work probably comes first to him. I have an idea he drives his workers like dogs."

They finished their lunch and the mill whistle blew its warning. And in a few minutes they could hear the mill's big saw singing as it cut its way along a spruce log. There wasn't much to do except sit back and wait.

Before the sun had set and the crews would be done for the day, Sterling and Wynola ate another hot lunch and coffee and Sterling then put the fire out. They shouldered their packs and carried their snowshoes in their hands. Snowshoe tracks would look to obvious.

Sterling found a deer trail and they followed that and worked their way down slope where they could watch if anyone left the mill yard on foot. It wasn't quite dark yet and they had to go slow and be careful about being seen.

The mill whistle blew, signaling the end of the work day and the workers would soon be filtering out of the woods to the dining hall.

Sterling found what he was looking for as they watched the last of the workers walk into the mill yard. He found a slight knoll far enough away so they would not be seen, yet they had a clear view of the dining hall and mill yard since here too they had electric lights and most of the exterior was illuminated.

"I need to pee," Wynola said.

"Okay." She went back behind some fir trees. She had a lot of clothes to undo.

When she was back Sterling looked at her and grinned. She nodded her head towards the mill. There were two men walking across the yard and one was carrying a rifle. Now Sterling had to pee. The adrenaline was beginning to flow. They followed a twitch trail up towards them for a short distance and then turned to the left where the newest slash would be.

"What do we do now?" Wynola whispered.

"We wait for a gun shot."

What seemed like an eternity was actually only fifteen minutes and there were two rifle shots about ten seconds apart. "Two deer. They'll both have their hands full when they come out. We need to get over on that twitch trail they went in on. I figure they'll use the same one to come out." They picked up their snowshoes and waded through the snow to the twitch trail. Then they followed that in for a distance until Sterling found what he needed for an ambush. Sterling whispered to his wife, "You hide in those thick jack firs. I'll be down the trail and when they go past you, I'll step out in front of the one in the lead. Then you step out and come up behind the last guy. It's hard to say which one will have the rifle. If my guy has it, I'll take it away from him. If your guy has it, watch him, if he starts to raise it at me...you already will have your handgun out, right?" She nodded yes. "Good. If he raises the rifle, hit him right here as hard as you can." He touched her collar bone. "This will break his collar bone and he'll drop to the ground and then put your .45 in his face. He won't move then."

"Is this how you got Griswold and Montague?"

"Yeah, shhhh."

They waited and they could hear each others heart beating. Sterling's was sounding like a drum Wynola had heard in her people's ceremonies.

"Okay, you get in here. Remember what I said."

"Okay."

Sterling went down the trail a short distance and stepped behind a huge maple tree. The sky was clear and the full moon was out. Visibility in the trees was good. They had time now to get both deer and they should be dragging them out now. Sterling was saying to himself.

Then he could hear them talking back and forth not aware of anything. Wynola saw them first and she noticed the guy in front had the rifle and like Sterling had guessed, they each were dragging a deer. She withdrew her handgun.

The first guy and deer were beyond her now and then the second guy. She silently stepped out on to the trail right behind the second guy. And at the same time, Sterling stepped out in front of his guy and he started to raise his rifle. Sterling grabbed the rifle and brought his handgun down on his collar bone. Behind him his friend saw what happened and he withdrew his knife and before he had a chance to bring it up, Wynola hit him in the collar bone and he went down. Then she stepped in front of him and put her .45 in his face and said, "Drop it." He did and his mouth was open in shock.

Sterling holstered his handgun and said, "You two are under arrest for illegal killing of deer and commercial hunting. What's your name?"

"Bill."

"And you?" he pointed at the other guy.

"Ted."

"And I bet both last names is Clemis. You okay Wynola?"

"I'm just fine. Hey, this is fun!" Ted looked at her and now he was more afraid of this woman, whoever she was, than the guy with the badge.

Sterling removed one blanket from his pack and tore a strip of cloth from it and tied a sling around Bill's left arm and then tied one around his shoulders to immobilize the broken bone and then he did the same to Ted and then handcuffed the two together. "Wynola, take his knife and cut both tails off and put those in my pack. Then throw the knife."

When she had done that, Sterling said, "Now gentlemen, we are going to walk out of here. If you raise your voice or give us any trouble at all we will hit both of you over the head and crack your skulls.

"Now, stand up." They did. "We can't drag those deer out of here and I'll explain to the judge why. Let's go."

They had to take their time as these two were handcuffed together and they each were hurting with broken collar bones.

Eventually they made it to the mill yard and instead of sneaking around to the tracks, Sterling was walking right towards the dining hall. Even Bill and Ted were wondering what was happening. When they were about fifty feet away, Sterling stopped and so did they all.

Then Sterling hollered for Doug, the boss, "Hey! Doug Clemis! Come out here!"

Wynola was shocked. She had no idea what he was doing. And Bill and Ted were equally surprised. And the two also knew there would be hell to pay for getting caught.

The dining hall door opened and Doug stepped out. "What's going on here?"

In a deep even voice, Sterling said, "Come here." Doug started walking, then stopped.

"We have Bill and Ted and they are under arrest for illegal killing of deer and commercial hunting. And I'm taking them to the County Jail in Farmington. If you think you and your boys are going to come after us, just remember what we did here tonight." Then in that deep steady voice again, "Do you understand me?"

"Yeah, I understand," Doug replied.

"Pa! Don't let him take us! Pa," now Bill was pleading.

Ted didn't say anything. He was still afraid of this woman who wore a wolverine vest.

They walked out of there and Wynola holstered her handgun. Sterling never had his out.

Bill and Ted being handcuffed together made it cumbersome

walking. When they reached the Dyer tank, Sterling stopped and asked, "Are you two going to make it?"

Bill answered, "Yeah." Ted didn't say anything.

"Are you cold?"

"Yes," Ted answered this time.

Sterling took his blanket out of his pack and drooped it around Ted's shoulders. Then Wynola did the same for Bill.

"If we stop, you'll only get colder."

"How far you going to walk us tonight, warden?" Bill asked.

"If the station house at Quill Hill is unlocked, then we'll stop there."

It was locked up tight, so they continued walking all the way to the Eustis Junction. The station house was open, and a fire in the stove.

When Bill and Ted started to sit on the floor, Wynola said, "I wouldn't sit on the floor. With broken collar bones, you'll never be able to stand up. You'd better sit in a chair." She was cold and tired and she knew Bill and Ted had to be, also.

Sterling noticed Wynola was getting tired. "Why don't you sit down and take a nap. I'll stay up and watch these two."

"No arguing here," and she sat on the floor in the corner and she was soon asleep.

Sterling sat by the stove watching Bill and Ted. They looked to be maybe in their early twenties. In an odd sort of way, he was feeling a little sorry for the two. They were sleeping, also.

As the sun was beginning to peak through the darkness, the station agent Howard Smith opened the door and was surprised to see four people in his work space. Then he saw Sterling was awake and he saw his badge. Wynola awoke then as did Bill and Ted. "What's going on here?"

"These two are in my custody and we're waiting for the train," Sterling replied.

"Well, the morning train from Strong was delayed this morning. It won't be here until 12:30 p.m."

"What do we do now, Sterling?" Wynola asked.

"We can't stay here in Mr. Smith's way, we don't have a choice. We'll have to walk to Redington. Come on you two, we have some more walking ahead of us."

* * * *

It was 10 a.m. when they came trudging into Redington. "Are you boys hungry?" Sterling asked.

"Yes, we're starving," Bill said.

Sterling took them to the boarding house for something to eat. "Sterling, why don't you wait out here with these two and I'll go in and talk with Bernice first."

"Good idea."

Wynola came back out and said, "You can bring them in, she said."

While Bernice was preparing a late breakfast for all of them, Wynola checked Bill and Ted's injuries. She had to tighten the sling around each of their shoulders. "Is that better?"

"Yes."

Sterling and Wynola were as hungry as the two prisoners. Baked beans, ham and biscuits washed down with plenty of coffee.

Already the story of Sterling and Wynola marching two culprits handcuffed to each other had circulated throughout the mill and mill yard. "Do you feel comfortable watching these two while I send a telegram to the Chief?"

"I don't have any problem." Then she turned her attention to Bill and Ted. "How about you two? Are you going to give me any trouble while he's gone?"

"No," Bill said.

"How about you, Ted?" He couldn't look at her when she was looking at him.

"No."

Sterling met the Swede outside. "Where's Wynola?" he asked.

"She's inside watching the prisoners while I send a telegram."

"Would you like me to stay with her until you get back?"

"From what I saw last night, I think she's okay. Actually, I think they are more afraid of her than me." Sterling headed for the station house.

Swede was wanting a cup of coffee any how, so he went inside. He looked first at the two prisoners and then at their captor, Wynola. He couldn't help but snicker, and he tried to suppress it until he was in the kitchen. "Do you see the expression on those two faces? And look at Wynola. It's no wonder they're so mellow. The fight has gone out of them. I don't think the Warden Service Department is paying Sterling double pay for his wife's help, but they sure should." He drank his coffee and then left by the kitchen back door.

The train from Strong arrived and picked up passengers for Rangeley and then left. The turn around to Redington would be about two hours.

"I think we should move to our cabin until the train comes back. We're taking up too much space here."

While Wynola watched their two prisoners, Sterling kindled a fire in both stoves and then Wynola made a pot of coffee. It didn't take long before the cabin was warm and comfortable. "Sterling, you need some rest. I slept for a while back at the Eustis Station, and you haven't had any."

He looked first at Bill and then Ted. "If I lie down for a few minutes, I'm assuming you won't give my wife any trouble." He laid down and was soon asleep.

Wynola busied herself while watching the two, so she wouldn't fall asleep. Bill and Ted were so played-out they probably weren't much of any threat. Two hours later the south bound blew its whistle signaling they were approaching Redington. Sterling heard the whistle and was up before they saw the train. And they were at the station before the train stopped.

Then engineer, Dana Aldrich, climbed down from the engine and went into the station house. "Hello, Sterling, it's all up and down the line that you have two more for the hoosegow, you're getting quite a reputation up and down the line."

"Well, I couldn't have done it without Wynola. She had as much to do with their capture as I did."

Dana looked at Wynola and said, "Don't get me wrong here, when I say you, I'm including your wife, also. People are talking as much about her as they are you, Sterling."

"We all loaded now Willie (Mr. Wilson)?"

"You're all set to go."

"Better get aboard folks."

Before they could board the next train to Farmington, they had to take Bill and Ted to the hospital to have Dr. Bell tend to their injuries. Alberta Probert was talking with Mary at the front desk when the four of them walked in.

At first Alberta didn't recognize Wynola dressed as she was and Sterling was taking up the rear. All Alberta saw was this woman with an animal hide draped over her shoulders and wearing a Colt .45 handgun around her waist and the two prisoners handcuffed together. "What's the idea of this? What do you three want?" Alberta asked.

"Alberta, it's me, Wynola."

Alberta opened her mouth and drew in a mouth full of air before replying. "Gracious, glory be, Wynola? I didn't recognize you dressed like that. What can I do for you?"

"Hello, Mrs. Probert," Sterling said. "These two fellows need some mending before we take them to jail. Is Dr. Bell here?"

"He is, I'll go get him."

Sterling and Wynola, after two days in the woods, looked pretty grubby themselves. Wynola had pieces of spruce and fir bough tips entangled in her hair, and her face was dirty. Sterling hadn't shaved now for two days and he wasn't looking much better than Bill and Ted.

"Bring 'em down here Sterling. More broken collar bones?" Dr. Bell asked.

While he was looking at Bill's shoulders, he said, "You're getting pretty good at setting bones and immobilizing the arm and shoulder. The only thing I can do is rebandage with clean bandages. You guys will be okay in two weeks. They're all yours, Sterling."

"Do you need me to come along with you? Or will you be alright alone?"

"You wanting to go home? No problem, I'll be alright."

"Good, I'll get the house warmed up and take a bath. I smell almost as bad as those two. I'll have supper ready when you get home."

He kissed her and said, "It may be late. I don't know about the train schedules."

"That's okay. I'll wait up for you."

She left the hospital and headed for home on foot. Sterling and his prisoners walked back over to the station, but the south bound had already left and the next train wouldn't be until mid-afternoon.

"There's a stage leaving from here in thirty minutes. Takes about an hour and a half."

"Well, I guess that'll have to do."

* * * *

The driver brought the stage to a stop on Main Street and Sterling and his prisoners got off and walked the short distance to the county jail. Once inside, he removed the handcuffs and Bill and Ted were put in a double cell and the door clanged shut.

"What are the charges, Sterling?" the deputy asked.

"Illegal killing of deer, both subjects, and commercial hunting."

"What did they kill?"

"Two deer," and he removed the two tails from inside his jacket and laid them on the desk.

"For a new game warden, you're sure making quite a name for yourself. Is broken collar bones your trademark?"

"What day is this?"

The deputy looked at him doubtfully. How could he not know the day? "This is Saturday, the 23rd."

"I thought maybe, but I wasn't sure. Providing these two can't make bail, which I doubt they will, they have to be in court Monday."

"That's right, Warden."

"Well, it's time I went home." He walked to the train station which wasn't that far away on Front Street.

The station agent said, "The north bound for Strong and then onto Rangeley is boarding now." Sterling boarded the train, found an empty seat and sat down, feeling exhausted. He was asleep before the train left the station and almost missed his stop at Strong.

The conductor knew Sterling and he woke him, "Excuse me, Mr. Silvanus, but this is your stop."

"Oh man! Thank you, Peter."

He was glad they had left their backpacks and snowshoes at the cabin. He wouldn't have wanted to pack those up Lambert Hill and all the way home. And he knew Wynola was not up to it, either. The sun was setting and he could see the lights were on at home as he walked by the Randall farm.

Wynola was in the bath tub when he walked in.

"I hope you aren't long in there."

"If it was bigger, you could come in with me. While I soak, there is hot food on the stove."

* * * *

They both had bathed and cleaned up, eaten, and now they turned the lights out and went to bed.

"Sterling?"

"Yes?"

"Are you horny?"

"Nope."

"I am."

"Can you wait 'til morning?"

Chapter 7

They spent two glorious days resting, sexual play and simply relaxing and enjoying being with each other. Sterling shoveled snow against the house and Wynola did some baking and put together a few cooking utensils they didn't have at the cabin.

Monday morning they boarded the early train to Farmington and then walked to the court house on Main Street.

Judge Butler was the presiding magistrate today. "The court calls Bill Clemis and Ted Clemis." The two stood up.

"Are these your cases Warden Silvanus?"

"Yes, Your Honor."

"Broken collar bones again?"

"Yes, Your Honor."

"Are the injuries warranted?"

"Yes, Your Honor."

"You two have both been charged with illegal killing of deer and commercial hunting to provide the Clemis lumber camp with meat. Did you kill two deer?"

"Yes, we did," Bill replied.

"And was this to supply meat for the camp?"

"Yes, it was," Bill replied again.

"Were you aware that lumber camps can no longer kill caribou, moose and deer to feed the crews?"

"He came to Langtown a couple of weeks before and said we couldn't any longer."

"So you knew you were breaking the law before you broke the law. Why did you?"

"Pa would have whipped us if we didn't."

Judge Butler didn't respond immediately, and when he did it took everyone by surprise. "I'm not going to sentence either of you yet. But you will remain in jail until I do. Warden Silvanus?"

"Yes, Your Honor."

"I am going to issue a warrant of arrest for their father and you are to execute the warrant at your earliest convenience, and to bring their father before me. Oh, by the way, for the record, what is the father's name?"

"Doug Clemis, Your Honor."

"Pa ain't going to like that sir."

"And why isn't he going to like it?"

"He don't like nobody telling him what to do."

"Well you let me and Warden Silvanus worry about your father. Warden Silvanus are you capable of bringing Mr. Clemis before this court?"

"Yes, Your Honor, I am."

Sterling looked at Wynola and shrugged his shoulders. She whispered, "Oh well."

Judge Butler remanded Bill and Ted to stay in jail until Mr. Clemis appeared in court.

Sterling picked up the warrant for Doug Clemis' arrest and he and Wynola boarded the train for Redington.

They would spend the night at the cabin and then catch the morning train to Langtown.

* * * *

It was Tuesday morning and Sterling and Wynola were up early. If they missed the morning train to Langtown then they would have to walk.

They met Swede on their way to the station house. "Where you folks bound for this morning?"

"Back to Langtown."

"Haven't you had enough of those folks?"

"This is a court order this time," Sterling replied.

There was enough time so he could send a telegram to Chief Perry advising him of the bench warrant.

Instead of riding in the passenger car, they rode up front in the cab with Dana Aldrich. "We'll be getting off in Langtown, Dana. And when will you be back at the Langtown Junction?"

"I'll have some switching to do at Skunk Brook and then again at the Berlin Mill. No stop at the Greene Farm this trip. It'll take three hours or so. This will be a non-stop return trip also."

"If we are at the junction will you stop and pick us up? There will be a third person going back."

"Sure, and if you aren't there, I'll wait twenty minutes. No more."

"Thanks."

The switch at the Eustis Junction was already set so their only stop was at Langtown. "Thanks Dana. We'll be waiting at the Dyer Tank."

It wasn't difficult to find Doug Clemis. As soon as they had been seen by the first person, word circulated like a Nor'easter. They headed for Clemis' office and he came outside before they reached it.

"Did you bring my boys back?"

"No, Mr. Clemis. The judge ordered them to stay in jail and for me to bring you in. Then he'll release the boys."

"Huh, what makes you think I'll go with you?"

"Mr. Clemis, you don't have a choice." Sterling removed the warrant from his pocket. "Judge Butler issued a warrant commanding me to arrest you for complicity for illegally killing deer and using the meat to feed your crews. When you are before him, then and only then will he release your boys."

"I can't just leave here, damn it!"

"Mr. Clemis, you don't have a choice." Sterling placed

his hand on Doug's shoulder and said, "Mr. Clemis, you are under arrest pursuant to this warrant." Then in a much more commanding tone in his voice, both Doug and Wynola noticed the change, "If you insist on giving us any trouble, I will... handcuff you behind your back. If you will give us no trouble, I'll handcuff your hands in front. This will make walking easier."

Doug surrendered and put his hands out front. Sterling secured the cuffs and looped one through his belt loop. "Okay, so far. Let's go."

Doug hollered to a worker on the chain, stacking lumber, "Tell my brother, Bill, I'm going to the county jail. He's boss until I get back! Let's go, damn it."

It was a slow walk to the junction. Doug kept dragging his feet. To spur him on, Sterling said, "If we miss this train, then we either walk to Redington, or we camp out in the cold tonight. Which would you prefer, Mr. Clemis?"

He didn't answer, but he did pick up his pace and they were at the junction an hour before Dana stopped to pick them up. "Thanks, Dana."

When they were seated in where it was warm and the train had picked up speed, Doug looked at Wynola and said, "What makes a woman as beautiful as you tramp around the woods following this guy and staying out in the cold?"

Wynola looked squarely at Doug and said, "Mr. Clemis, it is a hell of a thrill. It's fun."

Doug just shook his head. He couldn't understand how she could find anything fun out of a job that could take your life in a heartbeat. He didn't understand either of them. And he sure as hell wasn't going to cause any trouble. This guy acted so much like a gentleman, and then be so commanding.

The train only slowed as it passed through Redington. Redington was at the top of Sluice Hill and Dana had to be careful, even if there was only a few cars.

* * * *

They transferred to the afternoon train for Farmington and Mr. Clemis was in jail with his boys by 5 p.m. "What are we going to do now, Sterling, there won't be another train to Strong until the morning and then we have to be in court in the morning. I'm all for staying here tonight."

"That's a good idea."

The next morning, Sterling and Wynola were in the courtroom early and the deputy sheriff had already brought the Clemis family over.

When Judge Butler entered the courtroom, he took his seat and for several minutes he sat there apparently looking over some files. Then he said, "Mr. Clemis. Will you stand please."

Doug stood up. "Two days ago Bill and Ted Clemis were found guilty of illegally killing deer and commercial hunting since, as they said, the meat was going to be used to feed your crews.

"Bill and Ted, you have spent several days in jail, and I think you have been sentenced enough for your crimes. I am now releasing you both and you are free to return home."

Ted had never spoken up all during the process and he now stood and said, "Your Honor, do we have to go back? I'm afraid to go back," he was almost crying.

"What are you afraid of if you go home? You afraid of your father?"

"Yes, and other stuff," Ted said.

"What else?"

"Just stuff."

Sterling stood up and said, "Excuse me, Your Honor. I may have a solution to this dilemma. I recommend that all charges against Bill and Ted be dropped and their arrest record be expunged and suggest they look at the military as a life choice and a way to escape Langtown."

Judge Butler looked at Bill and Ted Clemis, "Well, what do you two think?"

"Really? You mean we can really join the military?"

"If that is what you want," the judge said.

"Yes," Bill said.

"Me too, Your Honor," Ted said.

"Do you boys have enough money to take care of yourselves?"

"No sir. We don't have any."

"Does your father owe you any money?"

"Yes sir, he does."

"How much?"

"We haven't been paid anything since we started up in the fall," Bill said.

"Would you settle for $100 each?"

"Yes sir!" Ted said,

"Mr. Clemis, do you have $200 now to pay the boys?"

"Yes."

"Then pay them each $100."

After he handed each $100 the judge said, "Okay, you are free to leave. Now I have some more business with your father."

"Now back to your problems, Mr. Clemis. It is obvious your sons are afraid of you. What else goes on at Langtown I can't even begin to imagine, but you, Mr. Clemis, I can do something about. It has become very clear you have never had any intentions of complying with the law which prohibits killing caribou, moose and deer to feed your crews. This law has been in effect since 1880, so it is nothing new to you or any timber contractor. I will not sentence you to jail, but I am going to fine you $200. If you do not have that much on you now, then you'll have to remain in jail until such time it is paid. If you don't have the money, the deputies at the jail will send a telegram for you to have the $200 brought in to the clerk in this building. The court bailiff will escort you to the clerk's window and if you don't have the $200, the deputy will escort you back to jail."

"Warden Silvanus. I want to commend you with your solution to get those boys out of Langtown. And is this your wife, whom I have heard so much about?"

Wynola stood and said, "Wynola Silvanus, Your Honor."

"A pleasure, I assure you, to meet you. You may not be aware of it but you two are the talk of the town. Good luck to you both."

"Thank you, Your Honor," they both said in unison.

Judge Butler left the courtroom and the bailiff left with Mr. Clemis and when Sterling and Wynola left the room, Bill and Ted were waiting for them in the corridor.

"Sir, could we have a moment with you?"

"Sure, what is it?" Sterling asked.

"We want to thank you for what you did in there. And we are sorry for what we did. We have a lot of respect for you and for you, Mrs. Silvanus."

It was Ted's turn now. "Are you sure we can get into the military?"

"There is an Army recruiter in town. If it will help, you can use our names for a reference."

"Are you sure, after all this I mean?"

"After all what, you have no criminal record now. The judge has expunged it, erased it as if it had never happened."

"You know sir, you're okay," Ted said.

* * * *

Sterling sent a telegram to Chief Perry telling him the Clemis case had been settled positively. And that he had received information of more illegal hunting coming from the Bigelow Station. And he would work on that as soon as weather conditions permitted.

Then they walked home for some well deserved rest. They both were mentally and physically exhausted. They needed time for themselves. Sterling rekindled both stoves and Wynola fixed a light supper then they took turns in the bath tub.

For three days they stayed at home, catching up with things that needed to be done. He shoveled snow from the roofs, except the barn. It was too steep to climb on.

The fourth night at home Sterling rolled over in bed, facing Wynola, "Are you getting bored staying home?"

She answered immediately, "Yes. I could have left two days ago, but I thought you were enjoying being home."

"I was, but I think it's time we went back to Redington. What do you think?"

"We haven't left yet?"

"Is in the morning soon enough for you?"

"Well, I guess it'll have to be," they both laughed.

He put his arm around her and pulled her close and soon they were both asleep.

The next morning Wynola fixed a huge breakfast of ham and scrambled eggs and the last of the muffins she had made two days before. While she was fixing breakfast, Sterling was fixing the house to leave. As soon as the breakfast dishes were cleaned and put away, he emptied all of the water containers.

"You ready?" he asked.

They closed the door and waded through the snow to the packed snow in the road. The air was crisp and frosty flakes floated in the air, but it wasn't that cold. At least they didn't think so. They both thought it was a nice start to the day.

When they arrived at the station, Pansy was just arriving for the day. "Good morning, Frank, did the north bound leave Farmington on time?" Pansy asked.

"Ed West left Farmington fifteen minutes ago. He won't be more than twenty minutes. He's a little ahead of schedule."

When the passenger car stopped at the loading platform, Sterling and Wynola stepped aboard. And much to their surprise, Doug Clemis was sitting by himself with a frown on his face.

They took a seat across the aisle from Clemis and Wynola sat next to the window. Sterling didn't want her so close to Clemis, just in case. "I'm surprised to see you here this morning, Mr. Clemis. I would have thought you would have made it home several days ago."

"My damned brother didn't bring the money in until

170

yesterday. The little bastard. I don't like you much, Sterling. After how you and your woman there beat my boys. Then what you did in court separating my boys from me. They'll never come back to work for me again. And what am I supposed to tell their mother? And I've been in jail for five days all on account of you, warden. No siree, I don't like you none at all, warden, but I can guarantee you one thing, there won't be any more animals shot illegally. So there won't be any need of you poking around my operations any more."

"Well, I'm glad to hear that, Mr. Clemis."

When they arrived at Redington, it was snowing. Nothing new in that country and when it stopped snowing the next day the weather turned and now it was unseasonably warm. And it stayed like that for days.

Even the men liked this warmer weather, but it wasn't good for the horse teams. Their twitch trails would warm up and break up by noon. So the horses were done for the day. The Swede knew that real cold weather would be here soon and not to be caught with his pants down, during the afternoons when the snow had softened up he would harness up his two strongest horses and make trails for the men to use to get in and around the spruce trees and twitch trails for the teams. So when the cold returned, everything would freeze solid as ice and make yarding the logs easier.

It was the following weekend when the God awful cold returned. At night the temperature would drop to -20° to -25°, and only warm up to -10° during the day. But the horse teams were able to yard more wood than they had been yarding. All thanks to the Swede's foresightedness.

One night after the cold temps had returned, Sterling said, "I have an idea how to keep the crews at Langtown on their toes."

"What are you thinking about, Sterling?"

"We can walk anywhere and stay on top of the snow. The crust is so thick and strong. I was thinking about you and I taking a hike through the choppings at Langtown, to see if Clemis is true to his word. If we don't find anything, then let a few of the workers get a brief glimpse of us. Clemis will get the word that we're back and I don't think we'll ever have any more trouble there."

"Dare the devil beware?" Sterling just grinned and Wynola said, "I'm seeing another side of you."

When the train arrived the next morning the usual engineer was not on board. "Good morning Mr. Leavitt, I was expecting to find Dana."

"The nice weather got the better of him. He came down with the flu, so I have his run until he comes back. What can I do for you?"

"My wife and I would like to ride up front with you to the Langtown switch. We're going in on business and I would prefer if a lot of people didn't know, in case any of the passengers get off at Langtown."

"Sure, no problem. What are you looking for?"

"Just witch hunting."

Sterling and Wynola jumped off at the Dyer tank and disappeared behind a cedar thicket before the passenger cars went by. There were three passengers getting off in Langtown. The crust was so strong they didn't have to worry about breaking through. They were going in light today. No backpacks and no snowshoes.

They were making good time and they could still see the train at the Langtown Station. They walked off the little knoll and headed first to the older harvest area. There were many ravens cawing and flying about. A tell tale sign of something dead. They found a dead moose or the remains of one, that something had dug up and the ravens were cleaning it up.

"At least it is old," Wynola said.

They continued on and saw many deer. Some lying down, others browsing and a few standing watch. None seemed to be too concerned about their presence among them.

Sterling made an arch up on the slope of Kennebago

Mountain. It was such a beautiful day for strolling. And that was mainly what the two were doing. While some loving couples might spend a beautiful day shopping in a large town, going from store window to store window and having a fabulous dinner in a nice restaurant or some couples might spend the day with family. Well, Sterling's and Wynola's family was out here in the wild and the wilder, the more at home they felt and the happier they were. For Sterling and Wynola there was no possible way of spending a more enriching, loving and fun filled day. This was a job, if you want to call it that, that they both enjoyed.

Sterling started working their way down the slope towards the active harvesting area. They had only found evidence of older kills and nothing recent. Maybe Doug Clemis was keeping his word.

They could hear an axe biting into the white meat of a tall huge spruce. The chopper was cutting the notch, while his partner stood back with the two man cross-cut saw. When the notch was cut, the two men grabbed the saw and found good footholds and began sawing back and forth and in no time at all the tall spruce came thundering down.

While the two men were cutting the logs into sixteen foot lengths plus six inches, Sterling and Wynola inched their way closer until one of the men saw them and then they ducked for cover.

The two sawyers were talking and not sawing logs. The one who had seen them was excited and trying to convince his partner.

They left the two arguing and moved on and found another crew and did the same and another crew and another. "There, tonight at the supper table we will have given them enough for conversations until morning and Mr. Clemis will be worried that we are out here watching every day.

"Come, we have done our work here. Let's follow the Dead River up where it goes under the tracks at the Eustis Junction."

During the thaw the river had opened up, but now in the

extreme cold it had frozen solid again, and the two followed the river, walking on the frozen surface, until they came to the junction. There were three men working there chipping ice out of the switch rails. Sterling recognized two of the men, but not the third. "Hello, Sterling and Mrs. Silvanus, what are you about today?"

"Oh, nothing much. Just looking."

When Sterling and Wynola were out of ear shot the new employee, the third guy, said, "Why don't they get a job like normal people?"

Lewis Bachelder said, "You don't know much about those two do you, kid?"

* * * *

The cold temperature was still hanging in and through the mountains and one morning Wynola asked, "When are we going to the Bigelow Station?"

"Before we go I'd like to take the train to the Greene Farm first and talk with the Reeds. Maybe even stay over there a night."

"I would like that; I like Mrs. Reed."

"We'll leave on the morning train tomorrow.

"I'm feeling restless and I think I'll go down to the mill and see if I can help out."

"I was feeling the same, but I didn't want to say anything. Think I'll go over to the boarding house and see if I can help Manette and Bernice."

It was mid-morning and still cold. The snow, what wasn't frozen, squeaked under foot. The Swede was loading railcars by himself. He had one almost full and there were three more to load with four foot pulpwood. "Do you need some help, Swede?"

"By-gory, you know I could. One man is sick this morning, and the other two I had to send up in the woods with another team. The boys are getting plugged up, up there. They have so much ahead of the teams now. You'd better get a pair of gloves in the mill and a pulp-hook." While Sterling was over to the mill, Swede kept throwing pulp. When Sterling returned he started at the other end of the same railcar and began loading.

He was feeling good and using muscles that had not been used much lately. After a few minutes Swede said, "You throw wood pretty good," and he started working faster. He didn't want to be outdone by Sterling.

Sterling was matching Swede move with move, stick for stick and he wasn't tiring as soon as Swede thought he would. Soon tossing pulp became a contest. Nothing was said about winning or losing. Just that neither man wanted to be out done by the other. Sterling did have a small advantage though. Swede had started before him.

After a while that railcar was full. Sterling mopped the sweat from his face and arched his back, stretching muscles. "You move down to the next car Sterling. I will load this one. I don't want you in my way."

Sterling moved down to the next car and before he started to toss pulp he stood and looked at Swede. He was standing facing Sterling with his hands on his hips, as if he was waiting for Sterling.

No one said go, the contest had started, but each went to work loading their own car. The larger sticks Sterling put on the bottom instead of having to lift them up any higher. Swede threw his on as he came to them.

Again, they were matching stick for stick. Working like this the cold air was better than if the air had been warm.

Bernice looked out of the window in the boarding house and said, "Manette and Wynola, come here. You've got to see this."

The three women stood at the window watching the contest between Sterling and Swede. Manette said, "This I know, Swede is enjoying himself. He likes to work hard. That's why he always pushes the men to work faster. Not many men, Wynola, can load the rail cars as fast as my Swede."

Wynola looked at Manette and she had a happy expression

on her face, because she was happy for her Swede. And Wynola was both proud and happy for her man.

The noon whistle blew and men were gathering to watch the competition between Swede and Sterling. Some were even taking bets. The two men didn't seem to notice that their loading had drawn a crowd. The women too had stopped their work and were now all watching. As the cars were getting closer to full, it became clear Swede was a little ahead. He threw on the last stick of pulp and he turned to look at Sterling. He was only three sticks behind. Swede wiped the sweat from his face and walked over to Sterling. He too had to wipe his face. They both were breathing heavily.

Swede put his arm around Sterling's shoulder and said, "We have one last car to load. Do you want to eat lunch first?" There was no alternative.

"You lead the way and I'll be right behind you."

They started walking towards the boarding house and the dinner table. "No one has ever come that close to beating me loading a railcar.

"I tell you what, Sterling, you quit wardening and come to work for me and I'll pay you double what you're making now."

"Thanks Swede, but I like what I do."

* * * *

The next morning, Sterling and Wynola boarded the train for the Greene Farm and it had to stop first at Langtown and drop off some empty railcars and pick up those that were loaded. While they waited in the passenger car, Doug Clemis walked by and recognized Sterling sitting by the window. He stopped and stared at him and the color was draining from his face. He hollered loud enough so Sterling could hear him, and so too could everyone else. "What the hell do you want this time, Warden?"

Sterling got up and went outside so he wouldn't have to holler through the closed window. He walked over to Doug and said, "Why, Mr. Clemis, we don't want anything. We're just on our way to the Greene Farm."

Doug walked away towards the mill shaking his head, and he was fuming mad. "What are you looking at? Get back to work!" he screamed at one of the yard workers.

The engine was turned around and recoupled to the train and now on its way to the Greene Farm and then to the Berlin Mill.

Sterling and Wynola were the only ones to get off at the Greene Farm and then the train left. They walked over to the farm and met Jim outside the huge barn. "Well, hello." His hands and arms were bloody.

"Oh, I haven't been butchering. I have a yearling heifer that needed help delivering her first calf.

"How about some coffee?"

"We never turn down a cup of coffee," Sterling said as they followed Jim into the shed next to the kitchen entrance. "While I wash this blood off…just go on in. Freda is right in the kitchen."

Over coffee and a turkey sandwich, they talked socially, mostly about the goings-on in the lumbering communities. "Two days ago I had to take a wagon load of hay and oats to Langtown." Jim started laughing then, "You two surely have stirred the hornet's nest there. Clemis workers are coming in every day from the slopes of Kennebago swearing to God that they see you two every day roaming through the choppings." Sterling and Wynola looked at each and grinned.

"Is there something to that? You two seem to know something I don't," Jim said.

They told Jim and Freda about their excursion on only one account through their works.

"I think you have really put an end to the poaching there."

Freda said, "I think it was good of you, Sterling, how you helped those boys leave that awful place."

"Ole man Clemis is afraid of you two. And in particular, of you, Wynola," Jim said.

"Why me?"

"Because you are a woman and his way of thinking women are only good for making babies and feeding the crews. He has never met a woman who is so capable as you are. And so attractive."

"And he has heard stories about a woman who wears a wolverine fur over her shoulders. Actually we have heard the same stories. That you are the *Carcajou* Woman who was written about in the New York Times paper. But when that article came out I was only a little girl then. If you were her, then you'd be older than me," Freda said.

Wynola looked at Sterling, "Go on, Wynola. Tell them about Rachael and her father. Just like you told me."

"The woman the article was about, her name was Rachel Morgan." Jim and Freda were glued to every word Wynola said. They had never heard such a story.

Sterling watched his wife as she told the story. He was happy for her, that these people were interested with her. He hated to always be the one that people they encountered were talking to or about. Now she had the attention.

They found the story about Rachel's father, the real *Carcajou*, fantastic. "I have heard stories when I was at college about someone called *Carcajou*, but didn't pay too much attention to it. I thought it only a story. And it seems the Indians also called him the Great Peace Maker."

"Yes, that is correct. He would be accepted into any tribal community or any nation."

"What happened to Rachel, Wynola?" Freda asked.

"She fell at home one day and hit her head which caused a cerebral hemorrhage. She died only minutes after. Her husband dressed her in her white clothes and took her back to Falling Bear's village. Only by now Falling Bear had died and his oldest son Wonnocka was now chief."

"When Kirby had taken her back to a special place that the two enjoyed, he gave this wolverine fur to Wonnocka and then he left."

"When Wonnocka gave it to me, he said to wear it whenever I travel and it would protect me."

"Kirby disappeared forever, didn't he? No one ever saw him again," Jim said.

"That's right," Wynola said.

"He was one of the first game wardens and when he disappeared, the Portland newspaper ran a long story about him. I still have the paper in my office. You both act like there's something there you want to tell us."

Wynola looked at Sterling and said, "Go ahead my husband. You were the one who found them."

Both Jim and Freda looked confused.

"When I first became a game warden last summer, my first assignment was to stop some poaching on Wonnocka's land. One day I accidentally stumbled onto both of their remains. After Kirby gave Wonnocka this vest he returned where he had taken his wife's body. Both skeletons were leaning up against a pine tree. He held his wife's hand as he sat there beside her, dying and waiting to be reunited with her."

"That's a remarkable story," Jim said.

"People are talking about you two all along the Narrow Gauge Railroad. Even along the spur to the east that runs up through Kingfield, Carrabassett and Bigelow. The station agents are doing a lot of the talking. Whenever you board the train to wherever, the agent sends a telegram to the agent in your destination and of course, all the telegraphers can copy the same message. So people generally have an idea where the two of you are."

"This isn't a game you're playing out here. I wouldn't trade jobs with you for anything. I think doing what you do takes a special kind of person. But on another note, you two have a lot of friends out here. People may be talking about you but they also respect what you do, as well as how you do it."

"Jim, it's time I started getting our supper ready."

"Can we rent a room tonight?" Sterling asked.

"You can have a room, but I wouldn't think of charging you for it."

"Can I help you, Freda?" Wynola asked.

"Yes, you can. Thank you."

When supper was over and the kitchen cleaned, the four sat in the living room close to the huge fireplace talking. The train from the Berlin Mill stopped and Sterling asked, "Why did the train stop?"

"The night train from the Berlin Mill always stops here to inspect the load before continuing on."

They talked on into the night, not realizing how late it was getting. Finally they said goodnight and they went to bed, 10:30 p.m. Sterling and Wynola lay in each others arms talking before going to sleep.

The next morning was about a repeat of the previous mornings. Cold—and their bedroom was cold—but they had slept well.

* * * *

They made it back to their cabin at Redington and started making plans for a trek to Bigelow via Caribou Pond, a township away.

"While you're putting up some food, I'm going over to the mill and see if I can find some canvas, so we can build a wikitup. I don't think we could stay warm in a lean-to."

Swede was at the mill. "Why do you want the canvas and how big?"

"We need to build a shelter, maybe a piece 10x30."

"I have a piece that big, but I'll have to charge you for it."

"No problem."

Sterling took the canvas back to the cabin and then went to the depot store looking for a light weight sharp axe. He found just what he was looking for. A light cruiser's axe and it was sharp.

"How do we get to Barnjum without everybody knowing where we're going?"

"Well, we'll tell the station agent that we're going to Strong."

When they had everything assembled in their cabin, Wynola asked, "What about snowshoes?"

"Good question. I'd hate to get caught out there without them if we needed them, but the crust is so hard and strong I don't think we'll need them. That'll be that much less weight we'll have to carry."

"Swede knows something is up, but he isn't asking any questions."

The next morning they boarded the south bound for Strong. 'Going home for a while, Mr. Silvanus?"

"Wife and I need a break, Mr. Wilson. We'll be back in a few days."

Fred Leavitt was still filling in for Dana. "Fred, alright if we ride up front with you?"

"Sure, but you'd be more comfortable in the passenger car."

"Well, we're only going as far as Barnjum and we'd rather get off without anybody knowing."

"Okay, I can help you there. When I'm disconnected from the cars, I'll pull ahead to the turntable and I usually turn it by myself. That would be a good time for your exit."

They were pulling into the loading platform at the Barnjum station and the engine was disconnected and Fred pulled it ahead to the turntable. "Wait 'til I have this side of the engine turned to the woods; nobody will see you."

"Thanks, Fred."

"Where you two going anyhow?"

"Keep it to yourself, Fred, we're going over the top to the Bigelow log operations."

"Aren't you taking the hard way to get there? I mean you could take the train to the operations at Bigelow."

"Yeah, but Fred, we don't want anybody to know what we're doing or where we're going."

"Oh, okay," Fred said, but he really didn't understand.

Sterling and Wynola jumped down and ran for cover in some nearby bushes before they shouldered their backpacks. Fred Leavitt was still turning the engine and trying to understand what Sterling had said.

As they were following the brook upstream where Sterling had his first camp, Wynola asked, "Where will we set camp Sterling?"

"Well, to get as far as I'd like to go would probably take all of daylight just to get there. I was thinking about using the Griswold and Montague cabin. Just for tonight."

The snow was frozen so hard they were leaving no tracks and there were no animal tracks anywhere. They reached the old cabin at mid-afternoon. Sterling had to break away chunks of snow from in front of the door before he could open it. He took his pack off and went after some firewood piled under the eaves.

There were mouse droppings on the sink counter and table. Wynola checked the bed and it seemed free of mice and other rodents. She wasn't happy about spending a night in this pig pen, but she understood.

When the fire was burning in the makeshift stove, the cabin seemed more comfortable.

Instead of coffee this late in the afternoon, Wynola fixed some natural tea she had brought from home. And she used some of her rolled aluminum foil to warm their food.

As Sterling was drinking his tea, he said, "You know, with a little fixing this would make a good cabin to use for details like this one."

"Maybe we can come back during the summer and fix it and clean it. And do something about the mice."

Sterling went outside for more firewood and Wynola put away their food and was cleaning up when a mouse ran across the top of the sink counter. The mouse made a mistake and stopped and turned to look at Wynola, who was holding her breath so she wouldn't scream. She slowly withdrew her gun, took careful aim and pulled the trigger.

Sterling came running back and saw Wynola standing there with her gun still pointing at the counter. "What in the world did you do?"

"I got tired of that darn mouse running back and forth on the counter."

"Uhm. Did you get it?"

"I don't know. I haven't seen it since I pulled the trigger."

Sterling looked at the big hole in the counter and there was blood and hair around the hole. He said laughing, "I guess you showed that mouse the outdoors. You blew him right through the counter top and out through the wall. Remind me sometime not to ever tease you about mice."

Sterling plugged the hole in the wall and Wynola washed the blood and hair off the counter.

As they laid together in bed Sterling said, "I wonder how many animal hides, and deer and moose those two shipped out of here?"

The cabin was cold and not very well built and Sterling had to keep getting up and put more wood in the stove. The third time he got up, he decided to stay up instead of waking Wynola anymore. Besides, it would be daylight soon. He checked his watch and it was almost 5 o'clock.

He boiled some water and made some coffee. He hadn't seen any more mice and decided the rest of them must have taken the hint. He thought about Wynola shooting that mouse with a .45 and blowing a hole through the counter and out through the wall, and he laughed and choked on his coffee.

Wynola heard him coughing and sat up in bed. "What's the matter? Why are you dressed? Is it time to get up?"

"No, go back to sleep. I didn't want to keep waking you every time I had to get up and put wood in the stove. I made some coffee."

"No argument here," she laid back and was soon asleep again. Sterling knew they would be doing a lot of hiking today and even though the crust made it easier, they both would be tired at day's end. And they had to make the wikitup, also.

As he sat there watching Wynola sleep, many thoughts were floating through his mind. The temperature had fallen during the night and the moisture on the roof was freezing and the roof boards kept snapping.

When the sun light started to filter through the tree tops he awakened Wynola and handed her a cup of hot coffee. "Thank you. Any more mice?" She looked around before getting out of bed.

"I think they all left."

"Good."

After breakfast they dressed and shouldered their backpacks and left. It was so cold, even the crust was squeaking with each step.

Shortly after leaving the cabin, they came out to the flateau overlooking Caribou Pond. "What body of water is that?"

"Caribou Pond." They worked their way through the cedar thickets and spruce trees to the ice. Sterling cut two walking sticks with his axe. "We might need these to keep from falling on this ice and I think the terrain gets steeper once we're away from the pond."

There were fresh beaver works on the left shore and about half way down the pond they found a large house with a larger feed-bed frozen into the ice in front of the house. At the lower end of the pond they found a small concrete dam. "This must be a reservoir for driving wood down the Carrabassett River." He noticed the removable flood boards were in place. "When they need more water in the river to float the wood down stream, someone comes up here and removes these flood boards allowing more water to flow towards the river."

They left the pond and dam behind, and trying to stay on high ground as they worked their way around Crocker Mountain. The crews would be working on the northeastern slope.

Without the walking sticks, they would not have been able to walk along the steep slope of Crocker Mountain.

By late morning they found what they were looking for. They had followed the contour of the land and traveled northerly from the pond. They had gone a long ways down the slope and found a small flateau with an abundance of small fir, spruce and cedar trees. And off to the side was a lot of dry wood. Some still standing, some sticking out of the snow.

Sterling broke up the pack snow with his axe and Wynola was clearing out the snow chunks. Sterling cut several fir and spruce trees and cut the limbs off. They made the framework for the wikitup and then wrapped the canvas around it, leaving a smoke hole at the top. While Sterling was cutting fir and cedar boughs for the floor, Wynola stacked the snow chunks up along the base of the canvas to keep the wind and cold out.

There weren't any rocks to make a fireplace inside and the ground wasn't frozen under the snow. So with sharp sticks they managed to dig out enough dirt to make a shallow fire pit. Now they could spread the boughs for a floor and not worry about them catching on fire. Sterling cut more boughs for their bed and then he brought in dry wood. When he was done he figured there was enough for three days. Wynola already had a fire going and was melting snow for water.

"I'm surprised how quick it warms up in here. And the smoke goes out the top." Then jokingly, he said, "You Indians were pretty clever to figure out how to make this, and so simple."

She hugged and kissed him.

"Are we going down tonight to look around? The moon is almost full again."

"No, we've had a long day as it is. We'll go down and look around in the daylight and see what we find."

Just then they heard the mill's steam whistle signaling the end of the day.

They ate and drank hot tea and talked about other things, besides catching poachers, until they both were too tired to stay awake any longer.

Sterling had brought in enough wood, so he wouldn't have

to go outside during the night. Even though it was cold outside, they were very comfortable inside the wikitup.

The wind started to blow during the night but inside the wikitup they were not bothered with it. By morning the wind was gone and the sky was clear and blue. They left their backpacks in the wikitup, but Sterling carried his axe. Since the snow was too hard to leave tracks, he would occasionally scarf the side of a tree for a marker for their return.

They were not as close to the harvest areas as he had thought they might be. They found an area that had been logged already and the crews had moved on. They started crisscrossing the area looking for signs of illegal hunting. Wynola pulled on Sterling's coat sleeve to get his attention and when she had it, she pointed off to the right side of the old choppings to a tree full of ravens. A sure indication that there would be dead animal remains close by.

They began circling the area in opposite directions and Sterling whistled to Wynola and she came over. He pointed to some moose remains, "Looks like something dug it out of the snow. There's the head and ribs, that's about all."

"Well, least we know they are killing animals illegally here," Wynola said.

They continued searching and found deer remains and then partially dug out of the snow was the nose of a moose calf. Wynola got down on her hands and knees and started breaking the snow away from it. Sterling saw what she was doing and helped with the axe. They soon had uncovered the complete calf. Nothing had been taken from it. "We'll remember where this is and come back to it before we go back to camp. This meat is still good. We can use this."

They continued searching and found where there had been something, but was unable to determine what. They searched the rest of that area and didn't find anything else.

They followed the main twitch trail out of there towards the mill yard and they followed that until they could see the yard and then they pulled back into the woods again. They set over and searched another harvested area and didn't find anything there. At least nothing had been dug up.

"I think we'd better pick up that calf and head for camp. If they shoot something during the night, we'll hear it. But I have a gut feeling the killing here is being done in the day light."

Rather than drag the whole calf back up to their camp, Sterling cut off the hindquarters with the axe. They each carried one and stopped often to rest. There was still some daylight left when they arrived at camp. Sterling made a rack to hang the two quarters in the wikitup to thaw, so they could remove the hide and slice the meat. "This will be good eating. I wish I had some herbs and onions," Wynola said.

Sterling went after more wood and piled it up under the spruce tree. He could see them being there for several days. "Do we have enough food for three or four more days?"

"With this calf, yes. Maybe more. You thinking we might be here that long?"

"I'm not sure. Mr. Parsons at the Berlin Mill told us he heard shots in the middle of the day, so I don't think they are killing at night. But I don't know how often or when they last shot something."

"Maybe we'll find something more tomorrow. You hungry?"

"I'm so hungry I could gnaw bark off a willow tree," he said.

When they had finished eating and everything was taken care of and they were sitting back watching the fire burn, Wynola asked, "What animal do you suppose is digging the remains out of the hard crusty snow?"

"I've been thinking about that also. Bear won't be out yet. Fox? Big cats? I don't know and there aren't any tracks on the crust."

* * * *

Wynola checked the two hind quarters and said, "We will be able to slice off some of this meat tonight for supper."

187

When they got down to the area they had searched the day before, they set over and found another area and here they saw ravens in a tree and found the remains of another small moose. Just the head and some ribs, like the other carcass. They didn't find anything else until they found new choppings and the crews had left that area also. Being careful not to be seen, they crisscrossed that area and found the remains of two deer. These seemed fresher than the moose they had found.

They sat down to rest and Sterling said, "I'm beginning to think that the kills are made in the areas where they are working at the time."

When it was time to start back for their camp, they had searched all the areas that had already been logged off. And they had not seen any live moose or deer. Which made him think the deer and moose were following the crews and feeding from the fresh browse and tops. So their work was narrowing down to the area where the crews were working.

While Wynola was preparing their food, Sterling cut more cedar boughs for their bed.

Wynola had added some moose meat chunks with the food she had brought and wrapped it in aluminum foil and heated it over soft glowing coals. When she opened the aluminum foil wraps, "Wow, does that ever smell good," Sterling said. Wynola was happy knowing he appreciated what she did.

"This is good," Wynola said. "Still wish I had some herbs. Maybe from now on I'll pack some herbs with my pack."

They ate their fill and then went to bed.

The next day they headed for the current harvest area. They watched each crew, trying to decide which crew was doing the killing. So far none of them had shown any interest with the numerous deer and moose in the fresh choppings. They were all hard workers.

When the noon whistle blew and the workers started out towards the dining hall, Sterling suddenly had an idea. They found a spot where they could see if anyone would come up from the mill yard. They hunkered down and waited. Wynola looked at Sterling and he knew what she was thinking. "Think about it. There's all kinds of deer and moose in these choppings. The crews are too busy to hunt, so that means someone else is doing it. And what better time than when the men are out of the woods and eating dinner." Wynola nodded that she understood. They waited in silence. And then they saw two men leave one of the cabins set back from the others. One was carrying an axe and the other a rifle. Sterling nudged Wynola and she nodded her head that she had seen them.

The two walked across the mill yard and up the main twitch trail. "We wait until they shoot then we'll move in slow." The two were out of sight only for about fifteen minutes when they shot a lone cow moose. Sterling and Wynola started to walk in that direction, staying to the cover of fir and spruce trees.

They could hear them talking and Sterling knew they must be close but he could not see them yet. There was a thicket of alder bushes between them now and he motioned for Wynola to circle below them and to come up to them and he would circle in the other direction.

Sterling watched Wynola only for a moment. She was staying low and out of sight of the two and silent. He was satisfied so he proceeded to the left. When he had cleared the alders he saw that the two were cleaning the moose. He could also see Wynola and he motioned for her to wait. When they had finished cleaning the moose one of them picked up the axe and quartered it and then they stripped out the tenderloins. Sterling figured they were done now and would return with a horse and sled to haul the meat down to probably the cook shack. He nodded to Wynola to proceed and he started walking towards the two.

They were so focused on taking care of the moose they had not seen either Sterling or Wynola. Sterling was only about ten feet away and he said in a soft tone, "Hello, boys."

They both looked up and as they recognized the badge Sterling was wearing they began to panic and the one with the axe threw it and turned to run, but when he saw Wynola walking towards him, he started screaming, "No! No! I give up!" and he dropped to his knees in the snow. "Don't hurt me! Don't hurt me! I give up!" Wynola had all she could to keep from laughing. He was terrified.

The one still facing Sterling dropped his rifle in the snow. "I give up, too! Don't hurt us! We won't give you no trouble, mister."

For now Sterling put handcuffs on both men, but not cuffed together. Wynola was smiling as she asked the one who had had the axe, "What is your name?"

"Sid Parsons, ma'am."

"And your name?" Sterling asked.

"Al, Al Thomston."

"How old are you boys?"

"I'm nineteen," Sid said.

"I'm twenty," Al said.

"What do you two do at the mill, besides shoot deer and moose?"

"We keep the mill yard picked up and clean, and we clean the mill every night after it shuts down."

"Plus you provide wild meat for the cook, is that it?"

"Yeah, that's right mister."

"Who's the boss of this operation?"

"Mr. Bigelow, Jim Bigelow."

"How much does he pay you for a moose?"

"He gives us $5 to split."

"What about a deer?"

"A dollar."

"Do you realize it has been against the law to shoot deer and moose to feed wood crews? And that there is now a season on each animal?"

"Yes, mister, we do."

"Are you two going to give us any trouble?"

"No sir, mister. Not after what we have heard you two have

done to others who did. No sir."

It was almost comical, but to laugh in front of them would be discourteous and not necessary.

Wynola had walked over and retrieved the axe and she was now standing beside Sid. He was looking at the wolverine vest and he said, "You're her, aren't you? You're the *Carcajou* woman."

She only smiled a beautiful smile and didn't reply.

"Well, Sid and Al, let's go talk with Mr. Bigelow."

"I thought you were going to," Al said. "We ain't gonna get paid for this one."

Sterling picked up his rifle and unloaded it. There were two shells, a Winchester .30-.30.

Wynola led the way down and Sterling at the rear where he could watch them. The mill whistle blew and workers were returning to the mill and the woods. Some saw Wynola first, and then Sterling bringing up the rear and even at a distance everybody knew who these two were.

Mr. Bigelow was still sitting at a table in the dining hall when they entered. His mouth dropped open and he sat there and couldn't find anything to say.

"Mr. Bigelow, I'm Sterling Silvanus, the game warden, and this is my wife, Wynola. We have, or I should say, you have a problem." Wynola indicated with a nod for Sid and Al to sit.

"I was expecting you to show up. Just not now. And I thought you'd come in on the train."

He turned to his wife and said, "Would you take Sid and have him get a horse and sled and you help him bring the moose to the station house?"

"Sure. Do you want me to take his handcuffs off or leave them on?"

"You aren't going to give her any trouble are you Sid?"

"No sir."

"If you do, she can out run, out shoot and knock you to the ground in a hurry."

"While talking with Sid and Al, I've decided that you are at fault here and not Sid and Al. You hired them to kill moose and deer which I'm certain you realize is against the law. It has been since 1880 and I also know you have been advised of this. It isn't my intention here to arrest Sid and Al because actually they are not the problem. But you are, Mr. Bigelow."

"I don't want any trouble, Mr. Silvanus. I will take all responsibility."

"I'm glad to hear that, Mr. Bigelow."

"So what are you going to do now?" Mr. Bigelow asked.

"What day is it?"

Mr. Bigelow looked quizzically at Sterling. How could he not know what day this is? "This is Friday, February 26th."

"Well, I have no choice but to arrest you and I'll have to take you to the county jail in Farmington. Court will be Monday morning. I suggest you bring enough money for the fine. So you don't have to sit in jail while someone brings it down. I am also confiscating your rifle and will return it when the fine is paid, and we are taking the meat with us. I'll give it to the school in Strong."

Mr. Bigelow was different from the others he had had to deal with. Jim was a gentleman and not a ruffian and he wasn't looking for trouble and he was taking responsibility. When Wynola and Sid returned, he took the cuffs off Al and said, "Mr. Bigelow is taking full responsibility, so I am not going to arrest either of you. But," and now his voice changed a little bit, "if I hear of either of you illegally killing anything, we'll be back." And he looked first at one and then the other.

"We won't, mister. I promise."

"Me too."

"Okay, go back to work. And Mr. Bigelow, I think the train will be leaving soon."

"I'll need to get some money from my office and leave word where I'm going."

"We'll go with you. Remember you are in our custody."

"Do you need to handcuff me? I mean I'm not going to give you any trouble."

"I guess we can forego the cuffs."

At the station house, Sterling said to the agent, "I want this meat tagged and sent to the Strong School System."

* * * *

The train left the Bigelow Station promptly at 3 p.m. They all settled in and Sterling and Wynola were enjoying the trip. Neither of them had ever been in this part of the country. It was an easy trip to Kingfield, the grade was almost level.

There were no transfers to other trains. At the Mount Abram Junction they picked up freight cars loaded with sawn lumber and two cars of pulpwood. Then it was on to Salem and the Summit Hill which was the steepest grade in the entire line.

At the Strong Station they had to switch tracks and pick up more cars from the Rangeley Line. Sterling left Wynola watching Mr. Bigelow while he talked with Pansy Newell about the moose meat.

"Pansy, can you contact someone from the school. We confiscated some moose meat that is sitting on the platform."

"Sure, I'll call someone on the school board and they can find someone who will take care of it. Until then, it'll be okay on the platform as cold as it is."

"Thanks, Pansy."

"The school kids will enjoy this, instead of canned baked beans three times a week."

The train was finally coupled and on its way to Farmington.

* * * *

Monday morning Sterling and Wynola were again sitting in Judge Butler's court. Mr. Bigelow had already been brought over by the deputy. When Sterling told the judge that Mr. Bigelow had not done the actual killing, in fact he had hired Sid and Al to do the hunting, the judge said, "When you employ someone to do something for you that carries the same weight of responsibility as if you yourself had done the illegal hunting."

"Where are Sid and Al, Warden?" the judge asked.

"I let them go, Your Honor. They were very corroborative and didn't give us any trouble and they told us all about Mr. Bigelow hiring them to supply wild meat for the crews. I decided to bring Mr. Bigelow in and he agreed to take full responsibility."

"That shows good judgment on your part, Mr. Silvanus. How many moose and deer have been killed since the first of this year Mr. Bigelow?"

"Oh, probably three moose and four deer. A full grown moose doesn't last long with a hungry crew."

"You were arrested and brought to jail on Friday and you have been in jail until today?"

"Yes sir."

"I'm going to sentence you to two days in jail. And time served. As for the fine, the court fines you $300. Do you have the money with you? If not, you'll have to remain in jail until someone can bring it in for you."

"I have the money, Your Honor."

"Good. You are excused and the bailiff will take you to the clerk's office."

"Mr. Silvanus and Mrs. Silvanus. You two have created quite the reputation for yourselves. People all up and down the county are talking about you two. You have done a remarkable job curbing the commercial hunting that has historically gone on in the wilderness logging operations."

Then on another note, Judge Butler added, "Be careful out there. $300 is probably a lot of money to Mr. Bigelow, as was the fine of your other recipients. But the law has been in effect for more than thirty years. It's time they were made to pay. Have a good day."

"Thank you, Your Honor."

Chapter 8

Sterling and Wynola stayed at their home for a few days before venturing off again. Sterling sent in a complete report and added that they were next going to check some of the lumbering communities along the Strong to Bigelow line. Maybe not all.

After three days, they both were feeling antsy and really needed to be out in the wild. Even if only at their cabin in Redington. So they put together a few things and walked to the train station and boarded the local for Rangeley.

"The telegraph is buzzing all day. The agents all over this state are talking about you two. I've even heard some stories that have been made up around you two. As much about you, Wynola, and *Carcajou* Woman, as about you, Sterling. You are being called the polite spoken game warden who isn't afraid of anything. Have a good trip and be careful," Pansy said.

They sat back in their seat and enjoyed the ride to Redington. On this run the train was not going to Barnjum first. The weather had started to turn and as the sun was rising earlier each day and setting later, the temperature was back to normal and although there was still crust to walk on in the morning, the warm sunshine softened it enough so you'd punch holes through it.

"What are we going to do with the canvas on the wikitup? And remember we left some moose meat, also," Wynola asked.

"Well, we could go get it, but I think we'd have to snowshoe."

Sterling walked down to the station house to talk with Mr.

Wilson. "Hello Sterling, what can I do for you?"

"I'm looking for a night train into Barnjum. Does the train ever make a night run there?"

"Yes, the schedules have changed a little. The 8 o'clock through here in the evening is now going to Barnjum to pick up loaded freight cars. You looking to leave tonight?"

"No, maybe tomorrow night. Thanks," and he walked back to tell Wynola.

That evening they ate supper at the boarding house. They were friends, family, with everyone there and there were no more curious stares towards Wynola.

They ate all they could and then topped it off with a freshly baked deep dish apple pie. Later Wynola helped with the clean-up and dishes and then all sat around the room sipping coffee and they all wanted to know what had happened at the Bigelow camps.

While Wynola was telling part of the event, Sterling looked from one to the other, trying to decide which one of them had left the goat on their doorstep in December. There was one among them who might have done it as a prank and not done as contempt. And that one person had to be Pearley Lablanc. He seemed to Sterling to enjoy a good shenanigan more than the others. He wasn't sure though, but when he was sure Mr. Lablanc would have his comeuppance. As Sterling was thinking about this, he was unconsciously smiling and Pearley saw the smile.

The next day Wynola busied herself with putting together some food supplies that she could use to cook up with the moose meat.

"Are we going to have to sleep in that awful cabin again?"

"Well, I was thinking about staying tonight at the Lax cabin that Mr. Barnjum said we could use any time we needed it. Then snowshoe over to the wikitup the next day. After a good breakfast at the boarding house."

With too much idle time on his hands, Mr. Wilson sent a

telegram to the Barnjum Station agent that the game warden and his wife would be coming in on the 8 p.m. train. He wasn't being mischievous; he was simply bored and needed someone to talk to.

So when Sterling and Wynola got off the train, Mr. Barnjum and several others were there to greet them and wondering what their business was this trip.

"We would like to use the Lax camp if we could, Mr. Barnjum. In the morning we'll be snowshoeing over Caribou Pond to our camp. And then in a couple of days we'll board the train at Bigelow."

"You two are going to snowshoe all the way over to the Bigelow Station?" Mr. Barnjum just shook his head in disbelief, not understanding why they would do that instead of taking the train all the way to Bigelow.

"The word is out, Sterling, all around the lumbering operations to stop shooting moose and deer to feed the crews. You two have done in one season what the law couldn't do in over thirty years. There aren't many, but I've heard there are a few who aren't happy about what you're doing. I for one am glad to see someone enforcing the law."

They walked up across the mill yard arm in arm, and it still seemed odd to see this little village way out in the wilderness, lit up at night with electric lights. Sterling was used to them in Washington, but out here they were quite a novelty. And as much noise as the mill made when it was running, now everything was so quiet.

They slept well and after a breakfast of ham and eggs and plenty of coffee, they shouldered their backpacks and carrying their snowshoes, they started the climb to Caribou Pond. This early in the morning the crust still held their weight and they were on top over looking Caribou Pond in less than two hours.

They sat down to rest and enjoy the view of the pond and the surrounding mountains. The sun was warm and it felt good as it shone on their faces. "I wonder what that tall mountain is off to the right?" Wynola asked.

"Well, on the map I have at the cabin, it should be Sugarloaf."

Sterling cut two more walking sticks and this time they stayed up higher, away from the steep terrain, and they had to strap on their snowshoes. That was okay too, as they were almost to their wikitup.

On the steep slope there were many nice hardwood trees; tall, plump and straight. Rock maple, yellow birch, a few white birch and beautiful ash, with an occasional beefy white spruce. This would be a lumberman's dream, except the terrain was too steep to log with work horses.

The air was so still they could hear the mill as the band saw sliced through the logs. When they finally reached the wikitup they were both tired. "We'll sleep good tonight," Wynola said. "My legs feel like rubber."

"That was quite a hike." They took their backpacks off and opened the flap on the opening. The moose meat was still there and intact. Wynola kindled a fire and put snow in the pot to melt for drinking water and Sterling went after dry firewood. He had to go far to find enough dry limbs to knock off the tree with his axe. He preferred dry pine limbs as these smoked less. Spruce was okay, too.

"Are you hungry?"

"I could eat a horse. My belly is scratching my backbone."

"Well, this moose meat has stayed frozen and it is still good." She sliced some off and put that in her aluminum foil, along with some potatoes she had brought and this time she had some small onions. "Now I wish I had some mushrooms."

She wrapped everything tightly in the aluminum foil and put it next to some hot coals to simmer slowly.

Sterling made two back rests with slabs of cedar he had split away from a huge cedar tree that had been ripped open by lightning.

When Wynola unwrapped the aluminum foil the smell of the cooked meat and vegetables smelled so appetizing. "This is really good."

* * * *

For two days they stayed at the wikitup before they moved on. The last morning as they lay awake listening to the wind rattle through the tree tops, Sterling said, "You know, when I'm the happiest, it is when we are camped out somewhere in a wikitup laying together on a bed of fir boughs with you in my arms. The world could stop and I wouldn't care." He turned over so he could look into her eyes. He cupped her cheek in his hand and said, "I really love you, wife."

They stayed wrapped in each other's arms and warmth and the sun was already above the tree tops. The world outside their wikitup had stopped, ceased to exist. The only thing of any importance was there with the two of them.

"In a way, Sterling, I'd like to leave this wikitup here so we could use it for another time when we might have to do some work here."

"You know Wynola, things are changing fast. Faster than we can imagine. Something tells me that we are seeing the end of this era.

"Do you know before I left Washington, there were several automobiles already in the city."

"I have seen pictures of these automobiles in the newspapers, and you think they are coming here in the wilderness?"

"I think in a few years we will see them in Strong. I think then that'll be the beginning to the end of the wilderness villages and people will ride more often in these automobiles than they will walk. I think even my job as a game warden will change way beyond what we do now."

"Have you had another vision, my husband?" Wynola was serious.

"No, I haven't seen this in a dream, it's just an inner feeling."

"Well, I have an inner feeling that if you don't let me up, I'm going to pee here in bed."

They relaxed for three days at the wikitup, until most of the moose meat was gone. "I'm torn between leaving this here or taking the canvas with us."

"Do you think we'll ever have to use it again?"

"Times are changing Wynola, and I doubt it. I'm not even sure about my future as a game warden."

"Then we should take the canvas and not waste it."

They unwrapped the canvas and folded it up and put it in Sterling's backpack. They left the poles as they were, just in case they did come back some time. They shouldered their backpacks and carrying their snowshoes, they started down the slope of Crocker Mountain towards the Bigelow station house. They walked right through where the wood crews were working and out along the main twitch trail, to the mill. Everybody stopped what they were doing and watched as they passed by. Mr. Bigelow was at the station house when they arrived.

Jim saw them first and stepped over to say, "We aren't shooting any more moose or deer," and he held his hands up to his chest and palms out. "Train is late today, you might as well leave your gear here and come over to the dining hall with me for a cup of coffee."

This surprised Sterling and Wynola. To see Mr. Bigelow so amiable. "We'd enjoy a cup."

Mr. Bigelow (Jim) was seemingly very chipper for someone who had just spent two days in jail along with a hefty fine. He poured three cups and they sat down at a table. "After what you two did here, I'm a little surprised to see you checking up on me so soon. How did you get here anyhow? You didn't come by train or somebody would surely have seen you. And how did you get here when you arrested me?"

"We came over the mountain from Barnjum," Sterling replied and then took a sip of his coffee.

"How long does that take you?" Jim asked.

"Ah, what's today?"

Jim just laughed out loud, "I'm beginning to think you two spend way too much time in the woods. This is Friday," and he was still laughing.

"Well, we left Barnjum Monday morning."

"You mean it took you four days to snowshoe over?" He had stopped laughing.

"Actually, we could have done it in a day. But when we were here before, we made a temporary camp on the north slope of Crocker. Far enough above your operations so the crews wouldn't discover us. We built a wikitup and wrapped a piece of canvas around it. We were there only a few days when Sid and Al shot the moose. We came back this trip to get the canvas and we've been up there since Monday afternoon just relaxing and enjoying being together."

"You mean you were sleeping out during that God awful cold?"

It was Wynola's turn to answer that. "Mr. Bigelow, a wikitup will keep you warm no matter how cold it gets."

"You know after all the work you two have done along the other branch of the railroad, I knew I should have stopped killing moose and deer to feed the crews, but do you have any idea how much food it takes to feed hungry men? You won't ever have to worry about this operation again. I didn't particularly like those days sitting in jail. And that $300 would have bought a lot of beef and pork. I do appreciate what you did for Sid and Al. They're good boys and were only doing what I told them.

"There's the train whistle. You'll be leaving and I need to get back to work."

* * * *

They got off the train at the Carrabassett Station and walked through the mill yard to talk with the operations boss, Bill Ledoux. "No, I stopped feeding the men the wild meat two years ago. I tell you what. I take and show you the food storage and lockers. You see for yourselves."

The only meat was pork, ham, bacon and beef. "Thank you, Mr. Ledoux."

"I don't want no trouble. You won't have to worry about Carrabassett operations."

They walked to the Spring Farm just down the tracks and were able to spend the night there. They stopped at Sanford's, and spent the night in Kingfield and the next day they took a stage coach to the Alder Stream operations and walked back to Kingfield. They spent another night and the next morning they caught the train to the Mount Abram Junction and walked to Soule's Mill at the base of the mountain. They stopped at Clint Starbird's cutting operation and caught the evening train finally back to Strong.

In all cases, the operators at the lumbering communities had cooperated and had already stopped using wild game to feed the crews. Some bosses had known that there were some operations who were still killing moose and deer and were glad when they had heard they had been arrested by the new game warden and his wife, the *Carcajou* Woman.

"The word is among the lumbering operations that they do not want any more trouble with you and will obey the law," Mr. Starbird had said. "I made my crews stop several years ago. I was here to run a logging business, not a sporting club."

That night in their own bed at home, Sterling said, "I think this year's work will probably stop the practice of killing moose and deer to feed the crews. You know, Wynola, it's kind of sad really."

"Oh, I don't understand, my husband."

"It's the end of an era. Times have changed. And some times people are a little slow about changing with them. It really concerns me because I'm not sure now if I'll be needed here. Maybe we did too good of a job."

"We did good. And I think the Chief will keep you around."

Sterling laid awake that night long after Wynola had gone to sleep. He was worrying if Chief Perry would be needing his services any longer. He did finally go to sleep, but not a sound rest.

The next day he wrote out a long report explaining what they had found at the farms and lumbering operations, serviced by the Strong to Bigelow Railroad line, and that they would be staying at their home in Strong for a few days and then back to Redington.

A few days turned into only one. As they were both feeling uncomfortable and bored. The life on the edge of the knife blade had become too comfortable and intriguing. It was fun, as Wynola had once told Mr. Clemis. On the train ride to Barnjum and then onto Redington, Sterling sat very silent and deep in thought. "Why are you so quiet, my husband? You act as though the world were sitting on top of your head."

"I was just thinking about our visit to the Skunk Brook camp."

"What about it."

"Do you remember how we had followed that crew down the twitch trail to the yard and when they had turned off the trail to the left towards the farthest cabin on the left?"

"Yes, I remember those two. They were talking in French."

"Remember how they both had stopped and watched as we passed?"

"Yes, they looked worried or concerned about something. And I could make out part of one conversation. One of them said, 'They are not following us.'"

"That worried look we saw has bothered me ever since. Now I can't help but wonder if we missed something. I also remember what the wood boss said about those two, that 'They stay by themselves pretty much and eat their meals in their own cabin instead of the dining hall with the rest of the crew.'"

"I remember the boss saying how he didn't care because they put out more wood than any of the other crews," Wynola said. "What are you thinking?" she added.

"I'm thinking maybe we missed something there."

"Well, let's make another trip there."

For the rest of that day, they were busy preparing to leave on the morning train the next day and get off at the Greene Farm and go in from there on foot. Sterling still had the piece of canvas and he put that in his backpack, sharpened his axe and helped Wynola with their food. She was again bringing along enough for three days. Sterling bought a two pound slab of bacon from the depot store and four pounds of ham.

Sterling met Swede as he was crossing the yard, "Where you off to now, Sterling?"

"Oh just some routine scouting," he hated to lie to Swede, but he didn't want anyone to know where they were going.

The next morning they boarded the train and people were watching and wondering where they were going this time and who they were after. The train didn't stop until they were at the Greene Farm and after switching cars it departed on route for Strong.

Sterling and Wynola shouldered their packs and carrying their snowshoes under their arm, followed the tracks to the Dago Junction. There they left the tracks for the cover of the forest and soon discovered the snow had softened enough so they had to strap on their snowshoes.

Their snowshoeing was still easy, as they stayed on top and not sinking. They found Skunk Brook and stayed on the south side away from the cutting operations and were soon beyond the active cut and found a nice spot to build their wikitup. They were almost a mile away from the camps. They went to work cleaning off the snow and cutting poles for the frame. Then they wrapped the canvas around it. As Sterling was cutting fir boughs for the inside floor and bed, Wynola dug out a shallow pit for the fire.

The sun was just beginning to disappear as they finished the wikitup and a pile of dry wood. And the temperature was dropping.

There was some open water in the south branch of Skunk Brook not far from their camp, and while Sterling went after water in the twilight, Wynola began to prepare food.

"Are we going to do anything tonight? I'm beat."

"Yeah, I'm a little tired, too. Maybe we'll stay put tonight and maybe do some reconnoitering tomorrow and see what we can find."

Wynola started laughing and then asked, "Where did you find that big word?"

"Oh, from a second lieutenant I used to know in Arizona."

There was only a partial moon out, but against the snow there would be sufficient illumination. The temperature had dropped but not as cold as it had been. And they slept quite comfortably that night.

Wynola woke up early the next morning and rolled quietly out of bed, so not to disturb Sterling. She kindled the fire and set coffee to boil and began to cook up some bacon. She wrapped bread dough around a stick and was roasting that over the fire.

The aroma of cooking bacon and coffee was more than Sterling could stand. He rolled out of bed and Wynola handed him a cup of fresh coffee.

"Wow, does that bacon smell good."

Fried bacon and fire roasted bread dough, washed down with fresh hot coffee was an excellent meal to start a day with a lot of walking and snowshoeing ahead of them.

Sterling watched as Wynola drank the last of her coffee and thinking how fortunate he had been to find her. And he was believing the Great Creator had brought them together.

"What are you looking at?" Wynola asked. She had been aware that Sterling was watching her.

"Oh…just admiring you and thinking how lucky I am to have you with me."

After everything was picked up and the fire was out, they started out towards the harvest area. Half way there they found a fox digging in the snow. When the fox saw them it ran off.

Sterling chopped away the frozen snow with his axe and found a pile of bones and hide. After examining the hair, "It's deer hair."

"Hide and bones, no head," Wynola said.

"Yeah, I don't think the deer died here."

They moved on, getting closer to the operations. They were amongst some of the old choppings, and they found a flock of ravens fighting over some food now buried in the snow. There was enough hide and hair lying about, and they knew it was another deer.

They started following an old twitch trail towards the log yard, some distance away and Wynola spotted a crumpled up piece of wire fastened about a small hardwood tree. The bark of the tree had been gouged and scraped. "Sterling, look at this," and she showed him the wire.

"In St. Francis, my people would use something like this, spruce roots, to snare small animals," Wynola said.

"Look at this," and he pointed to an old trail in the snow that went right by the hardwood tree. "I bet those two are snaring deer. All they have to do is find a well used deer trail and hang a snare above it. No noise, all is done very quietly. All we have to do is try to find if they have any snares out now."

They followed the old deer trail for a ways before they lost it in amongst some cutting slash and tree tops. They needed to find a trail in the snow the two men were using to check on a snare or that would lead back to their cabin, or maybe a working snare.

They spent the rest of that day searching through old choppings and found nothing else. "Let's head back to our camp. We're tired and hungry. We'll start over again tomorrow."

Even though it was warm they were not leaving deep tracks in the snow. It took an hour of steady snowshoeing to get back to their wikitup. Sterling had to get more wood while there was still a little daylight left. Wynola started the fire and then went after water from the brook.

Again the next morning Sterling awoke to the smell of bacon and coffee. It was promising to be warmer than the previous day; which wouldn't be good for traveling or for what they wanted to do.

They started looking where they had left off yesterday and

by noon they had searched all of the old cuttings where they thought the two had worked. Now that they were in the fresh choppings, they had to be careful not to be seen, not just by the two they were after, but by anyone at all.

They walked in well used deer trails as much as they could to hide their own tracks. Sterling led the way and Wynola followed, keeping a watchful eye of their surroundings. They knew they were quite a ways from the men but they could hear as their axe bit deep into the spruce trees.

By noon they had found nothing. Not even an old kill. When the two left the woods for lunch, Sterling and Wynola felt more comfortable searching closer to the log yard. They were now directly behind their cabin and Sterling saw another trail the two had been using that went back directly to the cabin. Still they had to stay back away from this trail, so not to leave their own tracks. And this new trail was following up along a deer trail when it suddenly turned to the left, right to the deer trail and there they found a wire snare hanging from a tree about eighteen inches above the trail.

Sterling tapped Wynola's arm and pointed at the snare. She saw what he was pointing at. Then he motioned for her to follow him away from the snare. When they were well away and in the older choppings Wynola asked, "How are we going to work this? If we stay and watch the snare for them, our scent will keep the deer away."

"I'm not sure. Let's go back to our camp and think on it over hot coffee."

While Wynola was making the coffee, Sterling sat outside in the warm sunshine.

"What if we don't watch the snare, but their cabin?" She began to draw a sketch in the snow with her finger. "We go in and circle high away from the snare and come in close to the cabin, about here," and she made an X in the snow. "Darkness will cover our movement."

"I think that is a good idea. I think maybe we should lie down and take a nap. We may not get much sleep tonight, depending on how this goes down."

* * * *

Two hours later Sterling opened his eyes and Wynola was still asleep in his arms. As much as he wanted to lay there with her, he knew they had to get up and eat before going down. He gently shook her and then he kissed her and she seemed to respond better to the kiss. "Come on sweetheart, it's time we were getting up."

She moaned and groaned a little, but she was up and fixing something to eat. "We'll have to leave everything. Even our packs. We can always come back for them."

The sun had already set by the time they left their camp and headed down. The moon was a little brighter tonight and that helped greatly. The air temperature was dropping and the snow was firming up. Once they reached the new cuttings they took their snowshoes off and walked in the deer trails like before.

They found a good place where they could watch the door of the cabin and still be in the woods and not that far from the snare. They settled in for a long night. They each had brought a wool blanket to wrap around them.

There were electric lights at the mill and at the main dining hall, but that seemed to be all. There was lantern light on, inside the cabin and they could hear conversations occasionally and movement inside. Apparently these two did not eat with the others.

"Sterling, I have an idea," she whispered. "Why don't I sneak down behind their cabin and listen to what they are talking about."

"Good idea. Be careful." He watched her as she stayed to the shadows and then to the back of the cabin where he couldn't see her.

She was there much longer than Sterling thought she would

be. He wasn't worried but he was getting anxious until he saw a shadow moving and knew it was Wynola coming back.

"They're going out later to check the snare. I think they intend to wait until things have quieted down and maybe the lights are out, also."

"Good work, sweetheart, I was getting anxious when you didn't come right back."

She only smiled, a smile she knew he couldn't see in the dark.

The lantern inside the cabin went out and all was quiet. "I hope we aren't wasting our time," Sterling whispered.

The lights at the mill went out next and the main dining hall. And then one by one the other cabins went dark and everything was so quiet. Sterling checked his pocket watch. "A little after 9 p.m.," he whispered to Wynola.

She pulled the blanket tighter around her shoulders and Sterling shifted positions.

Fir trees in the distance were beginning to snap. Sounding like a .22 rifle as the temperature dropped and the sap in the bark was freezing.

As he sat there waiting, he was thinking how could these two work all day after taking care of a deer at night. He checked his watch again. An hour and half had passed, 10:30 p.m.

It wasn't until midnight and the moon was overhead and the door squeaked open. There was enough light now to see one was carrying a lantern that wasn't lit and the other a knife and a sack. They were being very cautious waiting until the rest of camp was in bed and asleep. And just in case, they walked up back without lighting the lantern.

"How we going to work this?" Wynola whispered.

"We wait. If they have a deer, they'll probably light the lantern. If there's nothing, they'll be back soon. But I think we should follow this deer trail up a little closer, so we don't miss the lantern if it is lit."

They were close and could see a faint glow from the lantern.

And the two were talking excitedly, but also trying to be quiet. There was a lot of movement and Sterling had no idea what was happening. "Can you make out anything they're saying?"

Wynola got in front of Sterling with her ear turned towards the two. "It sounds like they're fighting. One is saying to the other to cut its throat. They must be trying to kill the deer. One of them is struggling with the deer."

"This would be a good time to catch them off guard. How do you say game warden—stop?"

"Garde chasse, arret."

"Don't let them know you can understand what they are saying. Maybe they'll really incriminate themselves. You watch the trail down to the cabin. I'll watch up ahead. You know what to do if they run or you feel threatened?"

"Oh yeah."

Sterling walked across straight to them while Wynola walked up their tracks behind them. Sterling was close enough now to see what was happening and it was really comical. It was a large deer and it had one of the men down in the snow and putting its feet to him. He was actually taking quite a beating. The other guy was trying to climb on the back of the deer and cut its throat.

Sterling motioned to Wynola to stop and wait. He wanted them to kill the deer before they moved in. Sterling had to muffle a chuckle as he watched as the deer continued to put his feet to the guy. After many agonizing attempts, the one with the knife finally managed to cut the deer's throat.

The two guys and the deer were all lying in the snow soaking wet, and in the glow of the lantern Sterling could see the guy on bottom had his face all torn up from the deer's hooves and now was covered in blood from the sliced throat of the deer.

Sterling waited until the deer was pulled off the guy and then he started laughing out loud. Shocked and surprised they stood there in awe, staring with their mouths open at Sterling.

"Garde chasse arret!" The knife was dropped. They both put their hands up. Wynola moved in now. There was blood all

over the snow and the guy who was on bottom, "Do you *parle Anglais?*"

"Nes pas, no Anglais."

He gave one set of handcuffs to Wynola and she handcuffed the bloody fellow and then Sterling cuffed the other. Then he picked up the knife and the lantern. He pointed towards their cabin and said, "Go!"

They knew exactly what he said, and they started walking. They had no intentions of giving them any trouble and it didn't take long. Wynola opened the door and they all stepped inside. Once inside Sterling turned the lantern up and lit another.

He pointed to the bench by the table and they sat. "I should look at his wounds, Sterling."

"Okay."

He looked at the wounded guy and asked, "What is your name?"

After much sign language and frustration, the guy finally understood and said, *"Je nom Jacque SinClair."*

"Monsieur SinClair," Sterling said. He pointed to the other fellow and said, *"Nom?"*

"Roland Gervais."

While Wynola washed SinClair's face, Sterling leaned against the sink counter looking at the inside. "By the looks of everything here, Wynola, I'd say they were going to can that deer tonight. There's the cutting board, Mason jars, and copper canner. These boys are either selling the canned meat or taking it out of here or maybe both, or selling it where they live, where ever that is. It's no wonder Mr. Phillips didn't know anything was going on the way these two have been doing it."

Wynola had his face cleaned up and had to wrap a bandage around his forehead. He had cuts on both cheeks and his right eye was turning purple. And his shirt and pants were still bloody but there was nothing she could do there.

When she had finished, Sterling said, "Watch these two while I look around." Behind the bed against the wall he found a box with eight, quart Mason jars with deer meat. He found two boxes of clean empty jars. He found almost $200 in small bills. But there were no firearms.

Sterling had an idea. Maybe if he left, Gervais and SinClair might start talking. "Wynola, do you feel comfortable here alone, while I go get Mr. Phillips?"

"No problem."

He left and no sooner had the door closed and Gervais and SinClair started talking. Wynola acted as if she wasn't understanding any of what was being said.

Sterling had to pound and pound on Phillip's cabin door. Finally a lantern was lit and, "Who the hell is there?"

"Mr. Phillips, this is Warden Sterling Silvanus and I need to talk with you."

The door opened and Phillips stood there trying to wipe the sleep from his face. "What is it, Sterling?"

"I need you to come with me to SinClair and Gervais's cabin." On the walk over Sterling told him about their activities.

"That's beginning to fit with something else now. All the other crews work Saturdays and take Sunday off. SinClair and Gervais always take it off and take the stage from Dago Junction home to Stratton."

"Then that must be how they are getting the canned meat out of here. They've been doing this all winter."

"Those bastards will never be allowed in this camp again. I don't allow any firearms here but my own shotgun. This is really pissing me off."

"How do you pay off the crews?"

"Mostly at the end of the season. If anyone needs some money, I allow them to draw a small amount."

"What about Gervais and SinClair? Have they had to withdraw any money this season?"

"No."

"Then the money I found, I can assume is the money they have made by selling the canned meat. It will have to be confiscated."

When Sterling and Mr. Phillips entered the cabin the two stopped talking. Wynola looked at Sterling and said, "It worked. They haven't stopped talking."

Before Sterling could answer, Phillips looked at SinClair and said, "Holy cow! Did you do this to him?"

Sterling began laughing and said, "No. The deer they caught in the snare did this to him before they could kill it. If you follow the bloody trail out back, you'll find a big deer. You might as well have it and feed the crews. No sense in letting it go to waste.

"So what have these two been talking about?"

"Tomorrow is Saturday and after working all night canning meat, they were going out by stage from Dago to Stratton. The meat does not go home with them but it is sold. I don't know who or how it's sold. And that $200 you found is how much they have made this season selling canned deer meat."

John Phillips looked confused as Wynola was talking and Sterling said, "Mr. Phillips, my wife is from St. Francis, Quebec and speaks fluent French."

"You know these two are the hardest workers here. I sure hate to lose them. But I won't put up with any tom-foolery. Wynola, can you tell them for me, that they are fired and will never work here again. And when they get out of jail, they can come and pick up their money and belongings."

Wynola rattled off in French and the expression on the two's faces was priceless.

"Now, tell them they are under arrest and we'll be taking them to the county jail in Farmington.

"After they appear in court, we'll have to come back and go up and get our gear."

"What do you mean, your gear?"

"We have been camping out about a mile from here and watching these two."

"Well I'll be damned. All the stories I have heard about you two are true. You're welcomed back here anytime," Phillips said.

As Sterling and Wynola left and walked across the log

yard towards the tracks, Phillips was thinking that as they encountered people on their way to Farmington, they are going to think Sterling and Wynola had beaten the hell out of SinClair. Others were up by now and watched as SinClair and Gervais were marched out of camp.

They had three hours to wait at the Dago Junction and already word had passed from station agent to station agent that Sterling and his wife were bringing in two more. One beat all to hell.

There was a two hour delay at the Greene Farm and Wynola talked with Freda Reed and she had food brought out for them and their prisoners. Word had spread to Strong and beyond and headlines in the next morning's paper were already type set. It was a long and tiring trip all the way to Farmington and all four were tired by the time they reached the county jail.

"Holy cow, Sterling, what did you do to him?" the deputy asked.

"Nothing, he lost a fight with a deer."

"Yeah, sure he did," the deputy said doubtfully. "What are the charges?"

"Two charges each. Killing deer in closed season and selling deer."

"This is Saturday and they'll have to stay in jail until court on Monday."

"That'll be fine."

Instead of going home that night, they stayed in a motel in Farmington. They both were exhausted. "That was a good piece of work, sweetheart."

She was tired and began laughing and soon Sterling was laughing also.

* * * *

Rather than going home and then having to come back for court the next day, they decided to spend another day in Farmington. They walked around a lot and did some shopping

214

and ate in fine restaurants. And everywhere they went, people would stare at them.

They were in court early Monday morning and soon after, the deputy brought SinClair and Gervais over. SinClair had his face wrapped in bandages and he was still wearing his blood soaked clothes.

When Judge Butler entered and saw SinClair's condition, he said, "He must have given you some real trouble by the looks of him."

"No, Your Honor. They didn't give us any trouble at all. A deer did this to him." Wynola translated for the two what Judge Butler had said.

After hearing all the particulars of the case and how much money they had made he sentenced them to three days in jail and a $300 fine each. "And you'll remain in jail until someone brings in the money. If you do not have the money to pay your fine, you will each remain in jail and work off the fine at $2 a day."

Wynola translated and they were not happy.

Gervais and SinClair were escorted back to jail and Judge Bulter had another case before him. As Sterling and Wynola were getting up the judge looked at them and very slightly nodded his head in approval.

* * * *

They returned home for two days and Sterling wrote another report about the Gervais and SinClair commercial hunting cases.

The cold weather was behind them and even the night air had a warm feel to it. April of 1915 came in windy and dry and on Wednesday, they were at the Strong Station House early to board the train to Redington. That is until Wynola handed him that morning's newspaper. On the front page was a picture of Barnjum's Mill on fire. The article said it was a total loss. But there were no injuries and sawn lumber had also been saved.

Instead of going directly to Redington, they got off at

Barnjum. The mess was worse than what the newspaper photo had shown. It was still smoldering in places. They saw Mr. Barnjum and walked over to talk with him. "Sorry to see this, Mr. Barnjum."

"Thank you. It's pretty disheartening. At first I was already to throw in the towel and move on. But I've had a couple of nights to sleep on it and I now plan to rebuild. I have the lumber."

"How did it start?"

"Not sure really. It was either a hot ember from the boiler igniting sawdust or a spark from the machinery. We were all eating lunch when smoke was seen."

* * * *

Sterling and Wynola returned to Redington. The weather was unseasonably warm and the wood cutting operation had to come to a close. The twitch trails had melted out and would soon be too muddy for the horses to drag the saw logs through. So the cutting crews were paid off and they gathered their belongings and left. The mill crew could work another three days, to the end of the week, and the mill would close until the yard was dry of mud.

The snow conditions now were too soft for travel, even with snowshoes, so Sterling and Wynola stayed at their cabin and made some much needed repairs.

At the end of the week, the mill crew all left. As well as the chief cook, Bernice, and Swede's wife Manette with her two small children. All that remained was Pearley Lablanc and Swede. With Bernice and Manette both gone, Wynola substituted as chief cook and bottle washer, until the two women were back.

Swede and Pearley loaded four freight cars each day with pulpwood and when those were loaded, they worked around the mill, cleaning up all the sawdust and wood scraps, filing saw blades and cleaning the boiler. When the pulpwood was gone, they loaded the rest of the sawn lumber. Swede was making a list of repairs to the carriage, deck, and saw. The edger and the boiler would require special technicians.

One day as Sterling was helping Wynola with the breakfast dishes, "I have an idea for supper tonight, sweetheart."

"What do you have in mind?"

He wanted to say a little devilry, but he would keep this even from Wynola for now. "That meat we canned last fall, let's have that for supper, along with potatoes and squash."

That evening when the four were seated at the big table, Pearley said, "My Wynola, that smells real good. Reminds me of my mother's cooking."

Everyone took large helpings, there was enough food for all. Swede was about half through his dinner when he said, "Wynola, you have outdone yourself. This is all so delicious. What is this meat?"

Sterling spoke up before giving her a chance to answer. "I'm glad you like it Swede. How about you Pearley? You haven't said much since we sat down."

"I agree with Swede. It is delicious."

"You really did outdo yourself, sweetheart. I'm glad you two are enjoying this meat. Last fall someone must have thought we were going to go hungry, because someone left a little deer on our porch."

He stopped talking and looking at Pearley grinning ear to ear. Pearley choked on a mouth full of meat and had to spit it out in his plate. "What's the matter, Pearley? Are you alright?" he said still grinning.

"Ah, uh, I'll be fine in a minute. Something must have gone down the wrong way."

Wynola looked at Sterling grinning like a Cheshire cat. And she noticed Pearley was not eating as fast as he was. "What's the matter, Mr. Lablanc, aren't you feeling well?"

"I'll be alright in a minute."

Sterling finished his meal and pushed his dishes back and then crossed his legs and said, "Pearley, I thought you were going home as soon as the wood crews were pulled out?"

"I'm afraid the old lady will still be there." No one asked him to explain.

That night when they were lying in bed, Wynola asked, "What were you up to, there at supper? You were grinning like a Cheshire cat, while Pearley was choking."

Sterling started to answer but he couldn't stop laughing. Finally he said, "That deer that was left on our porch?"

"Yeah."

"It was a goat, not a deer. And Pearley left it there as a practical joke. Having it for supper was a joke on Pearley, and when he started choking on it I almost burst out laughing. It was good though, wasn't it?"

Chapter 9

That following fall as the weather was getting cold, Pearley Lablanc showed up in Redington wanting to work the season again. The year before he had said he was there for just the one season. But when he had finally returned home in Strong, his wife greeted him at the door. Neither of them had been smiling. When Pearley had left her in the fall, he had not left her with any money and in order to survive, she had charged goods to every business in town. So Pearley Lablanc had gone back to Redington for another season to get enough money to finish paying off his wife's charges.

After that first year, Sterling and Wynola had so rattled all the lumbering communities along both branches of the Sandy River Railroad, that moose, deer and caribou were never killed and fed to the crews again and in most cases, firearms were not allowed except for the boss, and he usually had a double-barrel .12 gauge for nuisance bear.

They only made an occasional appearance in the lumbering communities and then those times were more a social call than job oriented. Sportsmen were flooding the wilderness and many lumbering communities were now providing room and board at the boarding houses. Many of the hunting sports were affluent and were willing to pay someone to shoot them a big buck.

The crews in the mills and woods soon discovered they could make more money guiding these affluent sports and the mill crews and cutting crews were soon being paid more. And these guides soon discovered they could make even more money if they shot their client a nice buck.

So Sterling and Wynola were still as busy now, but their attention was directed differently.

There was a new Chief Warden now, Gene Picotier, and Sterling was answering now to a regional supervisor, William Shaw, and not directly to the Chief Warden.

When Shaw was first promoted, he questioned Sterling about his wife accompanying him wherever he went. Sterling answered by saying, "If not for my wife, I would not have accomplished as much as I have. She is as good as any game warden. And besides, you are getting two for the price of one. She has never expected anything from the department. And if she doesn't go, neither do I."

Sterling was a valuable asset and no more was ever said about his wife.

Times were changing fast elsewhere, also. Automobiles were beginning to show up along Main Street in the populated towns and telephone poles were erected and wire strung from town to town and many businesses now had a crank telephone.

The war in Europe took its toll on the availability of young workers, and the contractors were having to employ more French Canadians.

Frank Barnjum did rebuild his mill. Bigger and better than before and then he sold to George True. But it was always called the Barnjum Mill, village and operations.

The Sandy River Railroad was sold to the Maine Central Railroad, but kept the name Sandy River Railroad.

In 1919, the owners of the Sandy River Railroad stopped passenger service to the Greene Farm, but freight trains kept rolling as they were needed.

There was a stage line now from Stratton to Rangeley and the Railroad lost many of its passengers.

Also that year was the most profitable of its existence, hauling 70,000 cord of pulpwood.

In 1916, the Starbird Lumber Mill burned and was rebuilt. There were many new faces in Strong now, that Sterling and Wynola did not recognize. They were still spending much of their time either in the woods or at the cabin at Redington. And many of the young men that they had known were now in Europe fighting in the war.

Both Sterling and Wynola were pushing forty. But no one would know by looking at them, and they still roamed the woods night and day, summer and winter, with the same agility of twenty-year-olds.

In May of 1920, they were relaxing at their cabin in Redington; it had been a difficult winter, with deep powdery snow and extreme cold. On the morning of May 25th, Swede came running and hollering to the warden's cabin. Sterling met him on the porch and asked, "What is the matter, Swede?"

"It's my wife, Manette. She going to have my baby, and too late to go to hospital and there's no doctor here. I need you wife, Wynola; she's nurse, she can help my wife."

"You go back to your wife, Swede, and I'll get Wynola and we'll be right over."

Wynola ran ahead of Sterling to the Haggan's cabin. "You stay out, Sterling. Now go down to the station and you can telegram Dr. Bell."

Sterling ran down to the station and Mr. Wilson sent a telegram and hopefully there would be a reply soon. Sterling waited there and fifteen minutes later his reply came in. Mr. Wilson handed it to Sterling:

> *Dr. Bell out of town. Not available. Suggest mid-wife in Rangeley. Elizabeth Pillsbury.*

"Any trains running to Rangeley, Mr. Wilson?"

"There's only the south bound that's at the Berlin Mill. There's nothing else. There is a hand car here though. It shouldn't take long to go six miles to Rangeley."

"Okay, I'll take the handcar to Rangeley and you get a message to Elizabeth Pillsbury and explain Manette's situation and that I'm coming on a handcar to get her. Also have someone tell Swede and my wife what I'm doing."

Sterling found the handcar and two guys helped him set it on the tracks. He didn't waste any time. He started pumping the handle and he was soon out of sight. It was a slight downhill grade all the way to the Marble Station in Rangeley. He had to be very careful about going too fast. Particularly at the Eustis Junction. He figured the tracks would be set for the Greene Farm. So as he neared the junction, he slowed and the tracks were set wrong. He would leave the tracks set for Rangeley until he came back and then he would switch them back for the Greene Farm line.

He was a little less than an hour getting to the Marble Station and Elizabeth Pillsbury was waiting on the platform. "Mrs. Pillsbury, I'm Sterling Silvanus. It'll be easier with two pumping the handle but it is uphill all the way."

"Then let's get to it."

Already Sterling liked her character. Having another person helping really helped and two hours later they were at Redington. "You go ahead and take Mrs. Pillsbury up, Sterling. I'll have the boys take care of the handcar."

Sterling waited with Swede and he was just as nervous. When they heard the baby crying, Swede jumped to his feet smiling. Wynola came out carrying the new baby. "How's my wife, Wynola?"

"She's doing just fine. I was sure glad to have Elizabeth's help."

Swede looked at his new son and said, "I'll call you Harold (Bud) Haggan."

Swede was too excited to stand still. He went in to see Manette and then outside to tell everyone he had a son after having two daughters, June and Floris. He was a proud father and Sterling and Wynola stood together happily watching Swede.

Shortly after Bud's birth, his mother with his two sisters moved to the green house at Toothaker Pond. The girls needed to go to school.

That night as Sterling and Wynola were lying in bed she asked, "Do you have any regrets, my husband, that I can not give you children?"

"Under the circumstances, how we live and work, that would be impossible. No, there are no regrets."

From then on, Carl and Manette Haggan could never do enough to show Sterling and Wynola how much they appreciated everything they have done to help those at the little settlement at Redington Pond.

During the hottest part of that summer, while Sterling and Wynola were fly fishing on Redington Pond, a telegram came in from Doug Clemis at Langtown, that his nephew had been missing for two days and asked that Sterling come to Langtown as soon as possible.

Ed Wilson could see Sterling and Wynola in a canoe on the pond. He tried hollering, but the mill was making too much noise. So he went to the boiler room and asked Steve to give three quick blasts and wait a bit and three more until Sterling came back.

Ed went down to the wharf just as the first three blasts were blown. This got Sterling's attention but he sat right there. Then there were three more and Ed began waving his arms. Then three more and this time Sterling swung the canoe around and headed for the wharf.

Ed handed the telegram to Sterling. He read it and said, "Uhm."

"What is it?"

"Mr. Clemis at Langtown is asking for our help. When is the train north, Mr. Wilson?"

"Not until tomorrow morning."

"Okay, send a return message that we'll be on the morning train."

"Mr. Clemis has a nephew who went missing two days ago and he is asking us for help."

They packed light. Wynola, being a nurse, took bandage material and Sterling brought food and water.

The train was not going to Langtown that day so they had to walk in from the Dyer Tank. The hot air was the only problem. The mosquitoes and copperhead flies were bad, too.

Everyone was gathered at the dining hall and as Sterling and Wynola entered, everybody went silent and they all stepped aside to allow them to walk through to Mr. Clemis. "Good morning, Mr. Clemis. This is the earliest that we could get here."

"Thank you for coming. Maybe we'd better talk in the kitchen where it is quieter."

People were gathering outside to see what Sterling was going to do. "My nephew, Jimmy, ran off three days ago and no one has any idea where he has gone."

"Why did he run off, Mr. Clemis?"

"Don't you think you'd…"

Doug Clemis didn't have a chance to finish that sentence and Sterling asked again in that deeper voice of his that commands compliance, "I asked you why he ran off!"

Even Wynola was caught off guard and Mr. Clemis was nervously upset.

"He and his sister Betty Jean were in the barn and they started squabbling and Jimmy pushed Betty Jean backwards and she fell on a pitchfork and one tine went up through her leg. When she started screaming, it must have frightened Jimmy and he ran off."

"How old is Jimmy?"

"Fourteen."

"Has he ever run off before?"

Clemis hesitated this time before answering. "Once before. Jimmy is ah…ah, a little slow. He doesn't think as fast as most people."

"Has anybody tried to follow his tracks?"

"No. That's why I asked you to come. I know you two are

good at this."

"Are there any out camps that he might go to?"

"I took him once when he was young to a camp up on the side of East Kennebago. The camp is on the brook by a large beaver pond. No one has used it for a while."

"Okay, we'll start with that. You keep your people out of the woods. We don't need people laying down more tracks for us to follow. Do you have any idea what direction he ran in when he left the barn?"

"I can show you how we used to hike up to that camp."

They followed Doug Clemis across the mill yard and bridge to the north side of the mill pond and then up along that until it turned into a brook. "We would follow this brook upstream. The cabin is about a mile from here. There's no food there. I don't know what he would have to eat."

"Okay, Mr. Clemis, we'll take it from here. You go back and if he should show up, send someone up this brook and fire three signal shots. This will tell us he is back and we'll come back."

Doug Clemis wandered on back to the mill and Sterling and Wynola started following up along the brook and looking for tracks. The ground was covered with spruce and fir needles and there were no signs anyone had passed through. But the softwoods soon changed to hardwood, and the ground was softer and easier to see tracks.

They found bent and broken weeds and grass but no foot tracks yet. And they weren't wasting any time trying to find any as long as their objective was the cabin. Tracks would be a good sign though. Wynola was following along the stream bank and Sterling was to her right about fifty feet. "I have tracks in mud in the stream bed. He must have stopped for a drink. He didn't cross the stream or up along the side."

"So he's probably still following along the bank." They continued on and soon Sterling found tracks in some black mud on a side hill where spring water was oozing out of the ground. "At least we know he came up here."

225

As they were following the tracks, Wynola said, "If Doug Clemis is an uncle, where is the father? We haven't seen or heard anything from him. I would have thought he would be more concerned than an uncle."

"I was wondering, too, where the father was. But I think I'll leave it alone, for now. We must be getting close to the camp; we have come more than a mile up the stream."

"Smell the air. I can smell smoke," Wynola turned her nose into the wind again.

"I can't smell anything. Are you sure?"

"I smell smoke. It isn't a strong smell, only faintly drifting with the wind."

They continued on, but slower now, not wanting to spook him. "I can smell smoke now. We must be really close," Sterling said.

"Look, there's a beaver dam. This must be the pond Clemis was speaking about. The camp must be close."

They moved in as if they were stalking a deer. One footstep at a time and silently. They had developed a routine after all the years. Sterling took the lead and was watchful of the front and Wynola checked, scanning, left to right. "There. I see reflection in a glass window." Inch by inch and then they could see the cabin. Smoke was coming out the chimney.

The door had fallen loose and hanging by one hinge. There was nothing to lose, so they walked up towards the door. "Jimmy? Jimmy, are you here?"

"Who are you?" a voice said that sounded like it had been crying.

"My wife and I have come to take you home. Can we come in?"

"Who are you?" he asked again.

"Sterling and Wynola Silvanus, Jimmy. We have come to take you home."

"Come on, you can come in. You're the game warden, aren't you, mister?"

226

"Yes, Jimmy, I am. I'm here to take you home."

"You going to take me to jail, mister?"

"No, Jimmy. We are only going to take you home." They stepped through the door and were surprised with the ramshackled appearance. It looked like a bear had gotten inside and torn it apart before leaving.

"Are you hungry, Jimmy?" Wynola asked. She noticed a dirty fry pan on top of the stove. "What have you been eating, Jimmy?"

"Frogs mostly. Some bunch berries. I didn't mean to hurt her."

Wynola sat on the cot beside Jimmy and said, "Why don't you tell us what happened."

"Do I have to tell you everything?"

"We would like to know everything, Jimmy, but for now you just tell us what you want to."

Sterling stayed back and out of the conversation. His wife was doing just fine interrogating Jimmy and making him feel at ease.

"Okay. Betty Jean and I were in the barn and we were doing okay. Then we started to fight with words and then I tore her shirt and she slapped me. It hurt real bad and I pushed her. She fell and landed on a pitchfork and it came through her leg and she began to scream and scream and I got scared and I run from the barn. I see others running to the barn so I run into the woods and come here." He was crying now and said, "I didn't mean to hurt her but she hurt me. I run off because I was afraid what her daddy would do to me."

"Who is Betty Jean's daddy, Jimmy?"

In between sobs, Jimmy said, "Uncle Doug."

"Well Jimmy, everyone at home is worried about you and would like us to bring you back with us."

"I'm afraid."

"What are you afraid of, Jimmy?"

"What my uncle will do to me."

"It was an accident, wasn't it, Jimmy?"

"Yes, I didn't mean to push her on that pitchfork."

"Well, if you come back with us, Jimmy, your uncle won't hurt you. He asked us to find you."

Jimmy finally agreed to go back with them.

* * * *

It was 3 o'clock in the afternoon when they returned with Jimmy. The mill was running and everybody was too preoccupied with their work to take much notice. Doug Clemis was having a cup of coffee in the dining hall.

While Jimmy ate some food, "He was more afraid of what you might do to him, Mr. Clemis, than anything else. It was an accident, just like Betty Jean had said."

"I won't hurt the boy. I was afraid with the way he ran out of here and thinking I'd get on him for what happened, that he might take his own life. That's really the main reason I asked for your help.

"Thank you both for coming here. I still don't like you none. Especially how Sid and Al just up and left. I don't like you, that's for sure, but I do hold a lot of respect for you both."

He finished his coffee and went back to work.

"Maybe we can catch the south bound," Sterling said.

As they were approaching the Dyer Tank, they heard the train roll by. "Well, we either walk back to Redington, or we camp out tonight."

"Either way, won't we still end up walking? Unless we want to wait here all day tomorrow," Wynola said.

"You're right. Me, I'd rather camp out and get a good night's sleep."

So they walked along the tracks until they found a nice spot to spend the night. There was a little knoll thick with moss covering the ground overlooking a deep pool in the Dead River. They made a lean-to with fir boughs and beds of thick moss.

228

While Wynola dug out a fire pit and gathered dry wood, Sterling went fishing for their supper.

A half hour later, he came back to the top of the knoll carrying two, two-pound trout. Those with what Wynola had brought would make an excellent supper and probably enough left for morning.

That night as they were sitting up watching the fire, Wynola asked, "How much longer do you think we can continue doing this?"

She didn't have to explain 'this'. He knew exactly what she had meant. "I don't know. There are rumors that the railroad might be slowing down. They have already eliminated their passenger cars to many areas. The only passenger service left I think is the once a day to Rangeley. Passengers still can ride the combination cars, but the only passenger car service is to Rangeley. Without the railroad we surely couldn't continue to work like we have been. Times are changing too fast for me sweetheart. I like, too much, I think, this wilderness life you and I have enjoyed together all these years."

* * * *

Changes were coming and Sterling also realized there was nothing he could do to stop it or even slow it down.

In 1922, cars, trucks and buses were starting to take a lot of business away from the Sandy River Railroad and in 1923, the Central Maine Railroad Company sold out to Herbert Wing and Joisah Maxcy, who held extensive timber contracts in the Sandy River Plantation.

Most of the timber had been harvested around the Bigelow Mill operations and what little there was left was now being shipped by trucks. So the line from Carrabassett was discontinued.

During the 1920's, there seemed to be more money floating around and it looked as if the Sandy River Railroad was going to survive. But with the increase in the sporting industry, sportsmen often rode buses to their destinations. Except sportsmen were still using the railroad to get to and from Barnjum and Redington. Even though Barnjum didn't have any fishing opportunities, the boarding house was almost always full with fall hunters. Redington had the pond and it was excellent fishing. Because of the dam the water backed up more than a mile with many spring holes where numerous large trout could be found.

Since Sterling and Wynola were living more at their cabin at Redington than their home in Strong, the sports were always careful not to catch more trout than was allowed. Fall deer hunting at Redington was as good as it was in Barnjum and an addition was built onto the boarding house.

Sterling and Wynola were spending much of their time each fall looking for lost sportsmen. It didn't seem as if any of these city slickers knew how to use a compass.

After one long and tiring search for a sport from Massachusetts, Sterling almost lost his patience. It had rained that night and all the next day and when he finally found the sport, he was too surly to sit well with Sterling. The guy said, "Why doesn't the state have marked trails to hunt from? Then maybe I wouldn't have gotten lost."

Wynola knew what was coming next. That change of tone in Sterling's voice. In that no non-sense deep voice he said, "Well, Mr. Massachusetts, I doubt if the deer would understand that they were supposed to stay within sight of the marked trails. It's obvious that you can not use a compass, so perhaps you should stay out of the woods."

The guy didn't like being talked to in such a manner. "What's your name? I'm going to complain to your boss how abusive you are."

Sterling removed a business card from his inside shirt pocket and said, "These cards are something new. My name is on it. When you complain to Chief Picotier, you make sure you get my name right!" And he handed Mr. Massachusetts his card.

"Now, do you want to get out of here or not? You can come

along with us, or you can follow your compass north to the railroad tracks and then turn east towards Redington." He didn't wait for an answer. He and Wynola started for home.

Of all the lost people he and Wynola had to rescue, most wanted to hug them and thanked them over and over again, for coming after them. Mr. Massachusetts happened to be the rudest.

In most cases Sterling felt compassion towards those who had gotten themselves lost. What would city folk know about the woods or compasses. He and Wynola were very good at locating lost people and there were times when she would have to go out alone for a lost person. It was part of the job that they excelled in.

* * * *

In 1926, there was something new added to the railroad and the first time Sterling and Wynola saw it, they weren't sure what they were looking at.

Leland Stinchfield was the head mechanic at the Phillips yard and he was ingenious to say the least. He had taken a gasoline motor, a radiator furnished by the Reo Motor Company, and the frame of a Model T Ford and built a gasoline railbus.

The first railbus was small and only had room enough for the operator. Lee later built a bigger model that would carry several passengers. And this new railbus transported passengers now instead of the train which was now hauling only freight. During the cold months, the railbus could not be used. The railroad superintendent Orris Vose had his own railbus called the "jetblack hot rod." He would often scare the track workers when he would take them out by railbus. He was known once to travel 60 mph with it. Mr. Vose also used it to transport Dr. Bell to the wilderness communities for emergencies.

Because the price of beaver pelts were high, any beaver problems had to be handled by game wardens, to ensure that beaver would not be killed for their fur and claiming they were nuisance beaver. In the spring and early fall there were a lot of beaver complaints all along the railroad. Sterling and Wynola would spend a couple of days in the spring and fall with Orris Vose with his personal railcar blowing beaver dams and shooting nuisance beaver. Sometimes when they would have to wait at a siding to let a train pass, Wynola would roast beaver meat over a fire. Mr. Vose was surprised how delicious it was. "I never supposed that beaver would be this good eating."

* * * *

Sterling and Wynola were at home in Strong working up some firewood and taking care of some needy repairs. "What are we going to do about our snowshoes?" Wynola asked.

"We have repaired them so much there just isn't any more repairing that can be done. Maybe we should take the train up to Joe Knockwood on the Salem-Kingfield Line and buy some new ones. Mr. Knockwood is a Norridgewock Indian. I've seen some of his work and he is good."

The next morning they boarded the train for Kingfield, except they rode in the cab with the engineer, Fred Leavitt. "Sure, you can ride up here. Where are you dropping off this time?"

"Actually, in Salem at Joe Knockwood's, if we could."

"Climb up. Not a problem. I thought you two might be after some more outlaws."

"Not this trip."

"To be honest with you, I'm not hearing that much of what goes on around here anymore. You two have everyone spooked.

"How are you getting back from Knockwood's?"

"We'll walk, and maybe we'll get a ride."

Summit Hill slowed the train down but as soon as it was over the top, its speed returned.

"We're coming up to the Mount Abram Junction. When I come back, I'll have to pick up three freight cars at the Soule Mill."

The train slowed enough and Sterling and Wynola jumped off. "Thanks, Fred."

Joe's cabin was right there near the junction and he was sitting outside in the shade with his dog. He sat right there in the shade and said, "No need for introductions. I already know who you two are. You two have carved quite a swath through the woods here-abouts.

"There are a lot of newspaper articles about you and they say you are a friend of the Indians. You have a beautiful Indian wife, you helped Wonnocka and his people and you saved the son of an Apache chief. I can see from your stature that this true. You two walk softly through the woods, but the ground trembles with each step. But in your wake you have left integrity and virtue.

"Now what can I do for you?"

"We need snowshoes for each of us."

"Yes indeed. I believe you will want the Alaskan Curl Tip."

"Yes."

"You are what, 200 pounds, and you," he was looking at Wynola, "about 130 pounds?"

"Not bad."

"I have the frames already curled, all I need to do is lace them and add the harness. It'll take two weeks to cut the lacing, lace them and time for curing. $35 each, with harness."

Sterling put the money on the table and said, "That will be fine. We'll be back in two weeks."

"You walking back to Strong?"

"Yes."

"Thought so. Enjoy your walk."

The graveled road had recently been graded and there was no traffic. No breeze either, and it was hot. They only had about nine miles to walk. Once they reached the top of Foster Hill, it would be down hill all the way to Strong.

There was a cool stream running off the side hill and they stopped for a drink. There wasn't a sound anywhere. They had a long ways to walk but they were together and enjoying the day. On the down side of Foster Hill they walked passed where Alberta Probert lived and didn't know it. There was some activity where Starbird was still dismantling the old box mill, but no one looked up as they passed.

As they were crossing Valley Brook there was a horse and wagon coming through the woods towards them in a cloud of dust, it was coming so fast. The driver, a young boy, saw Sterling and Wynola cross the bridge and he brought the horse and wagon to a stop. "Sorry about all the dust, mister, ma'am." Then he saw the uniform and badge. "Holy cow, you're him ain't you? And you're her, too! That everyone is talking about."

Sterling and Wynola both didn't know quite what to say; while grinning. Sterling started laughing and finally he was able to ask, "What's your hurry, son?"

"Trying to get home before it rains." Sterling looked at the cloudy sky, but the clouds were not rain clouds.

Then Wynola noticed the pig in back and motioned for her husband to look. "What happened to your pig?"

"My father sent me to town to get this pig and just as I was leaving Starbirds, it started to pour and I got the horse to running and I stayed just ahead of the rain. I could hear it splatter against the wagon. My backside got a little wet, but I outran that cloud burst."

"Son, your pig is dead."

"Holy cow! I stayed just ahead of the rain and dry and the pig must have drowned!"

Sterling noticed cuts on the young boy's elbow. "What's your name, son?"

Very proudly he said, "Albert Probert, Jr. But I prefer to be called Toby."

"Where do you live, Toby?"

"Oh, about one and half miles up the road. On the right just before Allie Durrell's house."

"Is your mother Alberta?"

"Yeah, do you know her?"

"Yes, we both know her. My wife used to work with her at the hospital. Who is your father, Toby?"

"Albert Probert, Sr. He built that new bridge in Strong across the Sandy River."

"Your father built that bridge?"

"Well, Ma says he was the straw boss. He's building another one in Fairbanks and then he'll go to Norridgewock and build one there, too."

"We walked right past your house. If we had known we would have stopped to say hello to your mother."

"What will you do with your pig now?"

"Probably eat it. I'd give you a ride if I was going to town."

"You say hello to your mother for us, okay?"

"Sure thing. Wait until I tell my sister Marie who I talked with." Toby slapped the reigns and the horse started up. Walking now.

As Sterling and Wynola walked on they were laughing about their encounter with Toby. "Did you see those fresh cuts on his elbow?" Wynola asked.

"They could be bites from that pig, you know. I'd sooner suspect that young Toby had to hit the pig over the head, to stop him from biting him."

"Yeah, and he hit him too hard. He sure was proud of his father, wasn't he?"

Just then, they could hear a rumbling on the road coming up behind them. They saw the dust rising above the road first. Percy Cook stopped with a Model T towing a trailer.

"By jinks folks, going right by your house. Jump on and I'll give you a ride."

They climbed on and Sterling asked, "What's all this stuff Percy?"

"I bought a maple syrup evaporator from Carl Weymouth on Gilkey Hill. I wanted to start tapping more trees and I needed a larger evaporator."

This was the first time that either Sterling or Wynola had

ever ridden in a motor vehicle, other than the train and railbus.

Two weeks later they returned and picked up their snowshoes from Joe Knockwood. He had done an excellent job. "I put on four coats of a special shellac made for the outdoors. If you'd use that shellac once a year before the start of winter, these lacings will last a long time."

"These are really nice shoes, Joe. Thank you."

* * * *

When 1929 rolled in, everyone thought it was going to be another good year. But when the stock market crashed, much of the country was out of work, money to buy food, and homes. But when you already live without many extras, life continued on, day by day, and no one at Redington even felt a ripple. The lumbering industry only slowed marginally and most of the operations along both branches of the Sandy River Railroad kept on working. Orders were slower but the railroad was able to continue business as usual. The new railbus was saving the railroad money and could operate with very little overhead. The Sandy River Railroad ownership was not affected as much by the stock market crash that had crippled many companies.

* * * *

One night, as Sterling and Wynola were laying in bed, wrapped in each others arms and warmth, Wynola asked, "Do you think, my husband, that we'll ever get an automobile?"

"I suppose we'll have to have one when we stop wardening. Right now it would sit in the barn and rust."

"How much longer are we going to chase after poachers? You know we're both pushing fifty."

Sterling squeezed his arms to hug her before he replied and then he was chuckling, "Seems to me we topped fifty a while back. Are you getting tired of traipsing through the woods?"

Train to Barnjum

"I can do it as long as you can," was her answer.

A couple of weeks later they were walking down from the Mount Abram Junction; it was September 9th, 1932 and they could see a black column of smoke from the bubbling spring below the Valley Brook Bridge. "That must be a bad fire," Wynola said.

"Yeah and it's either the Starbird Mill or Brackley's Mill." They were about a mile away and they quickened their pace to see if they could help. But it was useless. The fire was so hot no one could get near it. Ray Starbird's two boys were there, Virgil and Harrison, and Sterling and Wynola stopped and stood beside them.

"We're losing everything," Virgil said. "The saw mill, the planing mill, dryhouse, blacksmith shop, the stock sheds and there's 200,000 feet of lumber in those sheds."

Many of the workers from Brackley's Mill came to help, as did many in the town. But all anyone could do was stand by and watch.

* * * *

1932 was not a good year for the Sandy River Railroad. The railbuses were still taking passengers daily to Rangeley, but much of the sawn lumber was now being hauled out of the mills on trucks. The cutting crews at Redington were still going strong, cutting logs and pulp wood and the mill was running every day. But the Barnjum Mill ceased operations.

Maxcy and Wing were nervous and then in 1934 they sold the Sandy River Railroad to junkmen for $20,200.00, and the little railroad that had played such an important part in so many lives and opening the wilderness of North Franklin County, stopped operations forever.

Tracks were torn up and freight cars were dismantled and the wood was burned.

In 1935, when the last train left Phillips as the tracks were

237

being torn up, for the Farmington Station. Ceil Voter had a collie dog who had for all it's life ran beside the south bound train as far as the Voter property line and then returned home. On this day in 1935, the collie sat on the bank and watched as the train passed by. He had no desire to run with the train any more.

Chapter 10

The deer season was over for the 1932 season. There was a foot of snow on the ground and Sterling and Wynola had packed up all of their belongings at their Redington cabin and had taken their gear to the station and while they waited for the freight train from Langtown, they went up to the boarding house to have a last cup of coffee with Swede.

"It sure will be different around here with no trains. I don't adjust to change so well. No sir, it won't be the same around here anymore. I don't know if plows on these damnable trucks will be able to keep the road cleared up here in the winter. If not, we'll be stuck here.

"I'll sure miss you two, also. You're part of the family you know."

There were sad goodbyes as Sterling and Wynola boarded the train for the last time.

That night as Sterling and Wynola were lying in bed, listening to the stillness, Sterling said, "I honestly don't know what to do, sweetheart. Without the train, there is no way of getting back to much of the country we have patrolled for over twenty years. I really don't know what to do. We have saved most of the money we received from the Department. That, along with what we already had, should be close to $30,000. And the timber we have on our own land needs to be cut. Maybe the Sandy River Railroad closing its doors is telling us it's time for a change for us, too."

"You know, it would be nice to make this house into a home. If you retire, there's one condition."

"What's that?"

"We get an automobile so we don't have to hike up Lambert Hill any more."

Sterling began to laugh as he held Wynola's face in his hands and said, "Deal. Tomorrow we stop wardening."

They lay there in each other's embrace and each one full of thoughts and questions, but there was no doubt. Things had changed far beyond, to allow them to continue as a game wardening team. They each were sorry to see this lifestyle come to an end, and so too did many people all along the Sandy River Railroad.

"It has been fun, hasn't it?" There was a croak in his voice.

"Yes, it surely has been fun," there was a little croak in her voice, also. "We had some great times."

"We met some very nice people," he said.

She rolled over on her stomach and kissed him and whispered in his ear, "I'm horny."

* * * *

The next morning they both went to town and Sterling telephoned (for the first time) Chief Warden Armand Pelletier in Augusta and told him he was retiring and would be forwarding a formal written resignation.

While Sterling was doing this, Wynola stopped at the post office to pick up their mail. There was quite a bit since they had last picked it up. There was one letter from a childhood friend, informing her that an uncle and his wife and daughter and her husband had suddenly died from a sickness. The daughter's two babies had been taken to Wonnocka's village to escape the sickness. Now the twins, a boy and girl, are homeless.

Tears welled up in Wynola's eyes as she told Sterling about this. When she had composed herself, he held her hands and looked into her eyes and said, "We can adopt the twins, can't we?"

Wynola was so happy she burst out crying all over again.

"What are their names?"

"They will not have names yet. Indian children usually do not get names until they are about five years old."

"Then we can name them?"

"Yes, that is usually done by the father."

"Well, I'll name the boy, you the girl."

"What will you call the boy?"

Sterling did not have to think long. "I will call him Pierre Paul Silvanus, after your great grandfather. And we will call him Pierpole.

"What will you call the girl?"

"I will call her Rachel Molly Silvanus."

Epilogue

"How are we going to get to Wonnocka's village without the train service?" Wynola asked.

"Maybe it's time we bought an automobile. We're going to have to have something."

There was a bus service from Strong to Farmington and from the terminal they walked to the closest auto dealer.

"What are you looking for in an automobile?"

"I don't know, maybe we should walk around and look at what you have."

The depression was still being felt almost everywhere and the new auto lot was small. But they agreed on a forest green pickup. "This will come in handy around the farm," Sterling said.

"Do you know how to drive?"

"Nope. But I guess we'll learn."

The pickup cost them $800, "But that's only if you'll give us a driving lesson."

After both Sterling and Wynola had had a chance to drive, Mr. Smith said, "Now in snow during the winter, you'll have to use tire chains on the rear drive wheels, or you won't go very far without them in snow."

"How much for a set?"

"$10."

They left the auto lot and headed for home. First Sterling,

and Wynola, too, were having a bit of trouble getting used to the clutch and the stick shifting. But they each took a turn and they were home in surprisingly short time. "I could get to liking this," Sterling said.

"Wynola, I think we should bring along a gift. What should we bring?"

"I would suggest food."

"What if we get a side of smoked bacon and ham? It won't spoil on the trip and they might enjoy it."

While Wynola was busy packing, Sterling walked over to the Allens and talked with Freemont and Harry about buying some bacon and a side of ham.

That afternoon, they finished packing for a trip to Wonnocka's Village. "We still will have to go by canoe, but maybe we can drive the new pickup to Wilson's Landing on the Magalloway River."

It was going to be a long drive to Upton and they left early. When they drove by the Randall farm, Jim was down by the road and waved as they rode by. But he was waving them to stop instead. "Hello, Mr. and Mrs. Silvanus. Gee, this is a nice pickup. I just wanted to let you know, Mr. Silvanus, that I am all through with my hitch in the Army and I have applied to become a Maine Game Warden."

"Good for you, Jim. I'm sure you'll make it."

"Just think, Maine Game Warden Jim Randall."

"It has a nice sound to it," Wynola said.

As they were climbing up through Grafton Notch, Wynola said, "My, this is some awfully beautiful country."

"We'll be going right by Kirby and Rachel Morgan's house. We'll turn in so we can see it."

Just as they were making the turn into the Morgan driveway, Joe Chapman was coming out with his horse and wagon. When he first saw them, he started to snarl at them. Then he stopped and, "Oh my God! I knew you'd come back some time."

He had mistaken them for Kirby and Rachel.

He climbed down from his wagon and walked over to them. "But this ain't right! You haven't aged a day since I last saw you. In fact, you look younger." Then he bent down to look in the window at Wynola. "And Rachel died. I saw her body. But there ain't no mistaking that wolverine vest you're wearing. But you two look so much like the Morgans," and Joe's spirit and his chest dropped. He was disappointed that this wasn't his old friends coming home.

Sterling explained about the vest and Wynola and that he had met Joe when he was through here when he first became a game warden, "Oh yeah, I remember you now."

Sterling didn't have the heart to tell him his friend Kirby Morgan had died sitting beside his wife's body. There was no point in destroying his hopes.

They backed up so Joe could go around them. He had such a forlorn look on his face.

"I really feel sorry for him," Wynola said. "It looks like someone is still living here."

"Joe always took care of their house whenever Kirby and Rachel were away. I guess he expected Kirby to come home after he had taken Rachel's body back."

In Upton they talked with Ted at the canoe shop and Ted said, "If you'll tow this trailer behind your pickup with these four canoes on it, I'll give you a canoe to use free of charge. That is as long as you bring it back. You can leave it at Wilson's Landing."

Many people stopped to look at them as they passed. They reminded so many of Kirby and Rachel. They looked so much like them.

They made camp that first night and continued on in the morning. By noon they were at Aziscohos Falls and would have to portage from there. The rope was still there and eventually someone came down with a John Deere farm tractor and trailer.

"$2 to haul your canoe and gear. $1 each if you ride."

When they got to the dam, Sterling wouldn't believe what he was seeing. "When I was here before, it was only a driving dam. Now, instead of a deadwater, there is a lake behind it. How things have changed." He told her about his other trip up through there and having lunch with Taylor Bodreau and he had given him a red-tail hawk soup.

They paddled hard trying to reach the village before dark. They had many miles still to go, but there was no wind and the canoe glided through the water, as if it were on air. They canoed past the Parmachenee sporting camps and there was one person on the porch who saw them and waved.

It was late afternoon and they could see canoes pulled up on shore and smoke from the cooking fires and then excited cries as they were seen by children playing near the water. Some of the children recognized the wolverine vest Wynola was wearing and began shouting, "She has returned!"

By now, everyone in the village knew of their guests and were coming to greet them. Wonnocka was in front leading the others. He was so happy to see them both, there were tears in his eyes. Wynola was ushered off with the women who all wanted to hear about her exciting life, wardening with a Maine Game Warden. They also wanted to know about her life with Sterling and the white settlements.

Wonnocka placed his hands affectionately on Sterling's arms and said, "It is truly good you have returned. I have missed my friend."

"I have missed Wonnocka and his people and this life."

"Come, the women are done cooking and it is time to eat! We talk later and have all next day, too."

"Wonnocka, Wynola and I have brought you and your people a special gift of food. We should not leave it in the canoe."

Wonnocka summoned some young men and the smoked ham and bacon was taken up to the village.

Wynola saw what was happening and she walked over to stand with Sterling, and she said, "We have brought you some special meat, Wonnocka. Smoked bacon and ham."

"I have tasted bacon in St. Francis, but do not know ham."

"Ham comes from the same animal, Wonnocka, only prepared different."

"What is this animal?"

"Pig."

"I have heard of this, but not ever see one."

They all sat around the cooking fire eating and Wynola pointed to the two orphan twins they wanted to adopt. "When we talk with Wonnocka about adopting the two children, he will not give us his answer immediately. He will think on it, maybe for days before he tells us."

When everyone had finished eating and the food was put away, Wynola said, "Wonnocka, my husband and I would like to talk with you."

They followed Wonnocka to his wikitup. They sat and remained silent while Wonnocka lit his pipe and then passed it to Wynola first. "It not our way to have women smoke the pipe. But you, like Rachel, are special kind of woman."

Wynola took the pipe and drew a deep puff and handed it to Sterling. Not until the tobacco was gone did Wonnocka speak again. "Now, tell me why you have traveled so far to come here."

Wynola spoke, "Wonnocka, my husband, Sterling, and I would like to adopt my cousin's two children and raise them as our own."

He looked at Sterling and asked, "Do you want Indian children as your own?"

"Yes I do."

"I believe you. You have too much honor to lie to me. Wynola, you have lived with the whites for long time now. How do white people treat you?"

"My skin is darker than my husband, but everyone has always treated me with the same respect that they do Sterling. I have many white friends."

There was no more said about the two children. "Wynola, I need to talk with Sterling alone." Wynola smiled at Sterling and left.

"I have heard much about you and Wynola from our people in St. Francis. Your own people honor you both. When Wynola and then you came here so many years ago, I knew both of you were great people and I was surprised when she left by herself. But you are like this," and he held up his hand and cross two fingers together. "You are like one. This pleases me."

"Wonnocka, you seem to have a heavy heart."

"Many years, before you came to this village, I and my father, Falling Bear, traveled out to Upton and Grafton with Kirby and Rachel. They showed us many things we did not understand." He leaned over to reach for something and then showed Sterling a newspaper. "Last summer when the young people traveled to St. Francis, they brought this back to show me things the whites have."

He unfolded the paper and on the front page was a picture of an automobile. "I don't know the words on this paper but there are many such pictures. My young people have discovered a new world that offers many different things that we will never have here. Already there are those who want to leave for St. Francis. They want this new life.

"I can not live like that. I only know the old ways of our people."

"I understand what you say, Wonnocka, and I do not have an answer. Things are changing fast, Wonnocka. I understand you wish to live here like you always have, but maybe if you don't change, you'll lose your people and your land forever."

They talked until everyone else had gone to bed and Wonnocka's wife entered the wikitup and said, "Talk all done. You talk more tomorrow."

Wynola was waiting outside and she took him to their wikitup.

They laid awake a long time that night talking. "Wonnocka is afraid of all the changes in the world outside this village and afraid of losing his people who want more."

"It's truly sad when you're faced with losing your way of life," Wynola said.

* * * *

The next day Wynola and Sterling spent much of the day with the two children they wanted to adopt. And everyone was noticing.

The next day, after the noon meal, Wonnocka called for the two children to be brought to him. And then Sterling and Wynola. Everybody in the village now were standing behind them.

"Wynola and her husband want to take these two children and adopt them as their own. Is there any among who would be against this?"

Everyone was silent. "I think this is good thing. I have one condition. That you two bring them back for visits, so they do not forget us or our ways. If you agree, they are yours."

Sterling and Wynola both replied, "Yes, we agree."

The End.

R. R. Station, Strong, Maine.

Strong Station House with the Top of the Hotel/Hospital in the Background
Courtesy of Strong Historical Society

Forster Mfg. Co., Strong

Courtesy of Strong Historical Society

Main Street, Strong

Courtesy of Strong Historical Society

Brackley's Mill

Courtesy of Strong Historical Society

Strong Hotel - Hospital

Daggett Bros. Store, now Beal's Variety,
Owned by Troy Romanoski

*Courtesy of Strong
Historical Society*

Courtesy of Strong Historical Society

Starbird Mill - Strong

Courtesy of Phillips Historical Society

Phillips Station House

Courtesy of Roger Lambert

Redington Log Yard

Redington Mill

Courtesy of Phillips Historical Society

Courtesy of Roger Lambert

Redington Village

Barnjum Mill and Village

Courtesy of Phillips Historical Society

Barnjum Mill and Log Yard

The Greene Farm, 1956-1958

Courtesy of Dead River Society

The Greene Farm - 1971

Courtesy of Dead River Society

The White Elephant Restaurant *Courtesy of Karen Thorndike*
Once a Warehouse for Forester Mfg., Now owned by Thorndike and Sons

Drawing by Ed Palmer

Bigelow Mill and Station House

Author's Notes

While researching this book, I discovered some interesting information. There have been some writers who suggest that Pierpole was from the Norridgewock or Passamaquoddy Tribe. But I discovered that Pierpole's real name was Pierre Paul. A French Christian name. When Pierpole petitioned the Commonwealth of Massachusetts in 1812 to sell his land, he stated one reason he wished to sell this land was because his son, Iganoose, had died and he wished to take the body back to Canada (Kanada) for a proper burial. I believe he went back to his original Abenaki Tribe at St. Francis, Quebec.

There has also been a lot said about Pierpole's lead mine on Day Mountain in Strong. During the French and Indian War, 1754-1763, British surgeons were removing from many of their wounded, silver musket balls or an alloy of silver and lead.

In the book, *Abenaki Warrior* by Alfred Kayworth, Mr. Kayworth quotes a Benjamin Russell describing a hunting trip on Gooseye Mountain in Riley Township, west of Newry, Maine. Mr. Kayworth described the time, when the town of Berlin, New Hampshire was first settled (about 1771). Mr. Kayworth quotes that Mr. Russell was lost for a few days and finally walked out along the Bear River in Newry. That while he was lost as he had come to a steep drop off and he threw his hatchet down and then slid down on the steep embankment carrying his rifle and pack. He said that when his hatchet hit the rocks at the bottom, the blade had stuck into the rock. The rock was silvery colored and soft, and he cut away a piece that weighed approximately four pounds. When Mr. Russell returned to Massachusetts, he had the sample analyzed and discovered it was 60% silver and 40% lead.

This is what I believe Pierpole had found on Day Mountain. While on a moose hunt he may have found an out-cropping of quartz rock with a vein of silver. I don't believe in that time frame that Pierpole would have had the knowledge or tools to dig a mine.

* * * *

In 1880, the Maine Warden Service Department was created primarily because of the commercial hunting of moose, caribou and deer. Wagon loads of wild meat were going out of state and being used to feed hungry workers in logging camps. I created the characters Sterling and Wynola Silvanus to dramatize this commercial hunting, while creating a story to tell the history of the Sandy River Railroad and the lumbering communities and operations it serviced.

The Sandy River Railroad operated for 56 years from 1879 to the last train in 1935. It was an important tool to opening and taming the wilderness of north Franklin County. And townspeople depended on it for their well being.

It was not possible to introduce everyone involved with the railroad or every business in the towns along the way.

I used to hunt with the Haggen family on Carlton (Swede) Haggan's farm. The last time I saw Mr. Haggan he was 82 and still cutting wood on his own land in Phillips.

When the Sandy River Railroad stopped operating in 1934-35, operations at Redington continued until 1938. And then the mill was dismantled and everything was moved to a new sight near Toothaker Pond. All except for a couple of sheds, the buildings were either torn down or burned. Then in 1960, while the Navy was conducting survival training, the surrounding forest accidentally started to burn. The fire burned for more than a week burning 10,000 acres.

The Maine Forest Service with the help of hundreds of civilians finally brought the fire under control. Then in the fall of 1963, during a heavy rain storm, the dam on Redington Pond broke and washed out. Thousands of cubic feet of water started gushing down Orbeton Stream to the Sandy River, flooding much of the farm land lying adjacent to the river.

* * * *

Frank Barnjum's mill burned in 1915 and he quickly rebuilt it and sold it to George True. Mr. Barnjum quickly reinvested his profits and built another large sawmill, store and boarding house at Drews Mills in the Town of Jerusalem, which later became known as Carrabassett.

The mill at Barnjum now operated by George True closed its doors in 1932 with the stoppage of the Sandy River Railroad.

* * * *

When the last train left the Greene Farm, Jim Reed did not abandon his farm. There was by now a drivable gravel road connecting Rangeley and Stratton through the Greene Farm. It became a tourist attraction as well as an attraction for hunters and fishermen. Jim built a few small sport cabins for the sportsmen and tourists and he continued operating the farm. Then in 1971, the farm buildings, all except for the small cabins and the tower to the water tank, burned. The Reeds did not rebuild and soon the beautiful fields began to grow in with bushes. Today, all that is left is the steeple to the water tank and a couple crumbling cabins.

In the 1950s, my oldest brother, Gordon, Clayton Hinkley and Phil Richards (of True Hill) worked in the hay fields there at the Greene Farm.

* * * *

Sterling and Wynola are fictional characters I created to tell the history of the Sandy River Railroad and the lumbering communities it serviced. The poaching characters as well as the experiences at Langtown are also my creations.

Randall Probert

About the Author

Randall Probert lived and was raised in Strong, a small town in the western mountains of Maine. Six months after graduating from high school, he left the small town behind for Baltimore, Maryland, and a Marine Engineering school, situated downtown near what was then called "The Block". Because of bad weather, the flight from Portland to New York was canceled and this made him late for the connecting flight to Baltimore. A young kid, alone, from the backwoods of Maine, finally found his way to Washington, D.C., and boarded a bus from there to Baltimore. After leaving the Merchant Marines, he went to an aviation school in Lexington, Massachusetts.

During his interview for Maine Game Warden, he was asked, "You have gone from the high seas to the air. . .are you sure you want to be a game warden?"

Mr. Probert retired from Warden Service in 1997 and started writing historical novels about the history in the areas where he patrolled as a game warden, with his own experiences as a game warden as those of the wardens in his books. Mr. Probert has since expanded his purview and has written two science fiction books, *Paradigm* and *Paradigm II*, and has written two mystical adventures, *An Esoteric Journey*, and *Ekani's Journey.*

Acknowledgements

I would like to thank my Uncle John Gravlin for your help, and the following people: Carl Stinchfield and the Strong Historical Society; Dennis Atkinson and the Phillips Historical Society; Mary Henderson and Carol Van Hoosier and the Dead River Area Historical Society; Zelda Harden, Roger Lambert, Harold (Bud) and Cliff Haggan for your stories about Redington and Carlton Haggan (the Swede), and Conley Gould.

And special thanks to John and Regan Martin; without your computer skills, this project would not have gone so smoothly.

An additional thanks to Amy Henley for editing and Laura Ashton for formatting.

More Books by Randall Probert

A Forgotten Legacy

An Eloquent Caper

Courier de Bois

Katrina's Valley

*Mysteries at
    Matagamon Lake*

A Warden's Worry

*A Quandry
    at Knowle's Corner*

Paradigm

Trial at Norway Dam

A Grafton Tale

Paradigm II

Train to Barnjum

A Trapper's Legacy

An Esoteric Journey

The Three Day Club

Eben McNinch

Lucien Jandreau

Ekani's Journey

Whiskey Jack Lake

Made in the USA
Middletown, DE
02 February 2022

60332021R00156